THE SECOND BOOI

EARTHborn

J.L. Ormord

KINGDOM BOOKS

Published by Kingdom Books, an imprint of *CreativeJuicesBooks, Singapore (www.creativejuicesbooks.com)*

National Library Board, Singapore Cataloguing-in-Publication Data

Name(s): Ormord, J. L., author.
Title: Earthborn / J. L. Ormord.
Description: First edition. | Singapore: Kingdom Books, [2017]
Identifier(s): OCN 993850403 | ISBN 978-981-11-4170-6
    (paperback)
Subject(s): LCSH: Forgiveness--Fiction. | Families--Fiction. |
    Fairness--Fiction. | God (Christianity)--Fiction. | Good and
    evil--Fiction.
Classification: DDC 813.6--dc23

Contents

For my parents, John and Carol Peters, who taught me
how to put on the full armor of God.

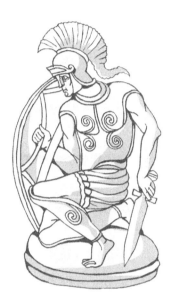

*And all things go to one place: of earth they were made,
and into earth they return together.*

Ecclesiastes 3:20, DRA

Humans and Their Guardians

Roni — Priscilla

Jeni — Samuel

Juli — Ariel

Zoei — Priel

Ryan — Oriel

Jason — Oriel

China — Neil

Allyson — Anastasia

Jared — Camiel

Jillian — Raven

Seth — Lorrel

Solomon — Saffron

James — Clayton

John — Daniel

Stephen — Heath

Victor — Jesse

Donavon — Delanny

Clara — Jordan

Madeline — George

Sarah — Rachel

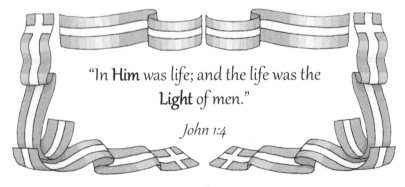

"In **Him** was life; and the life was the **Light** of men."

John 1:4

Last Day at the Firehouse

One Year Earlier

Beep, Beep, Buzz, Buzz, Beeeep. The early morning sound of the tones at Southwest County Fire and EMS roused Lt. John Chambers and the rest of B Shift from a deep sleep. The ambulances had been running continually through the night, and the third-up crew had just got back to sleep around 3:00am. It was now almost 5:00am, and the tones were going off again; but this time it was for a fire, and everyone had to respond.

Adrenaline was flowing fast as the six men and two women raced down the stairs to the ground level of the firehouse. The crew had jumped into their bunker gear and pulled up their thick red suspenders in less than 60 seconds.

John—or Padre, as his men had dubbed him—grabbed his helmet and coat and jumped onto Engine 46 with Brenda Valentine and Cody Sherman. Turning on their lights and sirens, they were the first out of the apparatus bay. But when they realized that the fire was at the county jail, located just next door to the firehouse, the fire and rescue trucks all came to a halt in the south driveway.

Stepping out of their vehicles, the firefighters beheld a curious sight. In the pre-dawn hours, it looked like large orange centipedes were exiting the jail. The prisoners pouring out of the smoking building were quickly corralled into large groups in a field across the highway. Traffic was blocked at least a half-mile back from the jail in all directions, and nearly every deputy in the city and county were there.

Officers with rifles and dogs were on guard, thwarting any hope of escape for the two hundred prisoners. The Fire Chief, Deputy Fire Chief, Capt. Michaels, Lt. Chambers, and several police officers—including the Police Chief—were huddled up, sharing information about the fire.

"The warden thinks the fire started in one of the boiler rooms," the Fire Chief began. "Most likely a gas water heater was sabotaged, since the facility is new and the fire isn't likely to have started from equipment failure. City Fire will be joining us as backup.

"Everyone keep alert! If this is an attempted jailbreak, I don't want to give these scumbags any casualties to gloat over. C Shift has been called back to the firehouse and A Shift has been put on alert. Now, the Chief of Police wants a few words with you guys."

A tall, dark man with a commanding voice addressed the officers. "We will be monitoring all communications from central command, which will be located in the apparatus bay of the firehouse," he announced.

"If you see or hear or even suspect prisoner involvement in this fire, you will communicate it immediately to the command center. 'All is well' will be the call for any suspicious activity. If imminent danger exists, you will call out 'the way is clear'. Does everyone understand?"

The group of firefighters nodded to indicate that they knew what they had to do.

"We don't want any heroes out there today. Stay with your partners!" said Capt. Michaels. "Padre, Val—you two take the south entrance. Randal, Mac—the north. Delanny, Coop—get up on the roof and try to vent some of the smoke. Sherman, I want you to man the pump. You are all the best at what you do, so let's get it done!"

John and Brenda looked over a floor plan of the jail, quickly plotting out the safest and most direct route to the south boiler room. The two firefighters put on their breathing equipment, then John grabbed the end of a one-and-a-half-inch hose, and Brenda picked up an axe and followed her Lieutenant into the building.

The smoke was thick. John turned on a flashlight clipped to his coat. The jail had been built mostly of cement, so he wondered what could be burning that would give off so much smoke. The first door they came to wasn't the boiler room, but it was obvious that the room was one source of the grey cloud surrounding them. He felt the door for heat. It wasn't as hot as he had expected it to be. The door was locked, so he signaled Brenda to use the end of her axe as a battering ram to break into the room.

He stood back as his partner forced the door open. Grey smoke billowed out. John got down on one knee and turned the nozzle of the hose to send out a gush of cold water. It took a few minutes for the fumes to clear enough for them to see what had been on fire.

A pile of bedding and prison uniforms were smoldering in the center of the laundry room. John and Brenda looked at each other. They knew at once that they had walked into a trap. John immediately pulled out his radio.

"This is Team One. All is well. I repeat, all is well in the south laundry room, over."

The radio crackled for a few seconds.

"We hear you, Padre. Report on your position, over."

"We entered the south laundry room and found a pile of clothes and sheets burning. The fire is out. No victims are present, over."

Almost a minute passed before they heard from the chief again.

"Uh... Padre, we will be sending assistance to help contain the damage. Proceed to the boiler room with caution. If the situation is too hot, exit the building at once, over."

"Understood, over." John looked at Brenda, who was frowning at him. He touched the rookie's arm and leaned towards her, so she could hear him through her mask.

"They probably think the ones who set the fire are long gone. Don't worry," he said calmly, trying to reassure the young firefighter. But John wasn't as sure as he seemed that the danger had passed.

Being a part-time minister had earned him the nickname "Padre" and the respect of his fellow firefighters. It was clear to them that he was a faithful Christian who walked what he talked. He lived out his faith every day, without judging his men and where they were on their spiritual journey. He and Brenda had talked about her salvation many times over the past few weeks, but she hadn't quite decided to commit her life to God.

They made their way cautiously down the corridor. Their senses were on high alert. The boiler room was only a few yards from the laundry room. They could see black smoke coming from underneath the door. John was just about to report that the room was too hot for them to enter when he heard a voice coming from behind the locked door.

"Someone, please help me!"

It was a woman's voice. The two firefighters looked at each other and made a unanimous decision. Once again, Brenda used the end of her axe as a battering ram. In one smooth motion, she made contact with the door and turned her body away from any potential explosion.

4

The firefighters positioned themselves on either side of the door. Surprisingly, no great torrent of fire came billowing out. John peered into the smoky room cautiously. He could see a pile of oily rags on fire. He opened up his hose again and extinguished the small blaze.

Brenda made her way over to the hot spot and kicked at the smoldering mound. They looked around for the woman who had called out for help but found no one in the room.

"Somebody is messing with us," Brenda voiced her suspicions.

John nodded in agreement. Once again he radioed to the command center.

"This is Team One. All is well in the south boiler room. I say again, all is well in the south boiler room, over."

"We hear you, Team One. Please state the conditions of the room, over."

"Just a pile of oily rags on fire. All fire appears to be out in the south wing, over."

"Alright, Padre, you and Val make your way back to base, over."

John gave the pile of rags one last good soaking with his hose before they turned to leave the room. As they walked toward the door, a man appeared in the doorway. Both firefighters stopped dead in their tracks.

"Well, hello, John," said the man.

His voice was like oil, slippery and smooth, but full of ulterior motives. "You're a hard man to track down."

"Who are you? What do you want?" John asked the stranger.

He moved forward, trying to put himself between Brenda and whatever this man might do.

The unwelcome intruder was tall and thin, with black hair. His full red lips, pointy nose and coal black eyes would have made anyone uneasy just looking at him. He wore a scarlet jacket and black gloves but no breathing apparatus. He reached into his pocket and pulled out a small caliber handgun.

John and Brenda backed up as the man approached them. He nudged them around the room and up against the wall near the door, so that no one coming in could sneak up on him. Then he pulled out a cellphone and pressed the speed dial button.

"I have him but he's not alone. What should I do with the other one?" he paused for a moment. "Ok, got it."

John didn't like the way the man's conversation had ended. He looked over at Brenda. She was shaking from head to toe. He could see a tear rolling down her cheek. He knew the man had been ordered to kill her, but he couldn't let that happen.

If he died, he knew that his soul would go to be with his Savior forever; but, if Brenda died, she would be separated from God for all eternity. John closed his eyes for a moment and asked the Creator for help. When he opened his eyes, it was clear what he had to do.

The stranger was fumbling around with his phone. John took the opportunity to push Brenda out and close the door behind her. He reached for his radio and, just before a massive explosion shook the building, his last words were heard over the radio...

"The way is clear. I say again, the way is clear."

CHAPTER ONE

Prisoners

*"See that you do not look down on one of these little
ones. For I tell you that their angels in heaven
always see the face of my Father."*

Matthew 18:10

Tuesday, 12ᵗʰ November

"Roni, start doing compressions!" Ryan yelled as he hit the code blue alarm button next to Sarah's bed.

In mere seconds, the hospital room was filled with a half dozen nurses and interns. Roni jumped up on the bed and straddled Sarah's body. As she began compressions, she could see Rachel standing by Sarah's head.

The guardian angel was calm as she spoke to her charge. "You are tired, my child. Come, I will take you to your Father."

"No!" screamed Roni. "She knows where MY father is!"

As Roni desperately continued the compressions, she felt her powers awakening. Ryan could see the faint blue glow coming from under her bandages.

"Roni, stop," Ryan said calmly. "The nurse here will take your place."

"No, I won't stop. She has to live!"

Ryan could see that she wasn't going to go quietly. He looked toward Michael and Priscilla, who were standing nearby. He nodded sadly in their direction, and the angels knew what they had to do.

Michael walked over to the bed and lifted Roni right over the heads of the hospital staff. A ball of blue light shot out of her hand, destroying the overhead lighting.

The angel held her tightly against his chest as they left the room. Her eyes were glowing as she struggled to get free. He had pinned her arms under his, so her hands were on his back. He began to feel the heat from them increasing on his back. He looked towards the heavens.

"Creator…" he began, but the Creator already knew what he needed, as Roni's hands released two explosions of energy directly onto the angel's back.

Michael cried out in pain as his skin was scorched by the will of this small human, but he did not loosen his grip on her.

"Priscilla, do it!" he ordered.

Priscilla looked helplessly at Michael.

"I know," he said softly as he looked into her watering eyes. He could only imagine the grief the guardian must be feeling, as she was about to cause pain to her own charge.

Priscilla stood behind Roni for a few seconds, hoping that the girl would give up and be at peace. But that peace never came; so she struck Roni in the back, right between her shoulder blades. Roni's screams stopped. Her body stiffened and then went limp in her guardian's arms.

As Michael released the girl, he himself went limp. Gabriel and Raphael came running into the room, sent by the Creator to support their injured leader.

"Wow! I thought the legions of Lucifer were attacking you," exclaimed Ralph.

Michael looked up, still trying to catch his breath.

"For such a small human, she has a mighty will. Remind me to thank Ezekiel for that kill switch later," he said wryly.

Priscilla carried Roni's unconscious body into the room next to Sarah's. There was a bed in there, and the guardian gently laid her charge on it. She was weeping as she stroked the girl's forehead.

"I'm sorry, baby. I had to do it. You weren't yourself. You were hurting everyone, and we had to stop you."

"Her pain runs deep. She will have to give it over to the Creator or it will consume her." Michael's blue eyes softened with compassion as he observed the sleeping girl.

Priscilla knew that he spoke the truth, but getting Roni to give up another thing in her life would be no small task. Her fears of loss and abandonment were like caged lions straining to be released. The knowledge of her father's possible imprisonment could tip the scale for her.

"Michael, is her father still alive?"

Michael stared directly into the guardian's brown eyes as he showed her the answer.

In her mind, Priscilla saw what looked like a dungeon. It was dark and cold, with metal doors lining a long corridor. She could see the faces of children peering through some of the barred prison windows: girls and boys who looked like they were between ten and fifteen years of age.

The girls outnumbered the boys by more than half. The boys all seemed sickly and malnourished, while the girls looked healthy but wore somber expressions on their faces. Most of the girls had bandages around their hands, like Roni.

Priscilla could sense the evil in that place. Dark angels were everywhere; they had taken charge of the humans who had rejected their Creator. These dark keepers were attached to all the guards and doctors at the facility.

A few slaves who were bringing food to the prisoners had guardian angels protecting them vigilantly. But some of these angels were weary of the constant assaults on their human charges. And, day after day and night after night, the evil keepers battled for the hearts and minds of the vulnerable children.

There must have been at least a dozen doors down the two sides of the narrow corridor. She peered into one cell that held a small boy on a little bed, curled up in a ball under an old, worn-out blanket. He was coughing badly, his frail body racked by an incessant hacking that was preventing him from falling into a deep sleep. An angel was lying on the bed next to the boy, covering him with her wings. Priscilla discerned that the boy was Sarah's brother Adam.

Turning her attention back to the hallway, Priscilla passed several more doors before stopping at the end of the passage. In front of her was one last door. A piece of plywood had been nailed over its window, so as to totally block its occupant from looking out. Just then, a slave came to deliver a food tray to the room. Priscilla took advantage of the moment and slipped through the open door. What she saw there sickened her.

A man, half starved, was sitting on a small, wooden chair by a rickety table. His hair was falling out from malnutrition. His skin and nails were pale and flaky. The maid left a bowl of what looked like watered-down chicken noodle soup, a piece of stale bread, and a cup of water. He thanked the slave graciously for the meager meal. Then he bowed his head and thanked the Creator for what he had been given.

After he had finished his meal—if it could even be called that—he reached into his pocket and pulled out two photographs. He smiled at both and began to pray over them. Priscilla gasped as she looked at the faces in the photos. One was of a middle-aged man and woman, smiling and holding each other close. The other was of four girls. Two of them had red hair. Priscilla knew she was looking at pictures of John and Carol Chambers and their four girls.

She looked at the ragged man before her. Reeling from shock, she realized he was John Chambers, Roni's father.

"Why didn't I know about this?" she cried.

"The Creator did not want it known," Michael explained. "I did not expect anyone except Ezekiel to know about his whereabouts. For this girl to inform Roni of his existence was very dangerous. As we now have proof."

"What in the world...?" Ryan had just come into the room and overheard the last part of the conversation.

"Calm yourself, Ryan." Gabriel put his hand on the doctor's shoulder. "Nobody but the Archangels had this information, and we were not allowed to share it with anyone because of the danger to Roni and the people around her."

"I think the reality of those dangers has been fully realized today," said Ralph as he looked over at Roni, who was still unconscious.

Ryan went over to look at Roni's hands. She had burned the gauze clean through.

"She is going to need skin grafts if she doesn't quit using her powers soon."

"The process of surrendering one's life completely to the Creator is a long and—most of the time—painful journey. It takes a lifetime for some of the most devout followers, and we are asking her to do it in a matter of weeks," Gabriel reminded everyone in the room.

"Gabriel is right," said Michael. "This child has had so much responsibility heaped on her shoulders that she will literally implode if she does not stop running from the Creator whenever she has a problem."

"She is doing the best she can," Priscilla said defensively.

Michael went over to the still-weeping angel and spoke kindly to her.

"Everyone knows this. We are all concerned about Roni's safety and wellbeing. You can only do so much as her guardian; she will have to choose the right path, if she is to stop destroying herself and those who love her."

CHAPTER TWO

John Chambers

Praise be to the God and Father of our Lord Jesus Christ,
the Father of compassion and the God of all comfort,
who comforts us in all our troubles so we can
comfort those in any trouble with the comfort
we ourselves have received from God.

2 Corinthians 1:3-4

John Chambers pushed his empty soup bowl to the side, as he looked at the two pictures of his wife and daughters. He smiled as memories of them filled his mind.

He could see Roni and her friends Ryan and Jason chasing each other, out at the old lake house. The sprays of lake water they had kicked up while running glistened in the sunlight. Roni's golden-brown hair streamed behind her. Her tanned skin made her look like she was from a country where people spent their whole lives on the beach. Her infectious laughter could be heard above the roar of the engines of boats that raced by. And her voice. Oh, that beautiful gift from the Creator to him. From day one she had filled their lives with joy.

He pictured Jeni and Juli building sandcastles on the shoreline. They looked like two ripened strawberries. Their fair skin could never be covered with enough sunblock. How many times had the two of them snuck outside without sunscreen and ended up looking like lobsters by lunchtime!

Jeni's passion for basketball was only matched by her love of reading. How many times had he caught her with a book in one hand while dribbling a basketball with the other! Never satisfied with a ninety-nine percent grade in school, she wanted one hundred percent and more.

Juli, his little sweetheart, was always singing and dancing. She could never have enough pink princess dresses or musical instruments. Piano, guitar, flute, violin, she wanted to try everything.

And then there was Zoei, their miracle child. The child all the doctors said would never be. He had been there watching when she was born. His awe and reverence for the Creator skyrocketed that day, as he held her in his arms.

Zoei's inquisitive nature and passion for life had blessed his days with wonder and excitement. Others had scoffed at his joy over having another girl, but he told his critics every child was a gift from God; every child was to be treasured. His eyes began to water as he thought of what he had missed in his girls' lives over the past year. His girls. His jewels.

He looked over at the picture of his beautiful wife and wondered how she was doing without him. He could see her so clearly in his dreams. Pale skin and hair as black as night. Her green eyes sparkled when she laughed. If his daughters were priceless gems, then their mother was his crown jewel, his one and only love. They had never been parted so long.

When Ezekiel took him from the fire at the jail, replacing his body with a convincing duplicate, his world had ended. After a year, he still did not know why he had been thrown into this dark, lonely place. What did Ezekiel want from him? Why were there so many children here with him?

He had made friends with a girl and her brother. Sarah reminded him of Roni. Same physical build and tanned skin—although most of her tan was gone after being locked away from the sunlight for so long. Her brother Adam always seemed sick. He coughed a lot like Greg and Sharleen's son Jason, who had died a few years back. He hoped the child would not die. He had passed Adam a lot of his rations over the last year. He thought the child could use the food more than he.

But where was Sarah now? He hadn't seen her lately, and Adam was getting worse. The next time he saw one of the doctors, he would ask if Adam could be transferred to his cell, so he could watch over him. John and the children had been moved to different cells recently, because of his contact with an employee of the facility, so they hadn't talked in a while. But he could still hear the boy coughing in the night.

He tucked the two worn pictures back into his pocket and slowly made his way over to the bed. It hurt him to lie down, as wounds were beginning to form on his hips. The once-mild case of scoliosis he suffered from had become a constant source of pain in the last six months. He eased his decaying body down slowly on the thin mattress. An old afghan was all he had to keep the cold off him. He could do nothing about the dampness in the prison.

No natural light ever entered his room. Trees and grass and sky seemed like a far-gone memory for him. He couldn't even remember the smell of fresh cut hay or his wife's favorite perfume anymore. His senses were dying along with his body.

His only comfort was that his wife and children were safe. Ezekiel had said that, as long as he was a model prisoner, they would be spared hardship. He often wondered what his family was doing. He had lost track of days and hours, but he knew it had to be close to a year since he had been gone. How the girls must have grown! He wondered if Roni had started college, if the twins were enjoying high school, and if Zoei was driving her teachers crazy at school with her thousand and one questions. He wondered if Carol, his beloved, had moved on. He prayed that they would be reunited someday soon.

This poor man had no idea that his wife had already been dead for more than six months or that his children were in constant danger of becoming Ezekiel's prisoners themselves. Had he known all this, he would have died a long time ago.

CHAPTER THREE

Reflection

*He makes me to lie down in green pastures; He leads
me beside the still waters. He restores my soul.*

Psalm 23:2-3a, NKJV

China could hear all the commotion going on in the room
across the hall. She and Juli had rested safely but not
soundly through the night. She had woken up several times
screaming and shaking violently. Each time, Neil held her
close and sang a song from the Book of Psalms. The words
wove themselves into her dreams and calmed her...

> The Lord is my shepherd; I shall not want. He maketh
> me to lie down in green pastures. He leadeth me beside
> the still waters.
>
> He restoreth my soul: he leadeth me in the paths of
> righteousness for his name's sake.
>
> Yea, though I walk through the valley of the shadow
> of death, I will fear no evil: for thou art with me; thy rod
> and thy staff they comfort me.
>
> Thou preparest a table before me in the presence of
> mine enemies: thou anointest my head with oil; my cup
> runneth over.
>
> Surely goodness and mercy shall follow me all the
> days of my life: and I will dwell in the house of the Lord
> forever.
>
> *Psalm 23, KJV*

Finally, around 3:00am, she fell asleep. During those few
tranquil hours before dawn, she dreamt of the Man... the
One Neil had called Jesus. In her dream, she found herself
in the place described in the song the angel had sung to her.

A large grassy meadow dotted with tall birch and cottonwood trees was before her, their leaves shimmering in the sunlight. She could smell mint and lilac in the air. Looking around, she saw lavender and white Shasta daisies growing in patches along the banks of a stream that babbled through the center of the meadow.

A cardinal was sitting on a rock in the middle of the water. It had been a long time since she had seen a bird this beautiful. She stooped down and touched the cold water and splashed a little of it toward the bird. He seemed to welcome the moisture and called for his mate to join him. The two birds chattered and whistled as they ruffled their feathers in the small shower. China laughed at the entertaining pair.

After a while, she decided to wade in the cool water. She was already barefoot, so she sat down on the bank and dipped her toes in the creek. A shiver ran through her body but, undeterred, she plunged both feet in, relishing the pleasure of the moment. She was leaning over to watch a minnow dart back and forth from behind some rocks when she caught a glimpse of herself in the water. She stilled her feet so the water would become flat. Like a reflection in a mirror, she gazed in wonder at what she saw.

A beautiful young woman with long, golden hair and sapphire eyes was looking back at her. Her skin was soft and velvety, with no scars or blemishes. Most importantly, the girl had perfect cherry lips and her teeth were white as snow. China reached out to touch the untarnished, celestial-looking being, but the water rippled, leaving the young woman untouched.

Succumbing to a nervous habit, China put her hands to her mouth. The girl in the water did the same. China furrowed her brow, watching as the lady in the water copied her.

"Is that... could that be... is she... me?" thought China. "No, it can't be!"

She kicked fiercely at the reflection in the water, but it would not go away. Suddenly she caught sight of a pair of feet standing on the opposite bank. Slowly she looked up and discovered that the feet belonged to the Man called Jesus.

"How are you, my darling?" said the Man gently.

China did not know how to answer.

"Didn't you like what you saw in the water?"

"I... it... I don't know who that beautiful girl was..."

"Why, it's you, sweet child. Maybe you didn't recognize yourself the way I see you."

She opened her mouth to reply, but she couldn't think of what to say. She looked back down into the water. The beautiful reflection was still there, but she turned away.

"Come with me."

Slowly she stood up and brushed the sand and grass off her dress. She hadn't noticed it before, but she was wearing the prettiest pink dress she had ever seen. It had a flowing skirt and lace around the neck. She looked up at the Creator and grinned from ear to ear.

"There's that smile I love to see," He said to her.

She jumped across the stream and into His outstretched arms. Once she had regained her balance, He took her by the hand.

"Let's go!" He exclaimed.

They began to run alongside the water. The ground was soft and cushioned her feet as she ran. Jesus held her hand tightly as they jumped over a few logs in their path. She laughed and squealed like a young child. When she was out of breath, He stopped so she could rest. She drank from the spring until she was satisfied.

"I have something for you, my Princess," said the Man.

He held out a golden apple to her. Her favorite! They sat down side by side at the base of a large willow tree while she ate her apple. The juice was streaming down her chin. The Man wiped it off her face with His sleeve. She laid her head down on His lap and began to doze off as He stroked her hair and sang the same song that Neil had sung to her.

"Neil must have told Him that I like this," she thought. She had a smile on her lips as she drifted off to sleep...

She awoke to the reverberation of Roni's screams that were filling the hospital corridor. She looked at Neil, who was right next to her.

"It's ok, my child," he said. "Roni is with Michael and Priscilla. They will protect her."

The sudden silence that followed Roni's shrieks made China even more afraid.

"Is she dead?" she asked Neil, gripping his hand as hard as she could.

"No. She is resting now."

***

Later that afternoon, a detective came to see China. He was tall and looked to be only a little older than Ryan. Behind a pair of taped glasses, his brown eyes were warm and they smiled when his mouth did. His messy blond hair fell in front of his face, and he stuttered when he spoke.

"Ah, M-Miss Miller, I'm S-Stephen Sanderson. I was w-wondering if I could... um... ask you a few... a few questions."

He pulled out a notepad and a pen and adjusted his glasses as he looked at the frail girl sitting on the hospital bed. China looked critically back at the disheveled man.

He had on a clean white shirt with a red-and-brown striped tie. His khaki pants were a little too short, and he had on one blue sock and one green one. He had taken off his long trench coat and laid it across the recliner at the foot of her bed.

"Sure," she said to the detective.

"Ok, thanks. What... um... is your f-f-full name?"

"China Sharleen Miller." She still wasn't used to hearing her name spoken out loud yet.

"And the child, what is her n-n-name?"

"Allyson Trinity Miller."

"Is there a f-f-father involved?"

"No."

"Can you tell me exactly w-w-what h-happened?"

China told the detective as much as she could remember and as much as she felt comfortable in sharing. After half an hour, she was feeling a little more relaxed with the man, and he was a little more at ease doing his job. He was not stuttering so much and was able to make China smile a little.

"If you think of anything else, m-ma'am, you can give me a call. I'll leave my card with you." He placed his business card on the table next to her.

Allyson started fussing and Anastasia handed the child to China.

"That's a cute baby," he said, stroking Allyson's cheek softly. The tiny tot reached up and grabbed Stephen's finger. She had his finger in her mouth before he could do anything to stop her.

"I'm s-s-so s-s-sorry!" he exclaimed as he pulled his hand away quickly. Allyson started to cry.

"It's ok," said China. "Maybe she likes you. You could wash your hands over there and then sit here and hold her for a few minutes, if you want to."

"Oh well, that's ok. I-I-I don't want to intrude."

"You're not," China smiled sweetly at him.

Although usually shy, she was also uneducated as to how to act in the company of strangers. She probably should have let the detective get back to his work, but she was enjoying his company so much, she didn't want him to leave.

Stephen went over to the sink and washed his hands as Allyson started to wail. He took the baby in his arms, and the nurse brought in a warm bottle for her. He held the baby like a professional. Allyson sucked down the bottle noisily.

"R-reminds me of a little piglet on a farm," he said.

China giggled a bit, and Stephen started singing a lullaby. Allyson drifted off to sleep. He put her over his shoulder, and she burped up a little formula onto his shirt. China apologized for the mess.

"No worries," he whispered. "My m-m-mom taught me how to get formula stains out. I'll come by and see you two tomorrow, if that's ok?"

China smiled at him, letting him know that she would like nothing better. She sat with a grin on her face for a full five minutes after he left.

"Well, someone looks happy," said Jeni as she walked through the door.

"Oh, yes. She is," said China, motioning toward Allyson.

Jeni laughed. "No, I meant you, silly."

China's face turned red.

"I think the good detective has made quite an impression on our girl," said Juli, who had been in the room the whole time. She had pretended to be occupied with a book, though she couldn't help but eavesdrop on their conversation.

China looked down at her lap. She felt embarrassed. Tears were beginning to well up in her eyes. She felt like she had done something wrong.

Jeni and Juli had not meant to upset their new friend. They were not privy to all the circumstances of her rescue.

They knew she had been held against her will, but they were too young and naive to understand all the ramifications of her imprisonment. They could not even begin to imagine the atrocities China had suffered in her eighteen years on earth.

"It's ok, China," said Jeni as she put her hands around her friend.

China held her tears in check and tried to brush off her distress.

"He was nice. Allyson seemed to like him very much," said Juli.

China still did not speak. Jeni decided to change the subject. "I think we need a movie."

China's face lit up.

"That would be great," said Juli. "Let's watch 'Tangled' again."

"Has she been torturing you?" asked Jeni. "I got us a real movie."

"You call 'Pride and Prejudice' a REAL movie?" argued Juli. "That stuff never happens in real life."

"Oh, and a girl with hair as long as a semi-truck does? The chameleon is cute but, if I have to hear you sing 'And At Last I See the Light' one more time, I'm gonna stick superglue on your lips."

The girls jested with each other for a while, but they ended up lying in the bed together, watching Lizzy and Mr Darcy fall in love in the England of the past.

China envied the two girls; they had each other. How she missed Trinity! But eventually she was able to put her friend and Stephen out of her mind and become engrossed in the five-hour BBC version of Jane Austen's well-loved book.

Were there men of such kindness and gentleness in the world? She wondered. If there were, she had yet to meet them. Ryan and Stephen seemed nice, but time would tell if that was their true nature—or if they had ulterior motives.

CHAPTER FOUR

Fairness

*In fact, the law requires that nearly everything be
cleansed with blood, and without the shedding of
blood there is no forgiveness.*

Hebrews 9:22

Wednesday, 13ᵗʰ November

The early morning light was peering through the frost-covered window. Roni's eyes were nearly swollen shut from all the crying she had done the day before. Her head was pounding and her back was killing her. She tried to reach up to rub her temples, but her hands refused to move. She started to panic. Then, by concentrating on her right hand, she managed with a great effort to raise it.

She wondered why her hands had fresh bandages on them. Then she remembered Sarah. Her heart began to race, and she called out for a nurse. Priscilla was by her side in an instant.

"Sarah. How is she?"

Roni wasn't really concerned about Sarah. All she was concerned about was her own father, John Chambers, and she only wanted the girl to give up information about his whereabouts. Priscilla knew this.

"She is ok. Ryan has put her in a deep coma, in an effort to slow down the nanites' destructive process."

Roni was happy that Sarah was still alive but disappointed because the girl would not be able to give any more information. She knew she was being selfish, but she told herself that it was ok because she missed her father.

"Roni."

Priscilla was speaking in her "mom" voice, and her charge didn't want to hear what she had to say.

"Roni," Priscilla said again.

Roni had been looking at the ceiling, but she finally turned her head to acknowledge her guardian.

"Think about what you are doing," said Priscilla.

"What do you mean?"

"Think about what you are willing to do to get what you want. Who are you willing to trample down, in order to find out where your father is? You know you would have killed Michael if he wasn't an angel. As it is, he's had to call on the Creator to keep you from blasting two holes completely through his body."

The angel and girl locked eyes for a moment. Finally, Roni spoke.

"I have lost both my father and mother in the last year. I have been denied a regular senior year of school. I am mother to three children who aren't even mine, and I could drop dead at any moment because the robots in my body don't like my heart! I believe I am entitled to a little trampling to find my father, who is most likely being held prisoner by a person who has tried to kill me and my sisters more than once." Roni was yelling loudly now.

A CNA had come down from the nurses' station. She stopped in the doorway of Roni's room. She made a noise and Roni look toward the door—and, to her horror, she saw Jeni standing behind the CNA with tears in her eyes.

Jeni tried to talk, but she couldn't. Upon overhearing Roni's selfish rant about being mother to three children who weren't hers, she was stunned. So stunned that she completely missed the part about her father.

"Jeni, I'm sorry. I didn't..."

23

But it was too late. Jeni let out a loud sob and ran away from her sister's room.

"Oh no! What have I done? Priscilla, go get her so I can apologize. I didn't mean to..."

"Didn't mean to what?" said Priscilla. "Didn't mean to sound selfish? I thought you said you were entitled to it."

Roni lay in bed, looking up at the ceiling again. Her selfishness had once again got the better of her.

"Just go away then, if you aren't going to be of any help."

Priscilla disappeared from Roni's sight but remained close by. Roni lay in bed for several more minutes and pouted.

"Here I am, flat on my back again. Why does this keep happening to me?"

"You know why."

Roni wasn't surprised to hear the Voice again. She decided not to insult the One whose voice it was by pretending she didn't know why she was flat on her back. Again.

"I know. Why does life have to be so hard sometimes? I'm a good person. Haven't I had my fair share of calamity? Why do I need another thing to be distressed over?"

"What do you think is fair?" He countered. "Should I have made one of your sisters the oldest, so all this responsibility would fall to her?"

Roni thought about His question. She wouldn't put that kind of responsibility on anyone.

"Should I have switched you and China when you were babies? Is it fair that she has never known real human love or that she suffered so cruelly at the hands of her captor?"

"Why do bad things have to happen at all? Can't we all just live good lives and not hurt one another?"

24

"Oh my darling, that was my plan all along. So many wonderful things that I meant for mankind's good... but they turned it into bad. My angel, the one I created to be so very beautiful, he betrayed me. His jealousy consumed him. The poison of his envy spread like wildfire through a dry field, until it devoured one third of my angels. Then he tempted the crown of my creation. One of my chil..." His voice choked up when He spoke of Adam and Eve.

Roni had never thought of humans as God's *actual* children before. Weren't people just here on earth to try to make the best life for themselves and their families while trying to do the right thing?

"But why did you even make that tree? If you hadn't put it in the Garden, they never would have eaten the forbidden fruit, and everything would be like you meant for it to be."

"Don't you see? I did not wish to force my children to love me. I wanted them to *choose* to love me; to *choose* to obey me. To trust that I, their Creator, knew what was best for them. But the temptation of the unknown lured them to the Tree, where the Dark One seduced Eve into disobedience. She could have turned and walked away or merely called out to me at any moment, and I would have rescued her in an instant.

"But Lucifer was tricky. He made them think I was keeping something important from them: the knowledge of good—*and evil*. I never wanted them to know evil or its destructive power; but they chose to disobey me and, in so doing, brought the blight of sin into the world."

He was silent for a few minutes. Roni did not know what to say in the presence of such sadness. The Voice continued.

"I actually knew all along what they would choose, but I chose to create them anyway. Walking and talking and sharing the few moments I had with them was better than spending eternity alone.

"I dared to hope that, perhaps at the last moment, they might desire to do the right thing and run away from the temptation of knowing... knowing everything. Good and evil. When they gave in to that temptation, I knew I had to make a way for them to escape the folly of their ways."

The knowledge of man's betrayal was a concept that Roni had never considered before. The Creator knew all along that humans were going to turn their backs on Him. Betray and curse Him. He knew that their unfaithfulness would cost Him dearly.

"I knew the only way to redeem my children was to come to earth myself. So I sent an emissary, my Son whom I had appointed as heir to all things and through whom I had created the universe. He would grow to be a Man who would be all human, yet have access to all the powers of His true deity. He would be fully God and fully Man, the radiance of my glory. He would live a perfect, sinless life, then consciously surrender Himself to be beaten and murdered for sins He never committed.

"When you speak of being fair, do you consider the sacrifice He made for you? That I made for you? Only someone perfect and blameless could stand in the place of all humanity and pay the price for the transgressions of the world. My Son. Was it fair for Him to die in your place? Sin demands a price, and that price is death... and the debt must be paid."

Why would someone as great as the Creator set Himself up for such heartache? Tears were falling down Roni's face as she communed in her heart with the Creator. She was so close to Him that she could feel His pain. She could feel the weight of His sorrow for the ungratefulness of His creation. But she could also feel the love that He had for those pitiful creatures who had doomed themselves to death.

She felt His sorrowful happiness in giving up a piece of Himself—His only Son—to suffer and die in the cruelest way. Could she give up a child who had come from her own body? To die for such wretched people? If indeed her father was alive and being held prisoner, was he giving up something of himself for her, an adopted daughter who wasn't even a part of his own flesh and blood? Could she give up one of her sisters to die for everyone else's iniquities? It would be easier to give herself up, rather than someone she loved.

She felt that an apology for her selfishness would not be enough to make up for her transgressions, but she said it anyway.

"I love you, my darling one," said the Voice. "Trust in me. I will see you through whatever you may face."

She felt that she owed someone else an apology too.

"Priscilla, are you still here?" she called out.

"Of course I am, baby."

"I'm sorry, Priscilla, for being so selfish again. Please forgive me."

"You know I will."

Roni asked Priscilla if she would get her a wheelchair so she could go and find Jeni. She loved her sisters with all her heart and had never wanted to hurt any of them. She went up and down the hallway on the third floor, looking for Jeni, and finally found her in a little chapel at the very end of the hall.

Her sister was kneeling behind the front pew. Her hands were folded, her eyes closed, and her face was lifted up. The sight of Jeni in prayer brought a lump to Roni's throat. How was it that her little sister had learned to run to the Creator when she was distressed—whilst she, Roni, kept turning inward to try to find answers to all her problems?

27

Roni got out of her wheelchair and left it at the back pew. She hobbled along each row until she reached her sister. She lowered herself down next to the praying girl.

Jeni wasn't even startled. A smile came across her lips as she realized Roni was kneeling next to her. She lowered her head and opened her eyes to look at her sister, who was weeping.

"I'm... I'm sorry, Jeni. I was whining and complaining, when I should have been thankful that I had sisters and that I didn't have to go through all this mess by myself. I am happy to take care of you and Juli and Zoei. It is my privilege."

Jeni put her arms around Roni.

"It's ok, big sis. Just remember we are here for you too. You don't have to pull the whole load by yourself."

The sisters stayed in one another's embrace for a few minutes. Then Roni pulled back from her and said in a grave tone, "Jeni, Dad might still be alive. The girl Sarah, who was trying to kill you and Ryan... well, she says she recognized me from a picture that a man in her prison had."

Jeni's face went white. The shock of hearing that her father might be alive was too much for her. She went a little faint, but her guardian Samuel steadied her with the help of Priscilla. When she had come around a bit, both girls decided they should get Juli, and then all three of them would go and talk to Ryan. Maybe Sarah had said more to him about their father's whereabouts.

They found Ryan standing outside Sarah's room. His eyes were closed and he looked like he was crying.

"Ryan, what is it?" asked Roni.

Ryan looked into the eyes of the woman he loved.

"Sarah's gone."

28

CHAPTER FIVE

Scars

"For if you forgive men when they sin against you,
your heavenly Father will also forgive you.
But if you do not forgive men their sins, your
Father will not forgive your sins."

Matthew 6:14-15

Roni could not believe what she was hearing. Sarah was dead, and all hope of finding her father seemed lost.

"I-I-I couldn't save her," wept Ryan. "I tried and tried, but I just couldn't do it. I'm sorry, Roni, I've failed you again."

"No, no, it's not your fault. I know you did the best you could." Roni put her arms around Ryan.

He lowered his head and cried into her hair. Her head was on his chest, and she could hear his heart beating. Jared had come out of China and Juli's room and seen Jeni crying as well. He tried to comfort her the best he could.

The humans and their guardians had been standing in the hallway, but now they decided it would be best to walk down to the chapel, where they could talk without anyone overhearing them. On the way, Roni stopped at a vending machine and bought herself a donut. She was famished and couldn't think straight until she ate something.

There wasn't anyone in the chapel when they got there, so they shut the doors. They comforted one another and then went on to discuss what should be done next.

"Obviously, the next plan has to be to go to Norilsk. We need to find out exactly where the children are being held captive and to see if John Chambers is still there as well.

"The vision you saw was old, Priscilla. The children and John Chambers have been moved since the last infiltration into the facility," Michael said as he eased himself down onto one of the pews. His back was still hurting from where Roni had grabbed hold of him the day before.

Roni looked up shyly at him as he spoke. She was still feeling bad about causing injury to the archangel.

"I can take Uriel with me on a scouting mission and see what we can find."

"Excuse me, Michael, but may I suggest that neither of you go at this time," said Samuel. The lower-ranking angel spoke in a tone of respect to his overseer.

"Go on," said Michael, curious as to the guardian's reasoning.

"Well, sir, first of all, you look a little weary and could use some rest to recover from your injuries. Secondly, the mission must be covert. After all, we will be trying to get past the Dark One's forces. We don't want to draw attention to ourselves and get into another situation, like when we went after China. If either of you are seen near Norilsk, the enemy may try to thwart our plans again. Sending two Watchers of lower rank will keep some of the suspicion off the bigger plan."

"Couldn't we make contact with some of the other guardians in the area?" asked Ryan. "I'm assuming that, since there are supposed to be a number of children in the prison, finding a guardian shouldn't be too hard."

"That is true," said Michael. "There will be many guardians. But there will also be keepers; and it would not be wise to contact any of the guardians, as the area will most likely have several enemy operatives residing there. We could be putting the guardians and their charges in jeopardy."

It was decided that two lower-ranking angels would go to Norilsk and check out the possibility of a prison rescue. They would report back to Michael as soon as possible.

When they were done with the meeting, Ryan asked Michael to go with him to one of the examination rooms so he could check on the wounds the angel had received the day before. Roni and Priscilla tagged along.

When they got in the room, Michael removed his shirt, revealing two large burn dressings on his back. Black blast patterns could be seen outside the bandaged areas. Michael winced as Ryan began to remove the tape carefully from the edges of the gauze. A smell of rotting flesh filled the room and Roni covered her nose, trying to escape it.

Ryan pulled the pieces of gauze back, exposing the worst burns Roni had ever seen: two black holes, each the size of her fist, on either side of Michael's lower back. The wounds were oozing a runny yellowish liquid. The skin around each hole was charred and flaky.

"Dr Young is probably going to want you to get back in the tub to debride the wounds again," said Ryan.

"What does that mean?" asked Roni, who was trying to control the urge to throw up.

"Well, the hospital has a large bathtub. We put Michael in it and basically soak the dead flesh off."

Ryan was pointing to the areas of dead flesh on Michael's back, and Roni could not contain herself anymore. She ran out of the room, looking frantically for a trashcan or sink, but none was in sight. Finally, she remembered that there was a bathroom right next to China and Juli's room.

She bolted toward the bathroom door, but it was locked. Unable to fight her body anymore, she threw up on the floor in the hallway. Priscilla came quickly to her aid.

"Child... baby... what..."

Roni continued to retch. The door to the bathroom opened and out stepped Jillian.

"Oh my gosh! What's wrong?" she exclaimed.

Roni couldn't answer. She dashed into the bathroom and tried to get the remaining contents of her breakfast into the toilet bowl. Fortunately, she hadn't eaten much of anything that morning, so by the time she got in the bathroom her body had finished clearing out her stomach.

She sat on the bathroom floor for a while. What had she done? Her temper tantrum the day before had done this to Michael! She hadn't even known that a human could injure an angel like that. How could she ever face him again? She didn't expect him to forgive her for what she had done.

What kind of curse had Ezekiel laid at her doorstep? It seemed that the wounds she could inflict were something neither Ryan nor anybody else could heal. She began to realize the terrible consequences of misusing her powers.

She decided she wasn't going to whine or complain about what she had done with this cursed power in her body. Instead, she would suck it up and own up to her sin. She was going to walk right up to Michael and apologize and then throw herself on his mercy.

She picked herself up off the bathroom floor and walked out into the hallway. Jared, Jillian and Jeni were standing there, waiting for her to say something. The mess she had made in front of the door had already been cleaned up. She said nothing but turned and walked back toward the exam room she had left so hurriedly.

Michael was still there. Ryan and Dr Young were examining his back and discussing treatments for him. She couldn't look the angel in the eye, so she stared at his feet while she talked.

"Michael, I just want you to know I'm really sorry for hurting your back. I was being selfish about wanting Sarah to tell me where my father was. I have no excuses... but I was wondering if you might be able to... if you might consider..." she wasn't sure why the last part was so hard to get out. "Can you ever forgive me for what I have done to you?"

The room was silent for a few moments, and then everything started slowing down. The doctors and the nurses weren't moving as quickly as they should be. Then everything stopped. Roni looked around in utter amazement.

"What is happening?" she asked.

"Come, take my hand."

Michael was standing next to her. Only he didn't look like a patient anymore. Instead, he was so large Roni could not even guess his height. His skin was golden, and he wore what could only be described as casual soldier apparel. All the protective parts of his attire were made of a leather-like material, instead of the gleaming silver metal he had worn in battle. As his six enormous wings began to flutter like those of an eagle, she felt herself being lifted off the ground.

They were not in the hospital any longer. She wasn't really sure where they were. They were surrounded by what appeared to be stars. Michael pulled her close to him and told her to hang on. The angel was so huge she couldn't fit her arms around him, so she just hung onto his arm with all her might.

His wings expanded to their fullest; and then, with a mighty force, they were propelled forward into what resembled a tunnel. Streaks of white light were all around them. How fast they were going or how much time had passed, Roni couldn't tell. After a while, Michael seemed to be slowing down.

They stopped suddenly in midair, and the angel lowered Roni down onto one of the many grassy hills in the area. It took her a few moments to get her bearings. Once she had regained her balance, she began to look around.

Downhill from where they were standing, a line of people stretched for what seemed like a mile. Roni wondered what they were doing; they looked like a mob waiting to get into a rock concert. Michael led her down the hill.

When she got to the bottom, she began walking alongside the crowd. Most of the people there were either sick or helping someone who was sick: a man with a crutch; a woman with a cleft palate; a child—with what looked like seizures—being carried by a parent. A man was being carried by four others on a pallet. A child of about ten was carrying on his back another child of five or six, who was missing a leg. Where were all those people going?

From the way they were dressed, it looked like they were in a third-world country. Men and women alike wore long robes. After walking for some time, Roni finally reached what appeared to be the front of the line.

A crowd was blocking her from seeing what was going on, but every minute or so she could hear a yell, and someone would run out from the throng of people, shouting, "I'm healed! Praise Jehovah!" She tried to press forward to get a look at who was attracting all that attention, but to no avail.

Then it was quiet. So quiet that not even a baby could be heard. Roni heard a voice she recognized. It was *His Voice*— the voice of the One who had come and spoken with her whenever she needed Him. She tried to get in close. She was desperate to see the face of the One who had got her through so many terrible times. But the crowd would not part for her.

People began shouting and praising this Man who could heal the sick and wounded; so grateful were they to Him that they followed Him all the way into the big city, shouting "Hosanna, blessed is He who comes in the name of the Lord, Hosanna!"

He was riding on a donkey, and people were laying their clothes on the ground in front of Him. Many were also waving palm branches in the air. It looked like what people at her church would call Palm Sunday. All those people praising that one Man; the sight was breathtaking.

Michael took her by the hand and they were flying again, but not for long. Suddenly they were standing on the roof of a large building. Roni could see a hostile crowd in the courtyard below. Over to one side of the enclosure was a clearing, where a lone man in a purple robe stood. He looked as though he had been beaten to a pulp. She wasn't even sure how He was still able to stand.

The crowd was shouting toward a high balcony, where a richly clothed man sat. He looked to be a judge of some sort. He was trying to talk the vicious crowd out of harming the man any further, but they would not be hushed. When it became clear that he could not curb their murderous appetite for blood, he called for something—and a servant appeared straightaway with a golden bowl in his arms. The judge went over to the bowl and washed his hands. The crowd erupted in thunderous applause.

Roni was speechless as she realized who the Man was. She was even more appalled when she saw some of the faces in the crowd; they belonged to the very same people who had rejoiced in their healing just a short time ago. The ones who had raised palm branches in His honor were now raising their fists in anger at Him.

Roni watched as the Healer carried His cross through the city and up to the place where he would be murdered. She hid her face in Michael's clothes as the soldiers nailed His hands and feet to the wood with long iron spikes. She looked with one eye when His torture device was raised high and its base planted firmly in the ground. She knew she was seeing Jesus, and He was dying on the cross, right in front of her.

Tears streamed down her face as she beheld what was left of His body. He was barely recognizable as a man. Then, all was quiet, and she thought she heard a sound coming from His lips. She strained to hear what He was trying to say.

"Father," He said, as He raised His bloodied face to the sky. "Father, forgive them. They do not know what they are doing."

Roni had heard this part of the Easter story a hundred times, but hearing it and seeing it were two completely different things. This Man, tortured and mutilated beyond recognition, was asking His Father God to forgive what those wretched people, to whom he had never been anything but kind, had done to him. She could hardly contain her feelings.

Michael turned and looked at Roni. "If the Creator could forgive the people who tortured and executed Him, I can most assuredly forgive you," he said gently.

Roni tried to control her tears, but she was so moved by what she had seen and what Michael had said that she fell to her knees and cried over the sorrowful beauty of the moment. Michael knelt next to her and held the frail human close.

When they returned to the hospital exam room, it was as if they had never left. Ryan and Dr Young were still discussing treatment options. Michael was sitting on the table with his wounds exposed, and Roni was standing before him.

"I hope the burns will not scar," said Roni.

"Who knows? The Creator still has the nail marks on His hands and feet."

CHAPTER SIX

Healing and Hope

The prayer of a righteous man is powerful and effective.
James 5:16b

Ryan was back in his office. He couldn't remember the last time he had slept. He stretched out in his cushioned swivel chair, closed his eyes, and kicked off his shoes. Sleep was instantly upon him like a warm blanket.

He wasn't sure how long he had slept before he was awakened suddenly by a shooting pain that went from the top of his foot to his hip. He tried to call out for help but couldn't catch his breath.

The pain was excruciating. He slid to the floor and lay flat on his back, staring at the ceiling. He saw Oriel hovering over him. Black spots began to float before his eyes, and he was shaking from head to toe. Then everything went black.

***

Roni sat in the hospital cafeteria waiting for Ryan. They had planned to have lunch together that day but, when he didn't turn up after some time, she thought he must have got stuck with a patient. She decided to go ahead through the lunch line. Chicken strips, potato wedges, applesauce and carrots.

She looked around for some ranch dressing and spotted several bottles of Yoo-hoo in a refrigerated glass cabinet. Snatching up two bottles, she paid for her meal and then sat down to eat it. She was still wondering where Ryan was; but she was so hungry after throwing up her breakfast earlier in the day that she ate her lunch quietly and put the whereabouts of her friend out of her mind.

***

Ryan was still lying unconscious in his office when Roni started looking for him. She searched everywhere. After thirty minutes of looking, she began to worry. She tried to call him several times and had the hospital page him, but there was still no sign of the doctor.

She finally found his office and ran toward the unconscious man. Trying to pick up Ryan's dead weight was impossible for her. She was able to cradle his head somewhat as she tried to revive him. She called upon the Creator for help, and He answered by sending two doctors and a nurse to Ryan's office. They immediately took charge of him.

Ryan was taken to an examination room, where his vitals were assessed and an IV started. As the nurse began to cut his clothes off, the medical staff could easily see what the problem was. On the upper part of Ryan's left foot was a horrific wound. It looked similar to the wound Roni had given Michael, except that this one wasn't healing at all. It was actually getting worse as the doctors looked at it. The circular laceration was bright red, and a mustard-yellow pus was seeping from it. The veins in his leg were also bright red and bulging from the infection that seemed to be spreading. It had almost reached his hip.

"His temperature is 104.5 degrees. His blood pressure is 147/85," said one of the nurses.

"This wound looks like a burn," the senior doctor said. "Get Dr Young in here, stat!"

Roni was standing near the door of the room. She was so used to being the patient, she didn't know what to do now. Ryan looked so helpless as he lay there on the exam table. The pain of loss began to creep into her heart. It was the same feeling of despair she'd had when Ezekiel was attacking Ryan out at the lake house, but this time it was stronger.

At the thought of Ryan's death, her heart started pounding in her chest. She wondered what she would do if he were taken out of her life once more. Tears filled her eyes. As his condition began to take a turn for the worse, a feeling of desperation came over her. She felt like she was losing a part of her own soul.

She could see the infection spreading as the inflated veins bulged all the more. The poison was traveling from his foot up to his heart. It didn't take a doctor to tell her that, if the infection reached his heart or brain, he would die. She was at a loss, not knowing what to do.

Suddenly she had a thought. *China!*

She raced down the hall to China's room. Ryan's sister was in the middle of feeding Allyson.

"China, quick, hurry! I need you to come with me right now. Ryan is sick and he needs you."

China was startled by Roni's sudden entrance. She had absolutely no idea how she could help anyone who was sick. She swung her legs around the side of her bed and stood up.

"I don't know what she expects me to do," thought China, as they hurried down the hall to the exam room.

China looked inside the room, and there was her brother, lying on an examination table. His clothes had been completely cut off. She could see the bright red path that the demon venom was taking, straight to his heart.

"You have to help him," cried Roni.

"I don't know what to do. I'm not a doctor."

"I heard about what you did for Allyson after she was born. You have a power. I beg you to use it before it's too late."

China did not know what to think. She remembered holding Allyson's hand and the soft yellow glow emanating from her hands, but she had no idea how to draw upon that power again—if it even was a power. She took a step back.

"Please, China. Please," cried Roni. "Please try!"

China saw in Roni's eyes a look that she herself had had when she was pleading with Joseph, her former master. She could not forsake another who was in sorrow too—a sorrow, she hoped, that would never match her own.

Reluctantly, the girl walked toward her brother. The doctors and nurses took no notice of her. She stopped at his feet, where a yellow discharge was running down each side of his left ankle. Slowly she reached out her hand and placed it on the wound. A soft glow came from beneath her hand. It grew brighter and brighter as she focused her energies on getting her brother healed.

The massive amount of power it was taking for China to heal her brother was exacting its toll on her. Her head was beginning to feel a little light. Seeing that she was weakening, Roni came up behind her and steadied the weary girl. Immediately, she felt some of her own power draining from her. She backed away, and China fell to her knees.

Roni and China now had the full attention of the doctors and nurses. They could not believe what they were seeing. They looked at one another, as if to say that someone needed to stop the two girls. But no one could move.

Roni realized that China could not only heal but she could draw on the strength of another person to aid her. Gingerly she stepped over to the weakening girl and offered up her strength to restore Ryan's body.

"Come on, Ryan," pleaded Roni. "Please. You have to live. You can't leave me again. How will I live without you? I lo..." She stopped herself before she could utter the word that was on the tip of her tongue. What was she saying? Did she love Ryan? After only a few short weeks, how could she imagine her life without him?

Ryan was regaining consciousness. Roni, still holding China's hand, went over to the head of the table. Ryan smiled as his eyes fluttered open and he saw the woman he loved looking down at him.

"My foot hurts," he whispered.

"China's trying to fix it for you," she whispered back.

He looked towards his feet and saw his sister concentrating very hard on his injury. He kicked himself mentally for not seeing Michael about his wound from the battle with the red demons, like Oriel had told him to. He had been so distracted with Sarah and Michael that he had forgotten all about his own injury. He could see that China and Roni were beginning to show signs of fatigue.

"China, it's enough," said Ryan. But his sister was concentrating so hard on healing the wound that she didn't hear him.

Roni let go of China's hand. The surge of power that the two girls had generated stopped as soon as the link was broken. China looked up and saw that her brother was awake and talking. He looked over at her.

"Thank you," he said gratefully.

"You're welcome," China smiled at him. She was starting to feel weak again. Holding onto the exam table to steady herself, she lowered her head and closed her eyes. Roni put her hand out to help her keep her balance.

"I'd better take her back to her room to rest," said Roni. I'll come back and see you as soon as I get her settled."

"If you see Michael, could you send him my way?" Ryan asked. Roni agreed to do so.

***

That night, Stephen walked up the stairs to his home. It was a little blue house in a rundown area of town. He wished he could make enough money to buy his mom a nice house in the country. As it was, he could barely keep the two of them afloat with his junior detective pay and her social security checks. She wouldn't need to be on oxygen so much if they lived out of town.

Because of his mom's medical condition, he had never been able to move out of her house. They had a nice house over in Pratt, Kansas, but the water pipes had broken a few years back and there was no way he could afford to fix them. Plus, they needed to be near his mom's doctor.

He was 24 and still living with his mother. He loved his mom, but he desired companionship with a wife. No woman would want to marry a man who still lived with his mother.

He smiled to himself as he thought of the beautiful girl he had met today. She was so sweet. He knew the kind of life she had lived, and he was sad for her. He wished he could be alone in a room with Joseph for a few minutes. Hopefully, the other prisoners would make him sorry for his crimes.

He loved her crooked little smile. And her blue eyes were like the Kansas sky on a cloudless day. He couldn't wait to see her tomorrow.

After he had put his mother to bed, he sat out on the front porch reading his Bible. Then, putting the book aside, he stood on the edge of the porch, staring up at the stars. He was always so lonely.

He repeated a prayer of petition to the Creator; a prayer he had prayed a thousand times before, asking for someone to love him, someone who would want to spend the rest of her life with him. And that she would love his mother too. He knew that one day his prayers would be answered.

CHAPTER SEVEN

Death and Disappointment

*God did not spare angels when they sinned, but
sent them to hell, putting them into gloomy
dungeons to be held for judgment.*

2 Peter 2:4

Thursday, 14th November

When China woke up on Thursday morning, she was happy that she was going to be out of the hospital. Happy, but anxious. Roni had invited her to stay with her family at their lake house. China of course had accepted gratefully, as she had nowhere else to go.

Madeline had decided that it would be alright for Allyson to travel with China to the lake house to meet up with Ryan's parents. The child was officially a ward of the state, but Michael had been given temporary custody. Madeline was surprised that the judge in the case had awarded Michael custody, but she didn't question it. Just another good thing happening, thanks to Michael.

China showered and got dressed quickly. Jillian had lent her some clothes because hers were so worn out. She looked at herself in the mirror. She had never had such nice clothes before. The blue cashmere sweater was soft against her skin. She brushed her hair, which was starting to look better. It wasn't falling out quite as much anymore—must be due to the good hair products Roni had bought for her.

Why was everyone so nice, all of a sudden? What did they want from her? Could these people really just want to be her friends? Or maybe they were expecting something from her, she wondered warily, waiting for the other shoe to drop.

"Time for a makeover!" said Jillian gaily as she came into the room. She had several small bags with her, which she proceeded to empty onto the bed. Out came a pile of makeup and hair accessories.

"I got up early and did a little shopping for you. I hope you don't mind. Since you look like me, it was easy to pick out the right colors for you." Jillian continued to babble on excitedly about what she had purchased. But China was still taking in the "since you look like me" part of what she had said.

"Is that the way this girl sees me?" thought China. "A beautiful princess with gorgeous hair and skin? My hair isn't even wavy like hers. It just falls down around my face like an old rag. My mouth will never be red and perfect like hers. It's ugly and crooked and..." China continued to think badly of herself until she felt Jillian touching her shoulder.

"Are you ok, China?" asked Jillian. "I didn't go out of bounds with buying this stuff for you, did I?"

China's blue eyes were filled to the brim with tears, and she couldn't contain her emotions any longer. She started to cry. Jillian put her arms around the girl and hugged her.

"Please tell me, what is the matter?"

"I... I just can't figure out why everybody is so nice to me. You say I look like you, but I don't. My... my hair is ugly, and my skin is pale and blotchy, and I'm ugly and skinny and..."

Jillian hugged the frantic girl again. "You are not ugly. You've been sick, so it will take a little while for you to get your strength back. And your skin and hair will start looking good too, I promise."

"But, my mouth, it's so ugly."

"Don't worry about that. As soon as Dr Parker does your surgery, you won't be able to tell there was anything wrong with it. She is a miracle worker!"

China felt a little better about herself after Jillian's pep talk. The girls spent the next hour happily doing their hair and makeup and nails. When Roni walked in, she could barely recognize China.

"Wow!" exclaimed Roni. "Is this the same girl who was brought into the hospital just a few days ago? You look wonderful!"

China smiled shyly and looked down at the floor. Roni was surprised at how different she looked. With adequate rest and nutrition, the little slave girl was turning into a woman—and a beautiful one at that, due to her selective breeding.

"Has Ryan been in to release you yet?" Roni asked. "I'm sure he is going to have a long list of instructions for you to follow. He told me he wants you to see a nutrition specialist to help you on your road to recovery. He's hoping to have you well enough so you can have your surgery before Christmas."

China put her hand to her mouth out of habit. She wasn't sure how she would feel without her deformity. It had been with her all her life.

Just then she heard a soft knock on her door. She turned around and saw Stephen standing in the doorway. Her face lit up when she saw him. He smiled at her.

"Y-y-you look great," he said.

Jillian took Roni by the hand. "We'll just be going now. We have to go... ah... find Jeni and Juli."

The two girls smiled at China as they left the room. She was alone with Stephen.

"I-I-I didn't m-mean to interrupt you and y-your friends."

"You didn't. We were done, anyway," she said timidly.

"How is Al-Al-Al... the baby?" Stephen couldn't get his stuttering under control, he was so taken with China's beauty.

"She's good. Anastasia has her."

"Y-y-you look wonderful."

China blushed again. She wasn't used to getting compliments from men, unless they wanted something in return. Somehow she felt easy when she was with Stephen. He had touched her damaged heart.

Stephen was kicking himself for acting like an idiot. This girl must have dozens of admirers and here he was, letting his heart get attached to her. He told himself that she was way out of his league. He couldn't even talk to her without his stutter showing. She was beautiful, and he was awkward and not even attractive. He had never even had one girlfriend. Who would want to be with him?

"Thank you," China said in response to his compliment.

It was quiet for a few moments as the two of them stared at each other.

"I-I was just wondering if you had remembered anything else about the other day?"

"No, I didn't."

W-w-well, I-I have some news about Joseph that I thought you might want to know."

China's face went white. She backed away from Stephen, as if just the sound of her former captor's name could hurt her. She was breathing rapidly, her whole being consumed by fear. The detective lunged toward her as she began to fall.

Stephen was able to get to her before she hit the floor. He sat on the ground and cradled her. Her eyes were open, but she couldn't move or speak. He could tell that she was having a panic attack, and he knew what to do. He held her like a child, speaking gently as he looked into her eyes.

"You're going to be fine. Joseph can't hurt you anymore. He is dead."

At that news, China grew calmer, but tears began to flow from her eyes.

"You are safe. Nobody's going to hurt you ever again. I will make sure of that," Stephen said as he stroked her hair.

As feeling began to return to China's body, she was able to lift her arm and grab onto Stephen's neck. She buried her head in his shirt. He smelled of clean laundry and spearmint.

She clung to him all the while that she was coming out of her panic attack. He didn't stutter at all while he was calming her. A feeling of peace swept over her as she lay there in his arms. She felt as though nothing or nobody could ever hurt her again.

Stephen stayed with China the rest of the morning, while she was going through the release procedures at the hospital. She never wanted him out of her sight, ever again. Peace began to fill her heart as the constant fear of imprisonment disintegrated.

Stephen held Allyson while China was signing papers. He had grown attached to the girl and her baby very quickly. He could not explain the bond he sensed was forming between him and them. He wondered if it was just him or if China could feel it too.

"It must be just me. No girl this beautiful would ever even look at me," he thought to himself.

He imagined what his mother would think if he showed up at their house with this beauty on his arm. He smiled to himself but then quickly dismissed the happy thought.

Roni had brought in the car seat that she and Jillian had purchased a few days before. Stephen made sure the baby was properly positioned in the carrier before he buckled up the five point restraint system.

"I-I give demonstrations at the police station on h-h-how t-to install car seats properly," he said. Then he thought, "That was a stupid thing to say. She doesn't want to know that I have credentials in car seat installation."

China smiled at him and thought he must be a very caring man to teach people how to keep their children safe.

Finally, around one o'clock, everyone was checked out and ready to head out to the lake house. Juli, Jeni and Jared settled into Jillian's car for the 75-mile drive. Roni, Ryan, China and Allyson were all set to ride in a minivan that had belonged to Carol Chambers but was now Roni's family taxi.

Michael decided it would be best if he drove, so he could keep a close eye on Ezekiel's prize. Madeline came along too, as she needed to pick up her car, which Ryan had borrowed several days ago. She couldn't afford a rental any longer.

"I will see that you get reimbursed for your rental car; and thank you for your patience," said Michael.

Madeline looked up at him. "I would do anything for you, Michael."

She had studied every chiseled feature of his face for years, so she knew it by heart. If she was lost in the dark, all she would need to do was touch his face and she would know that it was him. His voice moved her. It awakened a passion in her soul that could not be silenced. How much longer could she bear to be in his presence and keep her love for him veiled? She was sure that no one could ever fill the void in her heart but Michael.

Timidly, she reached out her hand to his and touched it with her fingertips. He did not pull away. He stared into the soul of this nearly-angelic woman. She had bewitched him as no other human had ever done. Her goodness was like mountain air. Everyone who breathed it in instantly felt better.

Michael had convinced himself that his admiration of her was one-sided and he was in no danger. He had attempted to keep his thoughts and feelings in check when he was near her, but this moment caught him by surprise.

For thousands and thousands of years, he had kept his mind clear of any romantic feelings for the Creator's children. He had seen the nightmare that could be unleashed when an angel disobeyed the laws set down by the High King of the universe.

Some beings have a desire to push the envelope of grace right to the edge. He remembered Samyaza and the two hundred other Watchers who had lusted after the daughters of man. They made a pact to take human wives—perhaps thinking that, if enough of them disobeyed, then the Creator would change His mind and let them cohabitate with the humans. They couldn't have been more wrong.

Their wives gave birth to giants who grew to be so enormous that there wasn't enough food on earth to sustain them. They began eating the animals and then the people, and eventually they cannibalized one another. The souls of the dead were crying out at the gates of heaven. Michael and the other archangels saw how much bloodshed was upon the earth, and they petitioned the Creator to put an end to it.

The Watchers were severely punished. One of Samyaza's lieutenants, Azazyel—who had taught the humans to make swords and other weapons—was captured and bound by Raphael. The Creator instructed Raphael to throw the Watcher into a pit and cover him with sharp rocks so that he would not be able to see any light. Azazyel was to remain there until the day of the Great Judgment, when he and his fellow Watchers would be thrown into the lake of fire.

All the giants—the Watchers' children—were killed and their souls bound beneath the earth until the Day of Judgment. Then they would be cast into the lowest depths of the fire and silenced forever. The disobedient Watchers mourned for their children as they turned on one another, killing each other like wild animals.

Michael could never forget the Creator's terrible pain and grief the day He sent the Great Flood upon the earth, killing all but eight of His beloved children. The flood had a two-pronged purpose: to destroy all the Watchers' children and their descendants; and to start all over with mankind, because humans had become so wicked that they were murdering their own children as sacrifices to false gods.

Michael never wanted to see his Master suffering such sorrow ever again. He pulled his hand slowly away from Madeline's.

"Madeline, I... it is prohibited... I mean, I... I am not what you think I am... I cannot..." he stumbled over his words, not wanting to hurt her, yet resolved to obey his Master at all cost. "Can we speak of this later?" he pleaded.

Madeline's face was red with embarrassment. She had let her feelings show, and she had been rejected.

"Um... no. It's ok. I shouldn't have said anything."

Michael could see tears forming in her eyes as she turned away from him. She got into the van quickly and shut the door. She fumbled with her seatbelt for a while until it finally snapped into place.

Michael looked towards the sky.

"Oh Creator..."

CHAPTER EIGHT

A Meeting, a New Bedroom, and a Report

*But know this first of all, that no prophecy of Scripture
is a matter of one's own interpretation, for no prophecy
was ever made by an act of human will, but men
moved by the Holy Spirit spoke from God.*

2 Peter 1:20-21, NASB

The group of people from the hospital arrived at the lake house around 3:00pm. Jillian's carload had a great time singing and telling stories all the way home. The van's occupants were less joyous on the drive, which seemed to them to last an eternity. Allyson cried the whole way, and Madeline was on the verge of tears. Michael was so absorbed in his thoughts of Madeline that he missed his exit and had to drive ten extra miles to turn around and get off the highway at the right spot. Roni and Ryan sat quietly in the back row, each wondering what the other was thinking.

As soon as the van stopped, Madeline made a beeline for her car. She got in the green Honda, started it, and was out of sight in less than a minute. Michael watched helplessly as she fled from him. Roni could see the distress on the angel's face, and she guessed what was happening. She pitied them both and wondered if he would be allowed to tell Madeline that being some sort of child placement agent was only a cover story for his real identity and mission.

China picked Allyson out of the carrier. She began to hum the simple lullaby that Stephen had sung to the infant yesterday, and the baby stopped crying. Already, she missed the detective and wondered if she would ever see him again.

51

Ryan was still limping from his injury. Michael had worked on the wound for about an hour the day before; but the doctor was in need of another treatment from the angel, who was nursing his own wounds—both physical and emotional. Ryan hoped that he could get a few hours of sleep and that Michael could recuperate too, while his fellow Watchers kept close guard over the house and its occupants.

Zoei came running out of the house, bombarding Roni with hugs and kisses. The little girl also invited her new friends, James and John, to lavish affection on her big sister Roni—which they gladly did. Jeni and Juli got a laugh out of the ruckus the children were making.

Jared unloaded the luggage with the help of Seth, Solomon, and another boy Roni didn't recognize. After everything was brought inside, Seth introduced his friend.

"Hey, everyone, this is Donavon Herrera. He came over and helped us put the family room back together. His dad owns the hardware store in our town, so we got a good discount on supplies."

Roni held out her hand to welcome the stranger. He was incredibly good-looking, with the same blond hair and blue eyes as Ryan, and she wondered if he could have had altered genetics as well.

"Nice to meet you, Donavon," she said. "I can write you a check for everything in a bit, if you have time to wait?"

"No hurry," Donavon replied in a silky smooth voice. He turned and looked at Jillian. "I'm sure I can make myself useful for a while."

Jillian blushed as the young man looked her over. She quickly turned her face away and began to pick up the smaller pieces of luggage that had been left on the floor. Seth elbowed Donavon, and Jared eyed the impertinent guest.

While the girls made their way up the stairs, Seth turned to his friend and said, "Hey, Amigo, easy with the ladies."

"Aw, man, I was just playing around," Donavon jested.

Jared stared warily at Donavon as he and Seth followed everyone upstairs. The hair on the back of his neck stood up. Something wasn't right with that guy, and he knew it. A small voice coming from just below him interrupted his thoughts.

"Listen to what you know, Jared."

Jared looked down and saw a child standing next to him—a little boy with eyes that were an unearthly shade of blue. Their brilliance caught Jared by surprise.

"Oh wow!" Jared exclaimed, taking a step back. "You're... um... James, right?"

James looked thoughtfully at Jared. "Yes, I am."

The vivid blue radiance in his eyes dissipated, and he turned and ran off to find his brother.

"Hey, wait, come back!" Jared called out.

But the child had already become engrossed in a game of checkers that Zoei and John were playing in the family room.

"Listen to what you know," Jared repeated the words to himself, trying to figure out what James had meant by them.

"James has the ability to see the future and John the past." It was Camiel—Jared's guardian—who spoke. "If Ezekiel were to get his hands on either of these boys, only the Creator knows what kind of havoc they could cause."

Jared looked quizzically at Camiel. "What about the future? What future was that comment about? 'Listen to what you know' could mean a ton of things."

"What were you thinking of, the moment James spoke?" asked Camiel.

"Well, I was trying to decide if I should pummel that guy for looking at my sister like she was a candy bar he'd like to unwrap." Jared was quiet for a moment. After a minute or two, he added, "I should probably watch out for that guy."

Camiel raised his eyebrows. "I would. I haven't spoken to Michael yet, but it's obvious that the boy is selectively bred. I don't know why he wasn't recruited earlier, and up till now I haven't seen his guardian."

"Until he's gone, I'm going to be keeping an extra close eye on my sister," said Jared. "And Jeni. And the other girls, for that matter. I think we should tell Raven."

"Oh, trust me, he knows."

***

Most of the items brought in from the van were for China and Allyson. They were carried to the upstairs bedroom, together with Jillian's things. Jillian had no problem sharing a room with China and Allyson; due to her genetic makeup, she needed only a few hours of sleep at night. Eventually, China would require less sleep as well, but for now she needed all she could get.

Zoei and Allyson were the only natural-born children in the house. Although Roni was mechanically-enhanced, she—like Zoei and the baby—needed at least eight hours of sleep at night and possibly a nap during the day too.

Roni was the last one to make it to the bedroom. When she walked through the door to her old room, she was taken by surprise. The walls had been painted a soft shade of pink. Multicolored curtains hung from the windows, and the twin beds had new sheets and bedspreads on them. The crib, which also had pink bedding, had been put together, as well as the matching dresser and changing table. She looked into the bathroom and saw that it had also been done over to match the bedroom.

"Oh, I hope you don't mind, but I had this room done over. Mostly for China and the baby, but honestly I had a hard time sleeping in a room so desperately in need of updating," said Jillian. "I came up with a design plan and put Seth and Solomon to work on it. They did a fabulous job, as you can see." The boys grinned as she complimented them.

"Oh no, it's perfect. I'm glad you thought of it," said Roni. "To tell you the truth, I did feel bad that you had to sleep in a room that had been decorated for a twelve-year-old."

China was standing near the door, holding Allyson. The room was so beautiful she wanted to cry. The pink walls were so totally different from the cinderblock ones that had imprisoned her for most of her life. And there were real windows. Three real windows! You could look out of all of them because the glass was clear—not blurry, like the glass blocks in her old room that distorted everything.

She laid Allyson down in the crib and walked over to the closet. There was a row of beautiful new clothes in there, and ten pairs of shoes and boots lined up on the floor.

"Now, that's your side of the closet and this is mine," said Jillian, as she walked over to a dazed-looking China. "And, if you ever want to borrow anything, just ask."

She pulled China over to the dresser. "I had to kind of guess your size; so, if any of the underclothes don't fit, we can exchange them."

Jillian then led her to the bathroom. "Here are some towels and washcloths, and these drawers are for you to put your stuff in. Do you have any questions?"

China was so overwhelmed by emotion, she was almost at a loss for words. "Thank you so much," she said, putting her arms around Jillian's neck. "This is the most beautiful place I have ever been in."

Letting go of Jillian, she went quickly over to Roni and hugged her too. "Thank you for everything. I don't know how I will ever be able to pay any of you back."

"Pay back? No way!" exclaimed Jillian. "You're just a great excuse to get my interior design degree going. I'm going to take pictures and send them to my mom. She will be impressed."

"Jillian and I did some shopping for Allyson too," said Roni. "Those bags on your bed are what we got. You can put them in her dresser yourself, or we can help you if you like."

China looked at all the bags on and around her bed. There were at least a dozen.

"I think I can manage the clothes, but I might need some help with the rest of this stuff."

Allyson started to fuss, and Roni offered to help feed the baby. China was happy for the break, so Roni gathered the little girl up and went out of the room to make a bottle.

"Oh, I forgot to tell you that there's a great rocking chair downstairs and Roni has ordered a gliding rocker for our room," said Jillian just before she left the room. "It should be delivered tomorrow."

China was still not sure what to think about all this. She looked around the room and marveled at her surroundings. These people hardly knew her, and yet they had welcomed her into their family. For the first time in her life, she felt like she might be safe.

She was supposed to meet Ryan's parents sometime in the next couple of days. Hopefully they would like her and Allyson too. She was still a little nervous about the whole custody thing. Were Ryan's parents going to take Allyson to live with them? Was she going to stay at their house? Ryan had promised that she and Allyson could stay together.

She looked through the items that Jillian and Roni had purchased. So much pink! She loved pink. Trinity had loved pink too. Trinity. Her friend would have loved this room. She hoped Trinity was looking down from heaven and could see that she and Allyson were doing fine.

A wave of exhaustion came over her, and she decided to rest on her bed for a few minutes. Almost as soon as her head touched the pillow, she was asleep.

Neil went over to the sleeping girl. He took her shoes off and pulled a blanket up over her shoulders. The guardian knelt beside the bed and kissed his charge on the forehead.

"Now may the Lord of Peace Himself continually grant you rest and peace in every circumstance; may the Lord be with you."

***

Downstairs, a meeting was underway to bring Michael up to date with everything that had happened while he was away. Jared asked Camiel if he could keep an eye on Donavon while the meeting was going on.

"Two eyes," said Camiel.

Once the door to the basement was closed, Seth and Solomon gave their report.

"We have some interesting news about China that we discovered at the house," Seth began. "We found paperwork that indicated she was actually married to Joseph."

Solomon interrupted. "We even called the courthouse to double-check, and it's true. China and Joseph Cardian were man and wife."

The room was silent. Everyone was in a state of shock. This was the last thing any of them expected to hear.

"What?" cried Ryan in disbelief. "That monster was married to my sister?"

Ryan's anger burned within him. Michael put his hand on his shoulder. He looked into the infuriated human's eyes.

"Joseph has his reward," the archangel said quietly.

Ryan was still upset by the news, but he told himself to focus on the rest of the discussion.

"Since China was legally married to Joseph, it means she is the sole beneficiary of his estate," Solomon explained. "The house and all the property and everything in Joseph's bank accounts all belong to China."

"It looks like he married her for tax purposes," Seth chipped in. "She actually has 1.6 million dollars in a separate account with her name on it. I know money can't make up for the terrible life she has had, but it sure can help to make her future a lot brighter."

"That is excellent news," said Michael. "Even better than I expected. What about the spies sent to Norilsk, any news from them?"

Gabriel stepped forward. "They found an entrance to an underground facility just east of the city. There is evidence that some children are being kept there."

Gabriel paused and looked over to Raphael.

"What is it?" asked Michael.

Gabriel took a deep breath. "We believe we may have found Carrick and Tinasophia," he announced.

Michael sat up abruptly. "What? Are you sure?"

"Not completely," said Raphael. "Some of the villagers claim to have heard... uh, signs of them."

"Where?" asked Michael.

"Down in an abandoned quarry," Raphael continued. "There are guards posted every ten yards, all the way around the pit. Some of the villagers say they have heard mournful songs in the night, coming from the direction of the quarry."

"It must be them," said Gabriel. "The singing, what else could explain it?"

The humans looked at one another. They were all asking the same question in their minds.

"Who are Carrick and Tinasophia?" Roni finally asked.

"They are Watchers of children," answered Michael. "They have been missing for almost a hundred of your earth years. We had thought them lost to the Dark One but, if there is a chance that they could be prisoners of Ezekiel, then perhaps they are not lost."

He paused for a moment, then continued, "This rescue operation is going to be much bigger than any of us had anticipated. We are going to need reinforcements. You children are going to need to immerse yourselves in the Scriptures and in prayer, to prepare for the battle ahead."

The angel stood up and looked around the room at the group of young people gathered there.

"I know you are all confused by some of the recent events that have taken place in your lives, and you have been asked to stretch your faith more than the average human. But do not fear; the Creator will be with you.

"When you see chaos and destruction going on, all around you, look up and know that your heavenly Father is watching you. The Creator has a destiny for each of His children, but it is up to you to choose to follow it. He will not force you.

"And there may come a time when you cannot see a way in front of you and you ask yourself: 'Why me? What is my purpose in this life?'" here Michael looked directly into Roni's eyes, singling her out, as he concluded, "I do not know the future, but *perhaps you have been born for such a time as this*."

CHAPTER NINE

Victor

Yet when I surveyed all that my hands had done and what I had toiled to achieve, everything was meaningless, a chasing after the wind; nothing was gained under the sun.

Ecclesiastes 2:11

Victor sat alone in his cell. The shock of the day before was still shaking him up. He had heard that a group of inmates had attacked and killed Joseph. He knew he was next. The other prisoners didn't take kindly to child predators, and he wondered if it would help at all if he told them he had never hurt a child. He was a victim himself and had only helped in the transportation of children who were sold to other dealers and customers... but that didn't make him sound guiltless.

As he sat in the 8 by 6 holding cell, he could sense them closing in for the kill; but he knew that, if his life was over, then Esperanza and the boys' lives would be over too. He had dropped her off at a house early Saturday morning, promising to come back for her that night; but then he had run into trouble at Joseph's ranch, and all hope of saving the boys was lost. They were probably already in the foster care system.

"O Espe! I'm so sorry!" he whispered aloud.

"Is that another one of your child prostitutes?" came a voice from above where he was sitting. A guard had crept up quietly on his cell and heard his plea.

"Hey, Philips, Mr Pedophile here wants his girl back."

Victor walked over to the door of his cell and, putting his hands around the bars, he pleaded, "Please sir, there is a girl locked in a barn back..."

"Don't go telling us all your sick fantasies," interrupted the officer, striking Victor's right hand with his baton.

Victor cried out in pain and held his now-injured hand to his chest.

"Just a few more hours, and me and my buddies are going to show you what we think of your lifestyle choices. Officer Bates and I got to help your partner understand how we feel about sickos like you." Turning to his colleague, Officer Philips asked sarcastically, "Did you tell our guest that his friend won't be able to do business with him anymore?"

"Let's just say that, when he was 'accidentally' put in the wrong cell, the other prisoners felt like they needed to question him... and, when they got done, he didn't have anything else to say!" Officer Bates replied.

Both officers laughed and walked away.

Victor sat on his bed, cradling his hand. He kept asking himself, "What could I have done different in my life? Why do things never work out for me?" He was supposed to be one of the *copii de aur*, the golden children, like everyone else born in the facility. Well, almost everyone, anyway, except for him. Instead of being perfect like his blond-haired, blue-eyed brothers, his hair was dark.

His eyes were mostly blue, but he had inherited a condition known as heterochromia that made his eyes look like one color was bleeding into the other. Orange lines of pigment shot out like the rays of the sun from around his pupils. With those genetic differences and the diamond-shaped birthmark on his neck, he just didn't make the grade. He was kept around the facility with a few of the other less-than-desirable children. They were simply known as *gunoi*, which means trash.

When he was nine, one of the guards took a special liking to him. He started bringing Victor candy and gum when he was on shift. Then one day the guard got permission to take Victor home with him.

At first Victor was excited. He had never been outside the facility for more than a few minutes at a time. As they drove away, he looked back and saw several dark-skinned girls being hurried along the outside wall of the facility by two large, well-armed guards. He wondered why the girls were there. Even though it had been Victor's only home, he had not been allowed to explore the facility thoroughly, and he could recall only seeing fair-skinned girls there. He was sure there were more people living there than just the few children who shared his small living space—because at night, if he was very quiet, he could hear someone singing through the vent in his room.

When they arrived at the guard's house, Victor was given a nice meal and allowed to play in a room furnished for a young boy. He had never seen so many Legos in his life. He thought he was the luckiest boy in the facility. The guard let him play for an hour. Then, after a bath, Victor was taken to another room with a large bed. He was allowed to jump on it for a while and, when he was tired out, he was tucked in. He dozed off to sleep quickly, only to be awakened in the middle of the night with the guard standing over him. That night, Victor lost what was left of his innocence.

As if being an unwanted and unloved child wasn't enough, now he was also marked by shame. And he went on bearing his shame. He became a regular visitor at the guard's house for several years, but eventually he grew too old and the guard moved on to another boy. Victor thought his own personal hell was ending, but he soon found out it was not.

He was passed around by many of the other guards and doctors there. One of the Swedish doctors had given him the nickname *diamant pojke*, the diamond boy, because of his birthmark. The more he protested against the attacks, the worse he would be beaten. So, he decided that he would accept his self-effacing designation as the diamond boy.

As he got older, he was allowed more and more outings. He partied with the facility guards and pretended to enjoy their attention. He would drink alcohol until he passed out... in the hope that, when he woke up, he would not remember what was done to him the previous night.

At eighteen, he began working for the facility. He started accompanying the adopted children to their new parents. He would watch as the parents welcomed the babies with open arms. Sometimes, after a delivery, he would sit in his van and cry. The love he saw flowing from the parents was something he yearned for. The thought of someone waiting so long for him—and the moment of finally being together—stirred within him dormant feelings, making him aware of a deep hunger within himself...

He began to search... but what he was searching for, he did not even know. He had a string of boyfriends that left him feeling empty. The one girlfriend he had didn't remain faithful to him, and it broke his heart. Alcohol and drugs only temporarily dulled his pain. And then, when he thought he could search no longer and he was ready to kill himself, he met a man, a prisoner at the facility. His name was John.

He told Victor there was someone who had open arms for him. There was someone who would love him and always remain faithful to him; who could give Victor hope to go on living. Day after day, he continued to talk to Victor about the uninhibited and unconditional love of the Creator and His Son Jesus. John read from a little red Bible that he had been allowed to keep when he was first brought to the facility.

The words of Jesus spoke to Victor's dying heart. He longed for a life with the Creator and His Son in it, so John baptized him. It wasn't a traditional baptism in any way. Victor sneaked a pitcher of water into John's small cell, knelt in front of the door, and repented of his sins. Then John dumped the water over his head. For the first time in his life, Victor felt God's love washing over him. It was as though the water itself had cleansed him—body, soul and spirit.

The guards heard the water hitting the ground, and they came to see what was going on. Before they reached his cell, John slipped the little red Bible into Victor's pocket. Victor tried to explain that he had spilled the water by accident, but the guards would not listen to him. They took John to another location, and Victor never saw him again. But he read the little red Bible every day. On the front of the Bible was an inscription: *My hero...my love.* On the inside page, John's wife had written:

> Love is patient, love is kind. It does not envy, it does not boast, it is not proud. It is not rude, it is not self-seeking, it is not easily angered, it keeps no record of wrongs. Love does not delight in evil but rejoices with the truth. It always protects, always trusts, always hopes, always perseveres. Love never fails.
>
> *1 Corinthians 13:4-8a, NIV*

The words had brought tears to Victor's eyes. He touched the page many times, trying to absorb the love between John and his wife. He had read in the Bible that the Creator's design for true earthly love and companionship was between a man and a woman. He doubted that he would ever find a girl who could love him despite his past.

Could humans love uninhibitedly like the Creator? Tears streamed unchecked down his face as he sat in his cell. He wondered if he would ever see Espe or James or John again.

The hall door opened and then slammed shut again. The voices of half a dozen guards echoed inside the jail, and he knew his end was near. He bowed his head in prayer.

CHAPTER TEN

My Sister's Keeper

Each of you should look not only to your own interests,
but also to the interests of others.

Philippians 2:4

The sun had gone down by the time China awoke. She had forgotten where she was for a moment but, upon hearing laughter coming from somewhere in the house, she remembered.

"I have a new life," she said to herself.

Looking over to the clock on the nightstand, she saw that it was after 7:00pm. She made her way to the bathroom and turned on the water. It was ice cold and felt wonderful on her skin. She grabbed a pink hand-towel and dried herself, enjoying the feel of the soft fibers on her face. When she turned around, she caught a glimpse of someone in the mirror. It was her own reflection but, every time she saw it, she marveled at the dramatic changes in her appearance.

Her hair was growing smoother, and it looked like it was beginning to curl softly like her twin brother's. The black circles under her eyes were almost gone, and the scars she had accumulated over the past eighteen years were shrinking too. Her crooked mouth was the same, but it wasn't quite so prominent; her sparkling eyes, rosy cheeks and soft skin far outshone the deformity. She remembered her dream of herself and Jesus by the stream. Was this what the Creator's Son saw?

Turning her eyes away from the mirror, she found a comb and began to brush her hair. Then she spotted, up on a shelf, a little basket holding a variety of hair accessories.

65

She picked each item up, one at a time, and examined it closely. Finally, she selected a purple headband and, as she slid it into place, she thought briefly of all the times she had dressed up for the customers Joseph brought to her. Not that they had really cared about what she put in her hair; but she had hoped that, if they were at least sober, she might get treated a little kinder. She quickly put Joseph out of her mind; she had a new life now, with the hope of family and love within her grasp.

Making her way downstairs, she looked at the Chambers' family photos hanging on the walls. There were so many pictures, most of them taken at the lake house. China felt sad as she touched a frame that held a picture of two boys and a girl splashing one another in the lake. She never had a childhood like theirs. She never really had any friends except Trinity and the old lady at the facility. They were the closest thing she had to a family, and now they were both dead.

"Oh, there you are," said a cheerful voice from the bottom of the stairs. It was Jeni. "I was just coming to wake you up. We are about to have dinner. Are you hungry?"

China's mind was still on the family photo gallery, so she only half heard what the girl had said. She stared back at Jeni.

"Oh... ah... sorry... what did you say?" she fumbled over her words.

Jeni was jovial as she repeated herself, "I said, are you hungry? We are fixing to eat."

"Yes. I could eat something."

"I just love your accent. I noticed the detective loved it too. Seemed like he hung onto every word you said."

China blushed and looked down at the ground.

Jeni continued, "I wouldn't be surprised if he made a personal home visit just to come see you."

They walked down into the family room, and all eyes were on China. The room fell quiet as it was plain to see that the ugly duckling was becoming a swan. Ryan got up from where he was seated and kissed his sister on the cheek.

"You look wonderful!" he exclaimed.

Her face flushed at the unaccustomed compliment.

"Alright, soup's on!" called out Priscilla as she walked to the center of the room. "Let's get the children's plates done first, and then the rest of you can go. Boys, try to leave some for the ladies. Michael, would you lead us in a prayer of thanks?"

"She's so bossy," said Raphael under his breath as he nudged Gabriel. "You would have thought she was the Creator's Number One."

Gabriel grinned and whispered back, "Is somebody jealous?"

Michael slowly arose from where he was seated, and the two angels stopped their jesting. Not because he demanded it, but because of the respect the archangel had secured over the millennia by his extraordinary deeds. China studied Michael closely as he stood in the center of the room. He closed his eyes and lifted up his hands.

"Blessed art Thou, O Lord our God, King of the Universe, who has created many living beings and the things they need. For all that thou hast created to sustain the life of every living being: blessed be Thou, the Life of the Universe. Amen."

China's eyes grew wide as she watched the mighty angel pray. His skin was luminous, and he looked both human and angelic at the same time. Even after everyone else began to get their food, she couldn't keep her eyes off him.

Michael walked over to her and took her hand.

"What is it, child?" he asked gently.

China took a step back from the angel and studied his cerulean eyes closely. She wasn't sure how to ask all the questions that were racing through her mind. She looked down at the hand that was still holding onto hers, trying to decide whether to pull away from him.

The angel spoke softly to her again. "You are troubled in your soul, little one. Please ask what you wish."

Timidly she spoke, "You are an angel, right? Like Neil and Anastasia?"

"Yes."

"Anastasia took Trinity to heaven?"

"Yes."

She paused for a moment. "When I die, will I get to go to heaven and see Trinity?"

Michael could see the tears forming in the corners of the girl's eyes and her bottom lip quivering slightly. He could feel the empty places in her heart.

"Yes, if you put your trust in the Creator, you will go to heaven when your time comes."

"How will I know when it is time and how will I get there?"

"The Creator knows when it is time for you and the rest of the saints to join him."

"Saints?" she said, bewildered.

"The saints are the ones who trust in the Creator and have fulfilled their purpose here on earth. They are the ones already worshiping at His throne."

She looked at Michael and tried to understand him, but her heart was so full of the present that she couldn't understand everything he was trying to say. Slowly she allowed the angel to draw her close to his chest and comfort her. Her heart was beating fast and she thought of running away from him; but the longer she stayed wrapped in his arms, the quieter her mind became.

"One day, daughter, you will understand," he assured her.

Juli came over to them. She held out her hand to China and said, "Come over here and sit with us." China allowed Juli to lead her over to where she and Solomon were sitting. The three sat quietly until it was their turn to get food.

China observed the people in the room closely. Most of them were talking and laughing. Jared and Jeni were sitting on the couch, chatting quietly. Three small children sat around a little table, in chairs that were just their size.

One of the older boys was talking to Jillian. China couldn't remember his name, but his presence made her uncomfortable. He was playing with a marble and it seemed to be suspended right in front of his face. China could tell that the boy wanted Jillian's attention, but she knew that her friend didn't want to be in a relationship with a boy who bore such a close resemblance to her brother.

Glancing around the room, it did seem kind of strange to her that all five of the young men in the room looked so much alike. Even the two little boys were like smaller versions of Ryan and Jared. As her eyes rested again on Jillian, she hoped her premonition about her friend's admirer was wrong.

After her little group had collected their food, they sat down at the dining table with Jared and Jeni to eat. Solomon tried to make small talk and asked if she liked chicken. China nodded her head, though she was having a hard time concentrating on anything but the tattoo peeking out from under his shirtsleeve. He noticed that she was staring a bit, so he pushed up his sleeve for her to see the rest of his ink.

"You can touch them. They don't hurt anymore," he said.

She reached out hesitantly, as if the flames tattooed onto his forearm could actually burn her. The skin on his arm was rough and uneven and completely void of hair. She noticed some words tattooed with the flames and tried to sound them out, but gave up after a while.

"What happened?" China whispered.

"Well," Solomon leaned back in his chair and grinned, "When we were eleven, my crazy brother got it into his head that it would be fun to set off some fireworks in our neighbor's cow pasture. The grass was high and dry, and he got himself surrounded by fire. I had to push him out of the way, and I got a little scorched. This past year, my folks finally let me get these tattoos to cover the scars. Seth has one too, kind of like it, covering a small burn on his forearm."

Seth, who was over by Jillian and Donavon, could see that Jeni, Juli and China were admiring his brother's tattoos. A mischievous grin, similar to his brother's, flashed across his face as he shouted across the room, "I guess it's a good thing I helped you get those tattoos, little brother, or you would have no way to impress the ladies!"

"Little brother!" Solomon roared. "By what, three minutes? And I never needed anything to impress the ladies. As I recall, you were the one who told Anita Fernanda that you were going to set off your own fireworks on Cinco de Mayo."

"Who is Anita Fernanda?" asked Juli.

"His *mami*," teased Solomon. "She won't let him do anything without her permission."

"I heard that," said Seth, "and she's not my *mami*. She's not the boss of me. I can do what I want, when I want."

"Oh, is that right?"

"That's right!"

The boys began besting each other in Spanish. No one else, except Jeni and Donavon, could understand what they were saying, but they both seemed to be having a good time. After a few minutes, they stood face to face. Seth put his hand on his brother's shoulder.

70

"*Yo soy el guardián de mi hermano*," he said.

"*Yo soy el guardián de mi hermano*," Solomon echoed.

Juli leaned over to Jeni and asked what they had said. Jeni smiled and put her arm around her sister.

"It means, *I am my brother's keeper.*"

Seth's cellphone went off. He picked it up and looked at the screen to see who was calling. His face went a little red.

"There's his *mami* now," laughed Solomon.

Seth gave him a playful shove as he answered the call.

"Anita, my dove, what... what? Oh, I'm so sorry I forgot to call you back," Seth put the phone to his chest and pointed at Solomon, "and you stay out of my head, little brother!"

He left the room to continue his conversation with Anita. Everyone at the table was laughing.

"What's that supposed to mean?" asked Juli, when Solomon was back at the table with them.

"Can you really get into his head?" Jared added.

"When we were younger, we discovered we could hear each other's thoughts," said Solomon. "We thought it was just a twin thing but, as we got older, we started hearing other people's thoughts too—which you might think was cool but, trust me, sitting in a classroom with thirty other people and hearing who did what with whose girlfriend over the weekend isn't the best way to spend a school day."

"So you can read my mind?" Jeni asked.

"Yes, I can, but I don't," said Solomon quickly. "I've learned to block out most of what people are thinking. All that seeps out now is kind of a general impression or residue of people's thoughts."

"Well, what's my residue?" Jeni asked impulsively.

"Hmph," said Solomon. "When I first met you, I got a lot of embarrassment; but I assume that's normal when you get invited to meet someone new and you are still in your PJs."

71

"Oh great," Jeni said. "I had a feeling you guys were going to remember that."

"Remember that? Jared never shuts up about it!" he laughed. "Anyway, not too long after that, I could hear a lot of random talking, mostly by people with British accents. Also the phrase *1-2-3 shoot*. Can you tell me what that means?"

Jeni looked sad all of a sudden. "I read a lot of Jane Austin novels, and the *1-2-3* thing was my dad's little free-throw shooting routine for me."

"Oh, I'm sorry. I didn't mean to upset you," said Solomon apologetically.

"What about me?" Juli asked timidly.

Solomon turned to face her. "When I met you, I heard music coming from you. Very sweet, soft music, like a string quartet."

Juli blushed.

"She does play the violin quite well. And the viola, and the cello." Jeni put her arm around her sister's shoulders.

"As do I," answered Solomon. "It would be a great privilege to play with you some time." He smiled at Juli as he picked up her hand and touched the calluses on the tips of her fingers. Juli smiled sweetly back at Solomon.

Jared thought it was time to change the subject.

"So, how do you know this Donavon character?" he asked Solomon. "From school or something?"

"No. My brother and I are homeschooled. The whole hearing-other-people's-thoughts thing got in the way of a normal education," said Solomon. "Our parents own a farm about an hour from here. Donavon's dad was a mechanic there a few years back. He worked on tractors and combines and stuff. Now he owns a hardware store in town."

"I see. Have you known him long?" asked Jared.

"Almost my whole life. Why?"

"Just wondering."

"My brother knows him better than I do," said Solomon. "Donavon was crushing on Anita when his family first came to church, but Seth set him straight on that right away. Donavon can be a little aggressive when he wants something, but we've never had cause to worry about him. I can see he likes your sister very much. I noticed him doing his levitating marble trick."

"How does he do that?" Juli asked.

"I don't know exactly. Maybe it's like me and Seth being able to read minds. I know he got teased A LOT in school. Wish we could have been there for him. It's kind of weird for a white kid to be adopted by a Hispanic family. Seth and I don't mind; we love our parents. But I don't think Donavon gets along with his dad very well. I've seen his dad slap him in the head for not doing his chores and stuff, so I guess we understand his anger more than most. They come to church regularly, but that alone doesn't make people good."

"So what kind of residue do you get off him?" asked Jared bluntly.

"Sorry, man, that's personal," Solomon replied. "I don't want to get into the profiling business. I can see that you are worried about your sister. Don't be. Donavon would never hurt anyone, especially a girl. He hates the way his dad treated his mom."

Jared did not look convinced.

"Listen," Solomon tried to reassure Jared. "If I or my brother suspect anything but gentlemanly behavior, we will let you know. Ok? We won't let anything happen to Jillian."

Jared could see the sincerity in Solomon's eyes, and he wanted to believe that Donavon's intentions were pure. But he was resolved to keep a close eye on Jillian. After all, wasn't he supposed to be his sister's keeper?

CHAPTER ELEVEN

Before Breakfast

*Religion that God our Father accepts as pure and faultless
is this: to look after orphans and widows in their distress
and to keep oneself from being polluted by the world.*

James 1:27

Friday, 15th November

Light was shining through the mini blinds and into Roni's
eyes. She sat up in her bed and stretched from head to toe. It
was early morning and chilly in the house, so she looked for
her zebra slippers.

"Not under the bed," she said to herself. "Maybe in the
closet?" She dumped out the contents of a laundry basket in
her closet and came up with one of the missing slippers.

"Story of my life, always one slipper short."

Downstairs, Priscilla was already hard at work preparing
breakfast for everyone. With twelve humans and an unknown
host of angels all wanting to indulge in her cooking, it was a
wonder the guardian ever had time for anything else.

"Morning, baby girl, isn't it a wonderful day the Creator
has made?"

"Um… yeah, it's great," Roni replied. She had never been
a morning person, so she was not yet ready to revel in the
beauty of the day. "Coffee, I need coffee," she said to herself.
"Or Yoo-hoo. I'd settle for a Yoo-hoo."

Music could be heard coming from the living room.
When she peaked around the corner, she saw Juli and
Solomon playing a duet. Her sister had out her violin and
Solomon was playing a cello. The sound was amazing. It had
been a long time since Juli looked so happy. She wondered
how the instruments had gotten there.

"Michael and Uriel must have thought we'd be in need of some music when they first brought Zoei and the twins to the lake house," she said to herself.

Jillian and Donavon were walking around the house. Roni could see them through the kitchen window. Donavon was obviously taken with Jillian, but anyone could see that she was merely trying to be polite as he tried to impress her.

"Poor boy," thought Roni.

On the counter next to Priscilla was a stack of pancakes almost two feet high. The plate near the stove held a mound of bacon, sausage and ham. Several of the early risers had already eaten their breakfast but, as fast as the food was consumed, it was replenished by the guardian, so there was still plenty left for the latecomers.

"Early risers," thought Roni. "I don't know how these people make it on four hours of sleep."

She could smell something sweet coming from the oven. She turned on the interior oven light and sighed in misery at the sight of five beautiful rows of homemade cinnamon rolls.

"Priscilla, you are going to make me fat with all this great cooking, and you are spoiling my sisters. They are going to expect this kind of cooking after you leave."

"Leave, huh! Baby, you ain't never gettin' rid of me! Besides, you've been looking a little scrawny lately. We need to put some meat back on those bones."

It was true that Roni had lost about ten pounds over the last month or so, but that wasn't a problem to her. It was a welcome change to her usual lot in life. It seemed that just looking at food made her gain weight. She wasn't worried about the loss of a few pounds.

The sound of little feet could be heard running from Zoei's bedroom to the stairs. Both Roni and Priscilla looked up at the ceiling.

"Zoei and the boys must be up," said Roni. "Might as well feed them first."

James, John and Zoei came running down the stairs and into the kitchen. The boys were right on Zoei's heels, like chicks following a mother hen.

"Something smells fabulous!" exclaimed Zoei.

"Yeah, fabulous!" echoed the boys.

Roni and Priscilla tried not to laugh when they saw the children. All three were dressed in nothing but their underwear, although Zoei was also sporting a bright pink feather boa that Roni recognized was from her childhood dress-up trunk. Trying to keep a straight face, Roni inquired where their clothes were.

Zoei, of course, had a completely viable explanation. "Nobody set our clean clothes out."

"Well, at least you didn't show up naked. Let's go see if we can find the three of you something to wear."

As Roni and her little chicks were leaving the kitchen, Ryan came upon the merry band of scantily dressed children. He looked at Roni and then at the children and then back at Roni again.

"Well, I'm glad to see that someone set clean clothes out for you today," she said to him and smiled.

He opened his mouth to speak his mind but then thought better of it and let the group pass by without comment.

"She is going to make a wonderful mother someday," said Priscilla, once Roni was out of earshot.

"She sure will," Ryan answered back.

He was lost in thought for a few minutes. Having Roni as the mother of his children would be like a dream come true for him. He smiled as several parental scenarios flashed through his mind.

"So, what are you going to do about it then?"

"What? I don't know... I mean, she doesn't even want to date me, let alone get married and have kids," Ryan said. "Besides, I really shouldn't even be thinking about marriage and family right now. I'm not even nineteen years old. Just because my selective breeding matures me faster than normal people doesn't mean I want to just jump into marriage and babies and... stuff."

"Oh really?" said Priscilla. "You mature faster? What is that supposed to mean? Who told you that?"

"I figured it out during my research. The papers and stuff that we got from Norilsk were mostly about the *AIRborn* children, but I did come across quite a lot of things about the selective breeding program.

"Not only were the scientists—if you can even call them that—breeding children for physical beauty, but whatever 'formula' they had come up with matures us twice as fast mentally, while our bodies develop at a slightly slower but still above-average rate. You could see how that would be an advantage to Ezekiel and whoever else he is working with."

"Interesting," observed Priscilla, a world of meaning in her tone. *Interesting;* not in a scientific or fate-of-the-world kind of way, but in a way that said, *I can draw many inferences about your life from this.*

"What? Why?" questioned Ryan.

"Oh nothing, just *interesting.*"

"I see that look in your eye, Miss Priscilla Matchmaker Angel. Don't you go meddling in—"

"I didn't say a word!" Priscilla threw her hands in the air. "I just thought it was interesting that you're supposed to be more mature than Roni. That's all. You can read whatever you like into it."

Ryan was about to delve further into the discussion when he heard a commotion out on the driveway. Opening the front door, he saw Jared and Seth out by Roni's van. They were struggling with something in the back seat. He walked toward the van, and Jillian and Donavon met up with him near the front of the vehicle. Walking up behind Jared, they could see immediately what the problem was.

An unconscious man was belted in, directly behind the front passenger seat. He was bleeding from a large gash on his forehead and his clothes were bloody and torn. It was difficult to make out his age because of all the blood.

Jeni came around from the driver's side and said, "We went out to get some milk and found him by the side of the road."

As Seth and Jared wriggled the man out of the van, Ryan checked his pulse. It was very weak.

"Ok, get him inside on the dining room table. Let me get my stuff and I'll meet you there."

Ryan sprinted to his room and was back in fifteen seconds. He shouted orders as he ran over to the kitchen sink and began to wash his hands.

"Is the table clear? Someone check his wrists and neck and see if he has a medical alert pendant on. Roni, get me your dad's old first-aid kit. Maybe there's some stuff in it we can use, if it's not too out of date; looks like we are going to need a lot of bandages. Can someone try to dial 911? Juli, I want you to assist me. Come wash your hands."

Juli went over to the kitchen sink and rolled up the sleeves of her sweater. She was shaking as she poured the antibacterial dish soap onto her hands.

"Don't be stingy with the soap," Ryan told her. "Anybody have an extra toothbrush? Juli, more soap. *Juli!*"

Juli jumped when Ryan yelled her name. Her eyes welled up with tears. She rinsed her hands off and ran out of the kitchen. Roni came up beside Ryan with a nailbrush.

"Hey, you hurt Juli's feelings."

"I don't have time to mess around, Roni. Besides, as I recall, she always liked to bandage up the cats when we were kids. She was always fixing Jeni's scraped knees. I thought she would like to help, but if she can't take the pressure..."

Roni scooted her way between Ryan and the sink and looked up at him fiercely.

"That was Jeni who used to bandage the cats and Juli's knees. Juli faints at the sight of blood, you big jerk!" She pushed her finger as hard as she could into Ryan's chest. "And, if you EVER, EVER talk to one of my sisters like that again, so help me, I will knock your teeth out of your head!"

If they hadn't been so pressed for time, the rest of the people in the room would have loved to see the conclusion of that fight; but there was a bleeding man on the dining table.

"I'm sorry, Roni." Ryan knew he had been a horse's rear. "I was being a jerk. I will apologize to Juli after I have taken care of this man."

Just then Seth came into the kitchen. "I'm not getting any service on my phone right now."

It was quiet and Roni looked like she wasn't going to let Ryan off the hook so easily.

"Hello, no phone service," Seth said again; but all eyes were on Roni and Ryan.

Roni backed down because she knew Ryan wasn't mean-spirited; he had got caught up in the moment, in the exigencies of attending to the critically injured man.

"Fine," Roni said without taking her eyes off him. "Jeni, Ryan needs your nursing skills. Wash up."

After Ryan had finished washing his hands, he grabbed a pair of nitrile gloves out of his medical backpack and made his way over to the dining table. Soft moaning sounds were coming from the injured man, but no one could make out what he was saying.

"Can anybody else help out?" Ryan asked in a much humbler tone. "His clothes need to be cut off."

"I got that," said Jillian.

"Me too," said Jared.

After they had all washed their hands and put on nitrile gloves, they began cutting the man's pants off. Rocks and dirt were falling off his clothes, which were almost in shreds. His knees had gravel crushed into them and were bleeding.

Donavon snagged a cinnamon roll and sat down on a bar stool to observe everything from a distance. He wondered why those people cared so much about a stranger.

"Probably just a hobo who had a few too many drinks," he thought to himself. He looked at Jillian. Her eagerness to get away from him and help this vagrant turned his stomach.

Jeni began to cut his shirt off. Blood had made its way from his hands down to his elbows. She noticed ligature marks around his wrists. Looking over at Ryan, she motioned toward the deep impressions in the man's hands.

"Who could have done this?" she said out loud.

"I don't know," the doctor said, shaking his head.

"Can someone go get my tweezers out of my bathroom?" Jillian asked.

China, who had just come down the stairs, turned around and went back to the bedroom she shared with Jillian. She found a purple set of tweezers in Jillian's bathroom drawer and hurried out of the bedroom with them, trying not to awaken Allyson.

She wasn't sure what was going on downstairs or why Jillian needed tweezers in the dining room. She wondered if one of the little kids had a splinter or something. When she delivered the tiny instrument to Jillian, she found out what all the fuss was about.

Ryan was at one end of the dining room, looking into the eyes of an injured man who was lying on the table. He kept shining a light in them and then away. She wondered why doctors did that.

Roni was cutting the man's shirt off. China cringed; she could almost hear the fabric being peeled back. Dried blood made the shirt stick to his arm and chest. The patient cried out faintly, but he was mostly in a delirious state.

Jillian and Jared were trying to cut the pants off, but they were running into the same problem as Roni. The dried blood was making it almost impossible to remove the clothing without causing more pain and suffering to the man. Skin was beginning to come off with the fabric.

"Stop! Stop! Stop!" screamed China covering her ears.

Everyone was looking at her now. Covering her mouth with one hand, she grabbed at her hair with the other hand and began twisting it nervously. She felt exposed.

"What is it, China?" said Ryan.

She was quiet for a moment as thoughts of her last beating from Joseph filled her mind. With tear-filled eyes she explained, "I was going to say, if you wet the clothes, then you won't hurt me... I mean him... so... um... much."

"Good thinking, Sis," said Ryan, and he smiled at her. "Roni, could you and Jillian make up some warm water to clean these wounds? Jared, there's some painter's plastic in the garage, above the washer and dryer. We need to put plastic over and under the table so we don't damage the carpet or the furniture."

After Jared had returned with the plastic, Solomon helped him lay it down under the table, while Seth moved all the chairs out of the dining room. Bowls of warm water were brought in, and the helpers began to soak the man's clothes off and wash his wounds, while the guardians kept watch close by.

Roni was cleaning the large gash on the man's head. Once the dirt and gravel were removed, it began to bleed profusely. Ryan called for more hand towels so that they could stop the bleeding.

Jeni was still working on removing the man's shirt. She tried to brush the soil gently out of the lesions around his wrist. As it was coming clean, something else began to appear: five circular scars on the top of his hand, all equal in size, although some looked older than others. She thought maybe they were acid burns or something like that.

"Jared, look at this," said Jillian.

"Wow," Jared exclaimed.

Jeni looked over at them. Jillian was pointing to the top of the man's foot. Jared was stunned as he looked at the foot his sister was working on and then back to where he was cleaning. Jeni stood up and went to the end of the table. The same marks were on both of the man's feet. She gasped and covered her mouth as the realization sunk in, of what the small, circular scars were...

"What is it, Jeni?" asked Jared.

Without looking, she reached back for the injured hand and held it up, so that Jared and Jillian could see it.

"What are they?" asked Jillian.

She looked at her brother and Jeni. The two were locked in each other's gaze. Jeni tried to speak, but no words would come out. Her eyes glistened.

"Jared, what's going on?"

"They are cigarette burns, Jillian," Jared said quietly. "This man has been tortured."

"Tortured!" exclaimed Jillian.

The room fell silent. Jared took his bowl of warm water and poured it over the rest of the man's lower leg. He then ripped what little fabric remained off the pants. He reached over and took Jillian's bowl. He poured out the remaining water and exposed at least a hundred more burn scars.

The rest of Ryan's impromptu medical staff gasped at the sight of the man's skin. Ryan wanted to be sick, but he knew he had to hold it together. He examined the scars closely.

"Jared's right," Ryan pronounced. "I'm pretty sure these scars were once cigarette burns. Not only was this man tortured, but it's likely the torture extended over a long period of time, possibly years."

Jillian could not stifle her tears any longer.

"Who...who would do such a thing?" she sobbed and turned away from the table. She hung onto her brother's neck and wept.

The girls were crying now. The boys tried to comfort them, but they themselves were having a hard time holding back their tears.

China was the only girl who was not crying. She knelt down next to the table and took hold of the patient's hand. She whispered something into his ear. Once again, everyone in the room was astonished as she called the man's name.

"Victor. Victor, can you hear me? Victor Green, can you hear me? It's China. Victor, wake up!"

CHAPTER TWELVE

The Valkyries

Satan himself masquerades as an angel of light.

2 Corinthians 11:14

"Victor Green?" said Solomon. "As in the man who tried to sell James and John to Joseph? What is he doing out of jail?"

"He must have gotten out on a technicality or something," said Seth.

Roni took a step back from Victor. "Well, I'm not sure I want to give aid to a child predator."

"Someone must have got to him after he was released," suggested Jared.

"What? This guy's a perv? Call the cops. We don't need his kind around here," Donavon declared self-righteously.

"Never mind about that right now," Ryan replied. "We need to get these wounds cleaned and patched up as soon as possible before infection sets in."

He began working on Victor again. The entire room was silent.

"Did anyone else try 911 again?" he inquired.

Nobody moved.

Ryan didn't even look up when he spoke again.

"I took an oath that, loosely translated, goes something like this—first, do no harm. So, unless you can put your prejudices aside and help me, then leave the room, please."

Reluctantly, the others started cleaning Victor's wounds again. China stayed close to his head and continued to try to rouse her semi-conscious friend.

"What is she doing?" thought Roni. "Why is she being so attentive to this man who sells children for a living?"

"I can't believe you guys are helping this child trafficker!" Donavon bellowed.

Seth grabbed his friend by the arm. "Amigo, chill! Let the doctor do his work."

Donavon stormed out of the house.

China started stroking Victor's head. A few pebbles, liberated from his matted brown hair by her fingers, fell into the puddles of blood and water underneath the table. The cut on his head was still bleeding. She reached over and tried to stop the blood flow with her hand, but it kept seeping between her fingers. Roni handed her a fresh cloth.

"Come on, Victor, wake up. It's your little teapot. Please wake up." China began to sing the familiar nursery rhyme about a little teapot softly into his ear.

He stopped murmuring for a few moments as the sweet song floated into the air. His mind seemed to quieten for the first time since he had been brought into the house. China removed the cloth from the cut. Blood was still coming from the wound.

Roni leaned in close to China and whispered into her ear, "We just can't get the bleeding to stop."

Then, as if a light bulb had been turned on in her mind, China laid her hand on Victor's head. She steadied her gaze on his face.

"Look!" exclaimed Jared. He was pointing at the soft yellow glow coming from beneath China's hand.

Victor began thrashing about.

"Hold him down!" exclaimed Ryan.

They did their best to restrain the man, who looked as if he was being tortured instead of healed.

He started yelling, "Esperanza! Espe! I'm sorry, I'm sorry! I swear I'll come back for you! Espe!"

Victor's eyes were wide open as he called out the name. He wrestled one hand free and reached out into the air. Ryan and Jared were trying hard to keep him from falling off the table.

Tears ran down Victor's face as he reached for the ceiling. Seth and Solomon hurried forward to help Ryan and Jared keep the patient safe. Then, just when it seemed like Victor was going to overpower them, he collapsed and was silent.

The room was quiet again. Everyone looked at each other, hoping the ordeal was over. Sweat was pouring down the faces of the young men who had tried to restrain Victor.

Then, just as everyone was starting to breathe a little easier, a gradual chill came over China. Fear gripped her heart. Sensing an all-too-familiar presence, she released Victor's head and started to back away into a corner of the dining room. She shut her eyes and covered her ears as she crouched down, trying to make herself as small and invisible as possible.

"No, no, no," she whispered softly. She began rocking back and forth.

Ryan knelt down beside his sister.

"What is it, China? What's the matter?"

"They are here."

"Who are here?"

"Them."

Ryan could not see or hear anything.

"China, I don't..." he began.

His words were cut off by a high-pitched scream that invaded every corner of his mind. He put his hands over his ears, trying to find some relief from the awful sound. Leaning back on his heels, he steadied his body against the wall.

He turned his head towards Victor and observed a shimmering figure standing over the injured man. It had the appearance of a woman. Her skin was white, almost like silver, and her wavy black hair hung down around Victor's head as she leaned over him. An orange mist was flowing from between her red lips and into Victor's nose and mouth. His eyes were half-opened, his eyelids relaxed.

All became quiet, and Ryan removed his hands from his ears. The mystical being turned her gaze upon him as she continued to direct her toxic vapor toward the man on the table. She gave him a saucy smile. Ryan thought she was the most beautiful creature he had ever seen. Dark eyes and perfect red lips. Her black lace dress hugged her figure in all the right places. Around her throat was a black ribbon adorned with a lace flower. He was dazzled by her brilliance and beauty.

After a few minutes, she stood up straight. Tipping her head back and closing her eyes, she breathed in deeply and removed from her head a helmet such as Ryan had only seen in mythological movies and books. She opened her eyes and, sauntering over to the young doctor, reached her hand out to him. Her other hand, gripping the hilt of a silver sword, flexed and then relaxed.

He took her hand and stood up. He was face to face with her now. She smelled of freshly picked strawberries.

"Hello," she said, flashing a smile at him. That one word resonated throughout his body—like a quiet stream, flowing gently down the twists and turns of a mountain meadow.

"H-hello," said Ryan nervously.

"You're so very..." she paused for a moment, then put her delicate hands around his neck. She ran her finger inside the collar of his shirt. The hairs on his neck and arms stood up.

Walking behind him, she whispered the rest of her sentence into his ear, "So very... human."

"Um... thank you?" Ryan wasn't sure how to respond.

"So vulnerable and exposed," she blew delicately into his other ear, "...and soft."

Ryan's head was starting to feel light and his eyes a bit heavy as she moved to stand face to face with him once more. She blew her orange mist gently into his face. The scent of wild strawberries was intoxicating.

"I'm... I'm...." was all he could get out.

"I'm Mist...or Misty, if you prefer. And you must be Ryan. Ryan Miller," she smiled ardently. "You're famous where I come from. I heard you and your... ah... girlfriend really stuck it to Ezekiel."

Misty leaned back on the corner of the dining table and crossed her arms.

"Well, we did what we had to," Ryan answered slowly. He was getting fixated on what appeared to be a red tattoo peeking out from the low-cut neckline of her dress.

Misty threw her head back and scoffed lightly. She was amused at the human's attempt to put a coherent thought together while fighting her fumes. She looked down at her feet and simpered as she began to reel Ryan in.

"I also heard an insane rumor that, even after all you did for her, she still won't give you the satisfaction of one... small... little... kiss... or anything. A girl like her should learn that a little gratitude goes a long, long way."

She stood up again and walked over to Ryan, who was almost in a state of complete disorientation.

"I... um..." He could barely put two words together.

Misty put her arms back around his neck and casually brushed her lips up against his.

"Now, I'm the kind of girl who knows how to show appreciation. I could offer you many pleasantries that...

would make you… extremely… satisfied." She kissed his neck intermittently, and her seductive powers began to take over his will.

"What? Wait…" Ryan protested.

"What? Do you have somewhere else to be?" she backed away, pretending to be bothered by his rejection. "Oh, it's that other girl; the *chubby* one. Well, if that's what you want… but just keep this in mind… I—"

She was cut off by the sudden interruption of someone throwing his body against hers. Both figures crashed through one of the dining room windows. When Misty regained her composure, she recognized her opponent immediately. Michael stood only a few feet away with his sword drawn.

"Back away, Katrina!"

"Don't call me that, you… you… subordinate drone!" Misty hissed at Michael as if she were a snake backed into a corner. She had her sword drawn and was crouched down in a position that told Michael she was ready to defend herself.

"What do you want here?"

"Only to claim what is mine."

"And what would that be?"

"The human lying on the table in there; he sold his soul to me, and I've come to collect it."

"Where is his guardian?"

Misty suddenly changed her demeanor. She knew she was outmatched in size and strength when compared to the massive archangel, so she decided to try a somewhat softer approach.

"He's busy right now," she said in a velvety tone, "and he asked me to look out for Victor until he gets back."

Michael knew she was lying but he hadn't quite figured out her game, so he decided to play along for a few minutes.

"What is he doing that is so important he would leave his charge with one of the Valkyries?"

"He didn't really have time to say. He was a little... ah... tied up at the time," she smiled shrewdly.

"I see. I will take over the care of the human. You may go on your way."

Misty's anger was beginning to boil over at the assertive presumption of the Watcher.

"No," she said firmly. "He is mine."

"You are mistaken, Katrina. He belongs to the Creator."

At the sound of her former name, Misty went wild and charged at Michael. She knew she was no match for the angel, but she rushed at him anyway. Her sword flashed in the morning sunlight as she felled one blow after another. But, though Michael was not completely recovered from his back injury, he easily defended himself.

When Misty had nearly worn herself out, she stopped to catch her breath. Michael was just about to speak when the Valkyrie lifted up her head and let out a high-pitched scream. Michael was taken aback by the noise for a few moments and closed his eyes to get his bearings.

When he opened them again, he wasn't completely surprised to see four more women of unspeakable beauty standing before him. They were what was left of the Valkyries. Michael had not seen or heard anything of their whereabouts for a few hundred years.

"Maybe you remember my sisters," said Misty with a sneer.

Michael looked the small group over carefully. He did recognize them. Eir stood next to Misty. She was tall, towering over her companions. She had the same silvery skin as Misty, but her hair was light brown and her eyes were sea green. Her entire body was covered in orange tribal tattoos.

Michael could see another of the bewitching figures behind Eir. He knew it was Prima because of the white dress that was peeking out from behind the taller Valkyrie. Not only was her dress white, but her skin and hair and everything else about her were white too. Even her eyes had no pupils or coloring in them. Though she looked peaceful, her mastery of the *Sai*, an ancient Japanese weapon, was paramount and more deadly than any other's.

Rota was on the other side of Misty. Her colorless face and scarlet hair were almost entirely covered by a hooded robe of blue velvet. The robe also concealed her clothes and any weapons she might be carrying; but Michael knew that she most likely had an entire arsenal of knives underneath her disguise. Her cool blue eyes glared from beneath her hood.

The final Valkyrie, Brynhildr, had long black hair. She wore a bodysuit of black leather with a luminous chainmail tunic. A ring adorned with a single sapphire hung from a chain around her neck. She gripped the hilt of her sword and stared violently at Michael, as if she could kill him with her violet eyes.

"Bryn."

"Michael."

"How have you been?"

"How do you think?"

The tension was building up, and Michael was becoming painfully aware that he was outnumbered. He could have taken on any four of the Valkyries but, with Bryn there, the fighting was going to be ten times fiercer. She hated Michael with a fiery rage that could not be extinguished.

"You are protecting a soul that belongs to us," Bryn snarled.

"I believe Katrina and I have already discussed this."

"Don't call me that!" Misty screamed.

"Where is Victor's guardian?"

"You will never find him," Prima stated coldly. "We have almost turned him to our cause. It cannot be long now."

"You cannot separate a guardian and a human so easily."

"Easy? You think what we did to him was easy!" scoffed Misty. "I had to use…"

"Never mind what we did," Bryn interrupted hastily as she stepped in front of Misty. "He left his charge unattended. He practically gave him up without a fight. You guardians, you think you're so valiant, so spiritually superior. But, deep down inside, you are just like us—always wanting more than what the Creator granted us. You love, you hate, you lust… you desire to have all you can…

"In fact, I was watching yesterday when that charming little social worker revealed her feelings for you. I almost fell down laughing when I saw your face. In all the centuries we have lived, no one has ever been able to tempt the great archangel Michael. For a second there, I thought you were going to kiss her."

"That's enough, Bryn! Go from this place while you still can." Michael was beginning to get angry. "You shall not have Victor, and you will release his guardian immediately!"

Bryn drew her sword slowly out of its sheath.

"Why don't you come over here, and we will discuss my terms of release?" she said.

Michael lifted his sword Adoni-Zedek in front of his face. "Very well."

CHAPTER THIRTEEN

Bryn

For though we live in the world, we do not wage war as the world does. The weapons we fight with are not the weapons of the world. On the contrary, they have divine power to demolish strongholds.

2 Corinthians 10:3-4

Michael and Bryn circled one another on the lawn, each trying to anticipate the other's movements. The conflict between them had been going on for almost a thousand years now and, though Michael had not seen Bryn for over two hundred of them, it was clear she had not got over what she called his unforgivable offense against her.

"I have not forgotten what you did on the island, Michael!" Bryn shouted.

Michael looked directly into the Valkyrie's blazing eyes. "Even though what happened was an accident, Bryn, you know the Creator's laws about cohabiting with humans—let alone trying to reproduce with them."

"I don't care about His stupid laws. I had love, and you took it away. Why couldn't you have just left us alone? We were on an island in the middle of nowhere. We weren't hurting anyone. Jade was a good man, and our daughter was the light of our life!"

Michael saw her eyes glistening in the morning sun and had a brief moment of pity for the fallen angel.

"Your daughter had already burned down over half of the island's vegetation by the time we found you and..."

"Don't you speak of Lilly!" Bryn screamed and lunged at Michael in one immense leap.

The Archangel barely had time to circumvent her sword. He dived to his left in an attempt to draw Bryn's attention away from the house. The pain in his back was excruciating.

Gabriel and Uriel appeared outside ready for battle. With their wings, Raphael and the other guardians formed an interlocking airtight seal around the lake house.

Rota's blue cape fell from her shoulders. Before the hood had even hit the ground, she had released two sets of knives. Her intended target was Gabriel, who would have dodged them easily if he hadn't been caught up in a too-close-for comfort struggle with Prima and her deadly *Sai*. One of Rota's knives nicked his calf. The sting distracted the angel long enough for the white Valkyrie to kick him in the chest, sending him soaring thirty feet across the yard. She gave chase, intending to put an end to him; but Gabriel was back on his feet, ready to go on the offensive.

Misty and Eir each took on one of Uriel's famous flaming swords. The more they dished out, the more competently he defended himself. Misty was becoming enraged with Uriel as her attack strategy became less and less effective.

Bryn continued to trade blows with Michael. For every two strikes he landed on her, she came back with three more. He was beginning to weaken quickly.

"Not so mighty now, Michael," she taunted. She was breathing heavily and the urge to lean over and catch her breath was almost too much for her to overcome. But she forced herself to stand erect in order to intimidate her foe.

"Come on! Is this how you fight for your woman? Thought you cared a little more than this."

Michael hung his head and leaned against a nearby tree. He could feel the wounds on his back burning through the bandages Ryan had just replaced that morning. A wound from a mortal should not be affecting him in such a perilous way.

Looking back at Bryn, he said, "I have no woman. You know this to be true."

"Well, she could be yours. Or, I could just make her pay for Jade, like she was your woman. You at least care for her."

Bryn walked around Michael and kicked him in the back of his leg. He fell to his knees. She continued walking around him cautiously, getting closer to him than she had ever dared. She pulled a small knife out of a scabbard strapped to her thigh and lifted the archangel's head with the tip of it.

"So the rumors are true," Bryn said.

"What rumors?"

"Well, a little bird told me that Ezekiel and his swarm have figured out how to put an end to you and your kind."

"Why do you continue to fight against the Creator?" Michael whispered. "You already know how all this will end."

Bryn threw back her head and laughed.

"Stupid angel, of course I know how the story ends," she said derisively. "But that doesn't mean I can't enjoy the middle of the book. Plus, I can insert a few lines of my own."

She flicked her knife from under his chin, leaving a deep gash on his jawline. Michael winced from the sting.

"This is going to be quite enjoyable. And, when I'm done with you, I'm going to pay a visit to your favorite social worker." Bryn put the knife away and heaved her weapon over her head.

Michael closed his eyes and appealed to the Creator for help. A moment later, a crash was heard coming from the direction of the house. Looking beneath his arm, Michael saw Roni and Ryan, along with Priscilla and Oriel, running towards him. While they were running, their swords reflected beams of light that caught Bryn in the eye. She stumbled back several steps, caught her foot on a tree root, dropped her sword, and fell.

Oriel reached her first. She shielded her eyes from his brilliance.

"Looks like you're all out of moves, Bryn," he said to her, pointing his sword at her chest.

Unfazed, she tried to get up but found herself pinned to the ground. She looked up at him and grinned slightly.

"And it looks like you brought a sword to a knife fight!" With that, she hit her heel on the ground, and a three-inch blade slid into place at the tip of her boot.

In a split second, Oriel realized what was about to happen. But he was a split second too slow to avoid Bryn's foot as it came into contact with the side of his knee. Oriel let out a roar and reached down to pull the Valkyrie's foot away from his leg. She rolled over and grabbed her sword. She would have liked to stay and finish the fight, but it was clear to her that she and her sisters were outnumbered.

Like a bottle rocket, she shot up into the sky, her shrill voice screeching out a summons to her troop to leave. And then the skirmish was over.

***

Ryan and Oriel tried to help Michael to his feet, struggling under the massive angel's weight, for he was almost unconscious. Several Watchers who had been guarding the house left their positions to assist their injured leader.

When Ryan and Roni saw Michael getting hammered by Bryn, they had begged their guardians to let them go and help him. At first, the guardians had resisted, pointing out that they were sealed in by a host of angels' wings. But, when a way past the airtight seal was suddenly opened, the humans had taken it as a sign and bolted through the opening, and their guardians had followed.

But now, as the humans and angels tried to get Michael into the house, a problem arose. Michael was having difficulty maintaining his human form. Transforming back and forth between a six-and-a-half-foot human and a nine-or-ten-foot angel was causing the humans to be shuffled forwards and backwards in such a way that eventually someone was going to get hurt. When Michael's feet went through the sliding glass doors in the family room, Ryan called a halt to the effort.

"This whole house is going to come crumbling down on us," he panted. "We have to come up with another option for Michael or find a new base of operations. Any ideas?"

"Can we stop whatever is happening to him?" asked Roni.

"Only when an angel is severely injured does this happen," said Priscilla. "We need a healer."

"First, we need a place to put him," Oriel added. "Some place where he can be well-hidden—and some place that he can't destroy in his present condition."

"What about the caves, Roni?" said Ryan. "If we can get him through the entrance, there's plenty of room for him to grow and shrink without injuring anyone or damaging anymore property."

Roni looked down at her feet. She knew this was her fault. If she hadn't been so selfish at the hospital and injured Michael, they wouldn't be considering putting the Creator's right-hand angel in a cave like an animal.

"Roni. Roni," Ryan was trying to get her attention.

A tear fell from Roni's eye and hit Michael's forehead. Her eyes were closed and she felt a hand take hold of hers. It was Ryan. She looked up, and he brushed the tears from her face.

"He's going to be ok. We will figure this out. Together."

Roni shook her head.

"Ok," said Ryan, "to the caves."

CHAPTER FOURTEEN

Donavon

*A hot-tempered man must pay the penalty; if you
rescue him, you will have to do it again.*

Proverbs 19:19

After Ryan and Roni had Michael somewhat settled in a big
cave, they and their guardians made a beeline back to the
lake house to check on their family and friends.

"Great, another hole in the house," said Roni, looking at
the dining room where Michael and Misty had blasted
through the window. Not only was the glass broken, but the
frame and part of the wall were missing as well. "Not to
mention that we are going to need a new sliding glass door
for the family room."

Ryan put his arm around her shoulders. "Don't worry,
Rapunzel, we'll get your castle back in order soon."

Roni rolled her eyes at the mention of his pet name for
her. Seth and Solomon came out of the house through what
was formerly the sliding glass door.

"Do you guys always have to make such a mess when you
fight with the bad guys?" Solomon asked.

"In this case, I think you mean bad girls, little brother,"
Seth said in jest. "And don't you dare tell Anita that I said
this, but those chicks were H-O-T!"

"Yeah, that was weird," Solomon added. "I thought all
the bad guys would be... you know... ugly."

"The Scriptures tell us that even the Dark One
masquerades as an angel of light," Saffron said as she and
Lorrel materialized next to Solomon.

"I suppose we should be used to that by now," said Roni,
who was startled by the guardians' sudden appearance.

"So, who were those girls... angels... or whatever they were," asked Ryan.

"They are the Valkyries," said Saffron.

"The Valkyries?" questioned Seth. "What? Like in the movie?"

"Really, Seth?" said Solomon. "I'm pretty sure none of those girls looked like Tom Cruise."

"The Valkyries," began Saffron, "are a consensus of fallen angels who have fashioned themselves into the most sensuous of all beings. Their beauty is said to have rivaled that of Lucifer himself."

"Humanly speaking," continued Lorrel," they are the most bewitching creatures man has ever had to defend himself against. But let us continue this narrative after we have secured this dwelling for the humans."

They spent the next two hours covering the new holes in the house with plastic and duct tape. A new window and glass door were order through Donavon's family store.

"If this keeps up, my father won't have to worry about paying for me to go to college," said Donavon. "What happened here, anyway? One minute you guys were in here helping the perv, and the next thing I hear is that big guy Michael going through the wall."

"Don't call him that!" Jillian exclaimed. "You don't know his life!"

"Oh, and you do?" Donavon lashed out at Jillian.

Jared was immediately in Donavon's face. "Hey! Don't you ever speak to my sister like that again!"

"Or else what?" Donavon spat back. "You gonna call your little angel friends to help you? Well, I got my own friends..."

Ryan put himself between the two enraged young men. Seth grabbed Donavon from behind, while Solomon tried to control Jared.

"Alright, that's enough, you two!" shouted Ryan.

Jared backed down, but Donavon continued to resist all their efforts to restrain him. Seth and Solomon tried to get Donavon to leave the area. Ryan motioned to Jared to go back inside, which he did. But he never broke eye contact with Donavon, who was yelling obscenities all the way around the side of the house. Only when the two brothers had him pinned tightly against the wall did he acquiesce.

"Dude! What's wrong with you?" Seth demanded. "You can't just come around here and start fights. We've got little kids here. Plus, it's not the best way to win Jillian over."

The brothers let Donavon go. He paced in a circle with his arms over his head, taking deep breaths in and out. His face began to drain of its scarlet color.

"Hey man," said Seth gently after a few more minutes had gone by. "This is what the school counselor used to tell us about, when we were in Junior High. You need to control your temper and not let it control you."

"I know," Donavon finally said. "It's so different now that you guys aren't at school anymore. We used to have each other's backs when Carlos and his posse harassed us. But now it's just me. My dad says I just gotta toughen up. He doesn't want his boy acting like a sissy."

"How's it going with your dad, anyway?" asked Solomon.

"The same," Donavon mumbled. "Worse since mom died."

The boys were quiet for a while. Then Donavon continued, "Only two more years. If I can just hold out two more years, I can rid myself of him."

Seth put an arm around his friend's shoulder.

"I'm sorry, man. I know having to go to that school alone kinda sucks, and I don't have all the answers to life. But I do know that we have to try to do the right thing, no matter what.

Remember that crazy Sunday school teacher we used to have? The one with the purple hair?"

"Mrs Smelt," said Solomon.

"Yeah, that's her, Mrs Smelt! What a terrible last name!"

The boys all laughed. Then Seth said, "I remember all those goofy skits she made us act out for the little kids."

"And the double chocolate chip cookies she would bring us every Sunday morning," Solomon added.

"Don't forget her pet dove, that left a surprise on your head the day everyone was supposed to have family pictures taken," Donavon laughed a little.

"Yeah, yeah, I remember," said Seth. "But the thing I remember most is her favorite Bible verse, *Colossians 3:17—* 'And whatever you do, whether in word or deed, do it all in the name of the Lord Jesus.'

"Her last Christmas, she made us all those bookmarks with the verse stitched on it. I still have mine in my Bible, and it reminds me that *all* my actions are important and, whatever I do, I gotta think about God the Creator and what He wants me to do."

Donavon pondered over what Seth had said for a moment. Then he said bitterly, "You know, I never quite bought into all that Sunday-school-Jesus-Bible stuff. I came to church 'cos my dad made me go; but, after mom died, it felt like we just went to keep up appearances. Honestly, I've found every reason I can to avoid that place.

"If this Jesus loves us so much, where was He when my dad was slapping my mom around? And where were the church members when my dad, deacon extraordinaire, chained me to the pole in the basement because he was tired of listening to me cry night after night about my dog that he shot? Tell me, where were they? Huh? Everybody knew it was happening, but nobody did a thing!"

"You know our parents tried to help out, Don," Solomon said defensively, "but, every time they called the cops or mentioned it to the church board, your mom would dismiss the charges or make up some excuse about falling down the steps. Seriously, how many times can a person fall in the basement of the house she's lived in her whole life!"

"You've got no right to judge me or my mom!" Donavon screamed as he shoved Solomon into the side of the house.

Solomon threw his hands up. "Ok, Ok, man. I'm sorry, Don..." Donavon had put his hands around Solomon's throat.

"Don! Stop, man, stop!" Seth tried to free his brother from Donavon's grip. Solomon's face was red and his eyes were rolling back in his head.

Suddenly a face superimposed itself on Solomon's. It was Saffron. "Let him go, Donavon!"

Donavon trembled as he stepped back and released his friend. Solomon dropped to his knees, clutching his throat and coughing violently.

"I'm sorry, I'm sorry!" said Donavon, walking away quickly.

Seth helped his brother to his feet. "Let him go. He needs to walk it off."

***

Back at the house, Jillian was still upset. She was crying and Jared was trying to comfort her the best he could.

"Hey, I'm really sorry about Donavon," said Seth sympathetically. "He's a good guy, really. He's just had a rough life."

"Well, I'm sorry about his rough life," Jared said, his tone slightly cynical, "but I don't want him anywhere near my sister. I don't like the way he looks at her."

"We get it, ok?" Seth replied. "But we aren't going to leave our friend hanging out to dry. He needs us, whether he thinks he does or not."

Ryan put a hand on Seth's shoulder. "You are right. Your friend needs you, but perhaps he should go home for now."

"Look, Ryan, I can't in good conscience send him home. His dad is..." Seth tried to get the words out, but his tears kept interrupting his plea. "He's just mean..." was all he could get out.

"We are his family," Solomon added. "He has no one but us to care about him."

Ryan was quiet for a few moments as he prayed for wisdom. He wanted to balance mercy and justice with grace and wisdom. His parents had always loved him, even when he was a prodigal son; so he had compassion for Donavon, a lost boy with no one to help him but these two young men.

"Alright, here's what we'll do," said Ryan. "He can stay, but he has to leave the girls alone. He must stay away from them, and he is not to go upstairs to their living space. Also, I never want to hear that profanity coming from him again. We have small, impressionable children here, and that's the last thing I want them to pick up. And, lastly, one of you two has to be with him at all times. He eats with you, he works with you, and he sleeps in your room downstairs with you."

"Can he go to the bathroom alone?" Seth said caustically.

Solomon put his hand on Seth's shoulder and moved in front of him. "Yes, thank you, Ryan. We will let Donavon know," he said as he hurried his brother into the next room.

"What's with you, dude?" Solomon whispered. "You know Ryan is in the right. Something is going on with Donavon. We both know it; I mean, he just tried to strangle me!"

Seth knew that his brother was right. He was just so frustrated that he couldn't seem to reach his friend; it felt like it was too late, like Donavon had crossed a line and couldn't find his way back. Solomon could feel his brother's thoughts and sought to comfort him.

"Don't worry, brother. We'll find him and bring him back."

CHAPTER FIFTEEN

Light Soup

In him was life, and that life was the light of men.
The light shines in the darkness, but the
darkness has not understood it.

John 1:4-5

It was dark by the time Ryan and Jared made their way back across the open field. Michael had been alone for hours in the cave while things were getting organized at the lake house. Victor was resting comfortably, and Ryan knew that Jillian and Jeni would see to his needs for the night. With the Valkyries and the local police after him, it wasn't safe to take him to a hospital. Juli and China still needed extra rest, so Seth, Solomon and Donavon were left to guard the house, along with a whole army of angels.

Ryan was anxious to get back to his patient. They had taken some medical supplies and bedding with them to treat Michael's injuries and also to get some sleep if the opportunity presented itself. Jared didn't like the idea of Donavon staying at the lake house overnight, but he would yield to Ryan just this once.

Upon entering the cave, they could see the glow of firelight from back behind the first bend in the cavern wall. Ryan, who was in the lead, put one hand on Jared's chest and the other to his lips, signifying silence. He peeked around the bend cautiously and then started making hand gestures at Jared. Jared raised his eyebrows and stared in confusion.

"Sorry, I'm not familiar with super-action-spy-commando-school hand signals," Jared said to himself.

In frustration, Ryan began again to signal to Jared.

"Oh yeah, doing it slower helps."

104

Finally, Jared waved Ryan off and bent forward to peep around the corner too. Two figures came into view. Jared backed up and put up two fingers. Ryan grabbed Jared by the shirt and they backed out of the cave.

"That's what I said!" Ryan whispered to Jared.

"No, you said this," and Jared began a comical string of crazy hand motions in front of Ryan's face.

"No, I said..." Ryan made the same signals as before, but this time he spoke the words as well: "Two people...no weapons ... you make distraction...I run to Michael...then circle back..."

"You left out the part about them making soup..."

Just then, they heard a twig snap.

"If you gentlemen would like to warm yourselves, you are more than welcome. We have prepared a light soup as well, if you are interested."

Both boys whirled around, and an unexpected sight met their eyes; a small, winged creature was looking up at them. She was no taller than Zoei and wore a dark orange tunic. Her little bird-like wings were tucked close to her body, and they were the same color as her clothes. They watched the tiny creature closely as they followed her into the cave.

Ryan glanced over at Michael, who was resting quietly a little way from the fire. He appeared to be holding his human form, which would make it easier for Ryan to examine his wounds. A soft glow was pulsing on his chest and Ryan wanted to make his way to the angel without delay; but his curiosity about the little creatures got the better of him and distracted him from attending to his patient.

Their escort made her way to her companion, who appeared to be similar to herself, only blue. All blue. In fact, as the humans approached the firelight, they saw that both creatures were entirely one color. Hair, skin, eyes, clothes and wings. One orange and one blue.

The look of shock on the young men's faces seemed to amuse the orange creature, and she smiled as she spoke.

"I am Carnelian, and this is Lapis. We are healers. We have come to look after Michael until he is restored."

Jared and Ryan continued their wordless gaze.

"Maybe they didn't understand you. This could be a non-English speaking cave," Lapis whispered loudly to Carnelian. "Try saying it in German."

Carnelian opened her mouth to speak again but was interrupted by Lapis. "Or maybe Scandinavian. You have to get the right dialect for some of these Europeans."

Carnelian shook her head and tried to begin again, but before she could get even one word out...

"Or French. They could be French."

"Don't be silly, Lapis," said Carnelian. "Of course they are not German or French. They are Ryan and Jared. The ones the Creator told us would come to help with Michael."

Lapis was quiet for a moment, then she came back with, "Are they from Scandinavia?"

Ryan finally found his tongue. "Ah yes, we understand you perfectly. We are just surprised to see you."

"Well, of course you are, my dears," said Carnelian. "Come and sit by the fire and warm yourselves."

Ryan and Jared sat down by the fire, and the healers served them each a steaming bowl of soup.

"How could you see the soup with such a quick glance?" Ryan asked Jared.

Jared smiled and pointed to his head, "Eidetic memory."

"Oh yeah, I forgot about that."

The soup, which was more like a broth, had a warm, soothing effect on the humans.

"It almost tastes like... like..." Jared tried to describe the taste and texture of the soup, but he was at a loss for words.

106

Ryan rolled the soup around in his mouth. After several minutes, he said, "Light?"

It came out as more of a question than an answer. He looked at Jared and, though they had reached a consensus as to the mysterious ingredient, they still wondered how anyone could actually eat light.

Lapis spoke. "I did wonder if the trace amounts of angel left in your blood would pick up the flavor."

"But how is this possible?" asked Ryan.

"Yeah," said Jared. "One does not simply eat *light*."

He laughed, but Ryan rolled his eyes.

"Come on, Ryan, that was funny."

"Hilarious, Jared," said Ryan, unmoved by his friend's attempt at humor. He turned his attention back to the healers. "How is it possible to ingest light, Miss Carnelian?"

"Oh, call me Neli," she said. "I will answer your question with a question of my own: what's the most important thing in the universe?"

"Ah, let me guess," said Jared in a jovial tone, as he slurped down his last bit of the soup. "Could it be *light*?"

"Jared, what's the matter with you? Be serious for a minute here," Ryan said.

"He's fine, dear. That's just the light talking," said Lapis.

"Yeah, Ryan, *light*-en up!"

"Jared?"

"Hey, Ryan... Ryan, would you call Roni's flaming sword a *light* saber?!"

"Alright, no more light soup for you," Ryan said, taking Jared's bowl. "You're acting like you've had one too many to drink. He's not going to have a hangover, is he?"

"Just a *light* one!" Jared giggled, slapping his hand over his mouth. He gave Ryan a muffled apology, trying to act sober.

"You are right, Jared," answered Lapis. "The most important thing in all dimensions of the universe is light. That is why it was created first. Spiritual beings as well as earthly beings need light to thrive.

"I'm not talking about the light you get from the sun, but true light; a part of the Creator Himself. He designed it to be in all spiritual things. It nourishes the *essentia* of angels and the souls of mankind.

"In the absence of light, wickedness attaches itself to a host and drains it of life. When an earthly being dies physically, what is left of their light is released into the atmosphere, and it can bring comfort to those left behind. That is why, when a servant of the Creator dies, many feel a sense of joy that the person is in eternal happiness."

"Well, what if someone dies, and they are not a servant of the Creator?" asked Ryan.

A look of sadness came upon Neli's face, and she choked on her next words.

"That... eh... hum... that is a most horrible and empty feeling. The Creator weeps every time one of His children is lost for all eternity."

"Can't the Creator make it so everyone can just go to heaven?" asked Jared, who was getting a bit more sober. "I mean, He's the boss, right? He makes the rules, doesn't He?"

"Yes, He is, and He does," Neli replied. "But true, pure light cannot exist in the presence of darkness, and that is a rule for everyone. Darkness and light will always be at war with each other; that is their nature."

Jared continued talking to the healers, but Ryan stood up and walked over to Michael. The glow on the archangel's chest was coming from two oval-shaped stones. One blue and one orange. Ryan reached out his hand to touch them.

"I wouldn't do that if I were you," a voice beside him spoke. Ryan staggered a few steps back.

"Another angel! They seem to have a knack of suddenly appearing out of thin air... Oh man! I just can't get used to this," he said to himself.

"Sorry, I didn't mean to frighten you," the newcomer said, "but, if you think that little bit of soup was heady stuff, direct contact with one of these light stones will knock you out for at least three days. The healers brought them straight from the throne."

Ryan was captivated by the speaker's gracious demeanor and gentle eyes that glowed with warmth and kindness—as though a light had been lit in them. Something was different about him, but Ryan just couldn't put his finger on it.

The stranger was holding an apple in one hand. He held the other out to Ryan, saying, "I'm John. And you're Ryan, right?"

"Yes," Ryan replied, "and that's my friend Jared over there." He pointed to his companion, who was trying to get Neli to give him more of the light soup.

"I hear you're a doctor," John said. "There's someone else I know who was a good doctor too; but he was an even better writer. World famous, if you know what I mean."

He winked at Ryan and ate a slice of the apple he was cutting with a paring knife.

"Oh really, what did he write? Maybe I've seen something in one of the medical journals I read," said Ryan slowly, not quite sure what that wink meant.

"Oh, he wouldn't be famous in medical journals," said John with a smile. "He's more of a historical biography person."

Ryan was beginning to feel like he had missed the punch line to a joke. "Well, does he have a name?"

"Of course he does!" John laughed. "Everyone has a name." He paused again to eat another slice of apple, offering one to Ryan as well. Ryan accepted it.

He thought he had never met such a peculiar angel... but an endearing one too! After another slice of apple, Ryan said, "Well, what is it?"

"Oh yeah, guess I should say that it's... um... Luke."

"Luke what?"

"Ah... Luke something or other."

"Where's he from?" asked Ryan impatiently.

"Ahh... you know, I never asked him that," John said. "Somewhere near the Mediterranean, I think. I know he likes the beach."

Ryan was now officially frustrated and decided to change the subject. "How is Michael doing?" he asked.

"Not too bad, considering," said John.

It was quiet again.

"Considering what?" Ryan asked.

"Considering your friend zapped him with enough volts to light up Atlantis," John answered. "She's quite scary when she does that, you know."

"Tell me about it," said Ryan. "I thought she was going to blow the hospital generator up. I know she's sorry and feels bad that Michael has to pay for what she did."

"Ah yes, but someone always does, don't they?" said John.

"Does what?" asked Ryan.

"Pay," replied John. "Sin always has to be paid for."

"That's true," said Ryan, and he hung his head, thinking about his brother Jason and how mean he had been to him when they were kids. "And sometimes you never get the chance to tell them you are sorry."

John placed his hand on Ryan's shoulder.

"He knows, Ryan. Jason knows you are sorry for your actions. Let me ask you this: have you asked for forgiveness?"

"Well, I can't really do that since he is dead," Ryan said, wondering why the angel didn't know this.

"No, I don't mean from Jason. I mean from the Creator," John replied. "I mean, have you really, truly repented of your wrongdoing and tried to do the right thing from then on?"

"I know I have tried to do the right thing, and I feel bad about how I was to Roni and Jason. But I don't know if I've ever really asked God to forgive me."

"Well, I heard it this way," John began. "If we confess our sins, He is faithful and just to forgive them. I had this other buddy, Paul. Great guy, used to be on his own personal holy war, and he did some pretty messed-up things too. But he became this great preacher after meeting with the Creator's Son.

"Anyway, long story short, he was able to turn his life around; but only because he accepted the forgiveness of the Creator. He could have sat around and tortured himself about all the horrible things he had done, but he didn't. He repented and got back in the game. He's written a bunch of good books too. I think he's got something like thirteen of them; you should look up some of his stuff."

"Sounds like I should," Ryan said sadly. "I always have this load of guilt on me, and I don't know how to get rid of it—or if I'm even supposed to get rid of it. Every time I look at Roni, I think about what a jerk I was; and that she could never love me after all I did. Maybe I'm supposed to suffer the rest of my life without her to pay for my sins."

"Hey, Ryan," John said, and he waited until Ryan was looking into his eyes, "You can't pay for any of your sins. The Creator's Son, Jesus... He's already paid for them. It's done.

It's over. He paid for everyone one time. You just need to ask for His forgiveness and accept His free gift."

As he checked Michael's wounds, Ryan pondered what John had said. He wondered if it was as simple as that. Just ask, and his guilt would be taken away. His thoughts were interrupted by Jared.

"How's the patient, Doc? Is he going to be back to flying around, kicking some bad guy's tail soon?"

"I don't really know," Ryan said. "These stones seem to be doing the job. I guess it's only a matter of time. The wounds aren't oozing anymore and the drainage is down to a minimum, so I'll take that as a good sign."

"That's good," said Jared. "I'm ready to get back to the house. I know we left Seth and Solomon in charge, but I don't trust that Donavon character. He's been creeping on my sister. On the way back, I'll tell you what happened at the house when you were out fighting those crazy chicks."

"Yeah, ok, we can go," said Ryan. "Just let me say goodbye to John."

Ryan approached his new-found friend, who was conversing with the healers near the fire.

"Hey, man—I mean angel—we're going to head back to the house. What did you say the name of your buddy was— the one who writes the self-help books? Paul something or other? You hang out with all these writers, John, maybe you should consider writing a book of your own."

John smiled at Neli and Lapis as he said, "I just might do that, Ryan, now that you mention it. And, oh, I have a copy of those books my buddy Paul wrote. I'll leave them up at the lake house in the morning."

"Ok. That sounds good. See you all later," Ryan said.

The sun was just coming up when he and Jared headed for the lake house.

112

CHAPTER SIXTEEN

A Visitor at the Lake House

The way of the wicked is like deep darkness;
they do not know what makes them stumble.

Proverbs 4:19

Saturday, 16th November

Jillian was sleeping peacefully next to Victor when the sun peeked over the horizon the next morning. It had been quite a feat to get him up the stairs and onto the bed in the master bedroom when the Valkyries commenced their attack on the lake house the day before. With only Juli and Solomon for help, it had been slow going.

By the time they made it up the stairs, Victor's head had begun to bleed again; and, when Jillian looked around the room for something to stop the bleeding, she came up empty handed. She could have used a pillow or the sheets on the bed, but in her panicked state she didn't even think to use them. Juli and Solomon had already left to find China and the baby, so no help would be coming from them.

She finally removed her shirt and used it as a first-aid bandage, but the fabric wasn't very absorbent. Being left with only her jeans and a thin cotton camisole, she was about to give up her last layer of clothing when Jared came running through the door with a pile of hand towels from the kitchen. Jillian was grateful for them, and she used the arms of her shirt to hold a towel in place over the wound.

As Jared turned to leave and join the battle outside, he stopped short right in front of Donavon—who had been standing just inside the door, quietly watching Jillian as she tried to control Victor's bleeding. In his hand was Ryan's first-aid duffle bag, loaded with gauze pads and bandages.

Jared looked into Donavon's eyes and knew that the boy had been waiting for his sister to take off her undershirt. No words were exchanged between the two young men, but each communicated a challenge to the other. Jared's narrowed eyes said, "Stay away from my sister," while the turned up corners of Donavon's mouth said, "Make me!"

Jillian's guardian, Raven, made a sudden appearance and positioned himself between Jared and Jillian, blocking Donavon's view of his alluring nightingale. Seeing that he was outnumbered, Donavon backed up, dropped the duffle bag, and left the room.

He crept up the stairs early the next morning and peeked through the master bedroom door, his blood boiling. Jillian was going to be his girl. He had seen her first. No useless pervert was going to move in on his territory. Seth had Anita, and he was going to get Jillian. He was so focused on the girl in the bed that he didn't hear Seth sneaking up behind him.

"Dude!"

Donavon jumped and a curse escaped his lips. Seth laughed quietly.

"Man, don't do that!" whispered Donavon.

"Dude, you should have seen your face!" said Seth, who was still laughing.

"Laugh it up, lover boy. I've seen you peeping through Anita's kitchen window."

"Yah, when we were like ten!" Seth exclaimed. "What are you doing up here on the girls' floor, anyway? You know what Ryan said. Girls up and boys down. Mingling is to be done on the ground floor only."

"What about him?" asked Donavon defensively, pointing to Victor. "He's up here."

"Really, man, he isn't even conscious!"

"Well, I think that Jared would be a little upset if he saw his sister in bed with a guy like that."

"She is taking care of him," said Seth. "Don't be so jealous. She isn't even your girl."

At that last statement, Donavon lunged at his friend, his face filled with rage. Seth ducked, avoiding his fist, but he was shocked by his lifelong friend's attempt to hit him.

"Whoa, man! What was that for?" Seth gasped.

Lorrel appeared and Donavon stormed off down the stairs.

"Problems?" the guardian inquired.

"Apparently," Seth answered. His voice was strained. "My best friend just tried to hit me—after he'd already attacked my brother yesterday."

"I have spoken with Camiel and Raven," said Lorrel, "and they are concerned about the young man's behavior towards Jillian."

"I know, Solomon and I are concerned too," Seth replied, "but I've known Donavon my whole life. He's had it rough, but he would never hurt anyone."

Lorrel remained quiet until Seth finally spoke again.

"Although he did just try to deck me, and he just about strangled Solomon yesterday," said Seth, who was feeling disheartened. "I'll go try to talk to him again."

"Very good," said Lorrel. "And I will continue inquiring as to the whereabouts of his guardian."

***

Everyone was cleaning up after breakfast when a knock was heard at the front door. Roni wondered who it could be. Since it was winter and the lake was usually abandoned until warmer weather came, random visitors were not expected. She looked through the small window in the front door and a grin appeared on her lips. Jeni and Juli, who had heard the knock as well, came down the stairs quickly.

"Who is it?" Jeni asked.

Roni stepped aside so her sisters could see who had come to call. The girls grinned at each other as she opened the door.

"Detective Sanderson, how nice to see you again," Roni greeted the nervous officer. "Won't you please come in?"

"Th-thank you," Stephen said gratefully, stepping inside.

Jeni whispered something in Juli's ear, and the girls excused themselves.

"How can we help you, detective?" Roni inquired.

"P-please c-call me Stephen. I-I was wondering if Miss Miller was available; a-and, if she is, c-can I t-talk with her?"

"Well, I don't know, detective," said Ryan, who had made his way to the front door, "that would depend. Are you here on official business or is it a personal matter that brings you all the way out here on a Saturday morning?"

Stephen was getting even more nervous. Roni elbowed Ryan in the ribs, and he stifled a groan.

"W-w-w-well..." was all Stephen could get out. Roni held out her hand.

"Of course you can see China," she said. "The girls went to get her. Let me have your coat. Please come in and sit down."

Stephen followed Roni to the living room. On the way, he noticed the plastic over where the sliding glass door in the family room should have been. When he sat down, the dining room window that Misty and Michael had fallen through was visible. Roni observed his surveillance of the damage.

"The... ah... wind sure did kick up around here last night. Was it blowing in Wichita?" she asked as smoothly as possible.

"N-n-no."

There was now quite an audience examining the visitor. Seth and Solomon, who were on dish duty, peeked around the corner to catch a glimpse of the stranger. Jared had been taking a cat nap on the couch but felt Ryan could use some back up. After all, he had only had a sister for a week and could use some pointers when it came to men interested in her.

Zoei walked right up to Stephen and climbed onto his lap. She looked up at him with her bright hazel eyes. "Hello, Mr Police Officer," she said. "I'm Zoei. I'm five. These are my friends, James and John. They are four.

"James wants to be a detective like you when he grows up, but John thinks firefighters are cooler. My daddy was a firefighter but he's in heaven now with my mommy. I don't think I want to be a police officer or a firefighter. Police have to carry guns and I don't like guns. Do you have a gun?"

Stephen nodded his head at the precocious child.

"Well, you'd better keep it hidden from James or he might try to use it to shoot at sticks out back. My dad said little kids should never touch real guns, and the way you could tell if they were real or not was if they were heavy. Heavy guns are real. Is your gun heavy?"

Stephen nodded again.

"Then it's real all right. Firefighters don't have guns but they have big trucks and hoses. When fires make smoke it makes me cough. I don't like coughing. I think I'm going to be a doctor and help people, like Ryan. He's a doctor and he saved my big sister Roni.

"I had a dream that Roni and Ryan got married and had lots of kids. Priel, my guardian angel, says that, if the Creator wants them to get married and have all these kids, I will get to be an aunt."

Zoei kept chatting with Stephen while James and John played with his shoelaces. Her comment about her guardian angel did not faze the detective in the least; his thoughts were on the beautiful young girl he had come to see. Occasionally, footsteps could be heard from upstairs. Roni guessed that Juli and Jeni were frantically helping China get dressed.

After about fifteen minutes, Jeni and Juli came down the stairs. China stopped near the bottom and tried to calm her frantic nerves before she walked around the corner to greet Stephen. When she finally appeared, Stephen tried to stand up; but Zoei was still in his lap and the boys had untied both of his shoelaces.

"Ok, Zoei, boys, let's let the detective talk to China," said Roni.

Zoei jumped up, and the boys took Roni's outstretched hands. As they were leaving, James looked back. He wriggled out of Roni's grasp and ran over to Stephen, who was retying his shoes. James' eyes were the same bright shade of blue they had been when he told Jared to listen to what he knew. He whispered something into Stephen's ear that made the young man's eyes widen and his cheeks flush a little pink.

"James," said Roni gently. "Let's go."

James obeyed and rejoined John and Zoei. Stephen looked like he had been hit with a stun gun. He stayed that way until he heard China's sweet voice lure him back to her.

"Hello, Stephen. You have come to see me?" she said quietly. Her soft Russian accent was easy on his ears and Stephen thought he could listen to her talk all day long.

"Uh... uh... yes. I just w-w-wanted to see h-how you were doing," he stuttered.

China looked at Jeni and Juli, her eyes pleading with them to get everyone to leave the room so she could talk to Stephen. They got the message.

"Alright, people, back to work," ordered Jeni. "Nothing to see here. This house isn't going to clean itself. You, too, big brother. I'm sure she's in good hands."

Jeni hooked her arm in Ryan's and led him over to the basement stairs.

"You and Jared need to go down and get some real sleep so we can get back to work on the Norilsk stuff," she said to Ryan. "Plus, I know you have patients that need to be seen."

She added the last part almost under her breath. They didn't need Stephen learning about Victor or Michael... who knew how much they could trust the detective? Ryan relented and headed to his bed, with Jeni's reassurances that China would be safe.

Jared and Ryan flopped onto their beds, exhaustion sweeping over both of them. "How is Jillian?" Ryan asked, his voice muffled by his pillow.

"She's ok," answered Jared. "She was sleeping next to Victor when we got in. Guess I should have been upset by that, but I wasn't. I'm pretty sure she woke up when Jeni and Juli were helping China get all dolled up for the detective. I'm surprised she was down in fifteen minutes. With my sister, a makeover could last all day!"

They both laughed.

"I have no idea what it's going to be like to have a sister," Ryan said apprehensively.

"A lot of posturing. You've got to let these young guys know you mean business when it comes to your sister and that you are prepared for a duel to the death should the situation call for it."

"Oh, is that all?" Ryan said sarcastically.

"And expect a myriad of responses from hero worship to 'meddling old fart' from the girls. Sometimes these girls don't know what's good for them."

"Well, I'll keep all that in mind... but for now I've got to get some sleep. See you in four, Jared."

"Yup."

And, with that, both boys were out.

CHAPTER SEVENTEEN

A Grand Entrance

*He trains my hands for battle; my arms
can bend a bow of bronze.*

Psalm 18:34

Stephen talked to China for almost an hour. She had never met anyone like him. He spoke to her like she was important, like she mattered. She got lost in his eyes, those beautiful brown eyes. But she knew he could never want her. She was ugly and deformed. The list of men she had been given to was endless. She knew that, if a man was really a gentleman, he wouldn't want a whore like her. How many times had Joseph told her that? Her attention was brought back to Stephen as he started stuttering again.

"W-w-well, the... uh... r-reason I came out w-w-was t-to see if... if y-you wanted to... I-I mean w-would like to..." he started fidgeting with the pens in his pocket. "You see, m-my m-mom, sh-sh-she likes... ah... babies, and I w-was wondering if y-you would like to c-come s-spend the... uh... day with us on Sunday? Tomorrow? For church and s-stuff."

China didn't know what to say. *This can't be right*, she thought. Maybe she had heard him wrong. She thought she heard him ask her to go somewhere with him and his mother. Somewhere out in public, where other people could see them together. She stared at Stephen for a whole minute before she spoke.

"You mean, you want me and Allyson to go out somewhere with you and your mom?"

"Y-yes."

"Somewhere other people will see you?"

120

"Yes."

"And people will see me with you?"

"Yes."

China stood up and faced the window. She grabbed the end of her long blond hair and began to twist it around her fingers. He had to be crazy to want to be seen with her. Maybe he didn't understand what kind of life she had lived. She had been Joseph's little rag doll, and no good person would ever want her as their companion… let alone want to be seen with her. She turned around and was about to object when Jeni came around the corner.

"Yes, yes, she would love to go to church with you and your mother tomorrow," she said. "What time should we have them ready?"

Stephen stood up. He wasn't quite sure what to say to Jeni. He certainly wanted China to say yes, but he didn't want to force her.

"Uh… uh… eight o'clock."

"Eight it is. Thank you so much for asking. They will be up and ready by eight."

"A-are y-you sure? I-I don't want to impose on the l-lady."

China looked at Stephen and smiled; and, although her mind screamed no, her heart whispered yes.

"I will go to church with you and your mother tomorrow," she said shyly.

Stephen's eyes beamed with delight. "O-o-ok," he said as he grabbed his coat. "I will s-see you at eight. Goodbye and thank y-you f-for your h-hospitality."

"Goodbye," Jeni answered and squealed with delight when Stephen had shut the door.

China wasn't sure whether to be angry at Jeni or not. She knew her friend had good intentions, but that didn't take away the shame in her heart. She would think more about all that later. Allyson had begun to cry, and she needed to attend to her. But there was one question she needed answered before she went upstairs.

She turned to Jeni and asked, "What is church?"

Jeni smiled and hugged her friend.

***

While Stephen and China were visiting, Jillian went back into Victor's bedroom. She filled a large bowl with warm soapy water and knelt down beside his bed. Gently she took his hand and began cleaning more of the dirt and blood from under his nails, careful not to cause him anymore needless pain. She dabbed the top of his hand with a soft washcloth and began to count the burn marks from below his wrist to his collar bone. She stopped counting when she got to his elbow because there were so many. There were at least sixty, and some looked as if they had overlapped one another.

Tears were clouding her vision, so she began to hum a lullaby to comfort herself. She knew this young man had once been a beautiful boy, and she wondered who could have been so cruel as to inflict that kind of hurt upon him.

Her guardian Raven appeared and handed her a handkerchief to dry her eyes. He took up the basin of water and began cleaning Victor's other hand. The human and her guardian sat in silence as they tended to their patient.

After a while, Jillian heard the front door open and close. She went over to the window and leaned her head against the glass. Looking out, she saw the detective walking to his car. She hoped everything would work out for him. It was obvious that he had feelings for China, but Jillian was unsure if China felt the same way about him.

What was it like to be held a prisoner your whole life and used as a sex slave? Could such a person go on to have any kind of normal life, with love and marriage and a family? She glanced over at Victor and tried hard not to speculate as to how he had ended up so torn and broken.

Her forehead was cold, and it had begun to stick to the glass. Placing her hand on the windowpane, she could feel the winter wind trying to come through. A low hum began to fill the room, and the glass in the window started to vibrate. The sound grew louder and louder. Raven stood up and drew his sword, and Jillian rushed over to Victor.

"What is it?" Jillian shouted over the noise.

"Another guardian approaches," Raven replied.

The bedroom door was flung open, and Jeni and her twin sister stood in the doorway with their bows drawn. They were quite a sight, with their flaming hair aglow with the Creator's power. Their guardians, Ariel and Samuel, drew their swords and took up their positions in the bedroom.

A small, glowing light appeared about five feet off the ground, in front of the bathroom door. It looked like a star, pulsating rapidly. Jillian covered Victor's body with her own and pressed her face into his chest. He was still unconscious and unaware of his surroundings.

Juli's eyes grew wide. She was not as brave as her sister, but hearing Jeni breathing alongside her helped to strengthen her resolve. She wanted to prove herself worthy of the Creator's weapons; she wanted to protect her friends. So she stood strong and whispered to herself, "He trains my hands for battle; my arms can bend a bow of bronze."

Jeni smiled when she heard Juli quote the scripture verse.

"Here they come!" Raven shouted.

The noise increased as the strange light grew larger. Then, just when Jillian thought her ears were going to burst, a loud roar shook the house and the glowing star collapsed on itself.

The windows in the house shook violently, and the large picture window in the living room exploded into a zillion tiny pieces that rained down on the front lawn like glitter being shot from a cannon.

When their eyes had adjusted from the flare of the explosion, Juli and Jeni walked over to where Raven, Samuel and Ariel were standing. On the ground lay an angel. His wings were tattered and torn. His face and hands were bruised and he had a large abrasion over his left eye. He looked like he had been in a fight and lost.

Samuel knelt down and touched the angel on the shoulder. "Jesse, Jesse, are you ok? Are you hurt?"

The angel slowly pushed himself up into a sitting position. He looked up at Samuel and gave a sheepish smile.

"Never better," he replied and promptly passed out.

"He always was one for a grand entrance," said Ariel.

"Oh yeah," Samuel replied with a grin. "The fun has begun."

A commotion could be heard at the bottom of the stairs. Looking down the hallway, Juli could see Roni trying to distract Stephen.

"Oh no," she whispered loudly. "It's Stephen!"

Jeni peeked around the corner. "And he's got a gun!"

Stephen came through the doorway with his gun drawn, and all the humans put their hands up.

"W-what... what... what," was all he could get out as he surveyed the room.

Jeni, Juli, and the three guardians were still clothed in their battle gear. Jesse was sprawled out on the floor, wings and all.

Then Stephen noticed Victor lying in the bed.

"Who... who...?"

China came up behind Stephen and put her hand on his shoulder. Startled, he turned around quickly and pointed his gun at her face.

"Stephen, please, we can explain," she said softly.

"Who... who are you people?" he demanded.

China stepped forward and softly touched Stephen's shaking hands that were gripping his gun very tightly.

"W-why is this man here?" he motioned with his head toward Victor. "He... he's a ch-child predator!"

"He's not, Stephen," China answered. "He's my friend."

"Y-your friend?"

"Yes, we were both born at the facility."

"But-but I just busted him for trying to s-sell those kids."

"I don't know what he was doing exactly, but you can't imagine the life he's had. Please put your gun down and we can talk about it."

Stephen began to lower his weapon. Ryan came through the door looking frazzled. Roni had rushed downstairs and awoken him from a sleep so deep that not even Jesse's grand entrance could interrupt.

"What the..." said Ryan, surveying the room. Then he noticed Stephen. "Who let him up here?"

"Well, it seems angel boy here decided to make a very loud arrival before the good detective could leave the property," Jeni offered, pointing to the ragged-looking angel on the floor.

"Like I said, a grand entrance," Ariel added.

Ryan walked over and knelt down next to Jesse. He touched the angel's shimmering wings that were splayed across the bedroom floor. They looked like bird feathers but felt like silk. After a few moments, the wings disappeared. Ryan stood up and told the angels to move their broken brother onto the bed, next to Victor.

125

Ryan half expected Jesse's appearance to fluctuate between human and angel, like Michael's had done; but the angel held his human form. He was not as tall as the other guardians, so moving him was less trouble than it had been when Michael needed to be carried to the cave. When placed next to Victor, it was obvious that the two were somehow linked, as they had corresponding head injuries. Jillian even noticed a few circular scars on Jesse's arms.

"W-will someone p-please explain what's going on?" Stephen asked.

China took Stephen's hand and led him out of the room. He followed her reluctantly but continued to look back over his shoulder. Standing in the hallway, she looked up at him with moist eyes and began to speak with quivering lips.

"Victor and I grew up at the facility together. He was a few years older than me and was the closest thing I ever had to a brother. We were the *gunoi*, the trash of the facility... failed experiments left to fend for ourselves. We were supposed to be golden, like the rest of the children born there, but I had a broken mouth and Victor's hair and eyes were the wrong color.

"I was given to a nurse who was kind to me; but Victor, he... he..." tears began to fall unchecked down her face as she recalled her friend's terrible life in the facility. "He was given to the guards, who did unspeakable things to him.

"I haven't seen him in many years, but I know that whatever he has done is not something he ever wanted to do. He was only trying to survive, just like me. So, please, I beg you not to make up your mind about him from the few days you have known him."

Stephen was overrun with emotion as he listened to his sweet dove relay her friend's heartrending story to him. His own life was not so different. He had survived an abusive, alcoholic father, and he remembered what he had done to survive. He looked at China tenderly and wiped a tear from her face.

"I-I will not judge, f-for I too am in need of the Creator's mercy."

China smiled at him, grateful for his understanding. They turned their attention back to what was happening in the room. Ryan had finished examining the still-unconscious angel and decided he could do nothing for him but bandage his external wounds. He spoke quietly to the other angels in the room, making sure the detective could not hear him.

"We should get him to the cave with Michael. Two of your 'little friends' are there, and I think they will be able to help him more than I can... though I get the feeling that this angel is Victor's guardian."

"You are very observant," Raven said.

"I'm assuming we should probably not separate the two of them," Ryan inquired.

"In most cases, you would be correct," said Samuel, "but, in this instance, a temporary guardian can be assigned to Victor until Jesse is healed."

"Why doesn't he already have a backup?" asked Ryan almost indignantly. "Don't you guys plan for these types of emergencies?"

Oriel, who was still nursing his leg wound, made his way past Stephen and placed his hand on Ryan's shoulder.

"Sometimes, it is unknown if a human has rejected their guardian or if the guardian is being prevented from protecting their charge," the angel explained.

Ryan looked a little confused.

"If a human no longer wishes to be under the protection of the Creator, then he is free to reject his guardian, who is thereafter relieved of his duty."

"Also, guardians can be involved in battles on behalf of their charges and can be delayed in rendering aid to them."

"So is there a kind of protocol manual for angels?" asked Ryan.

Oriel smiled. "Yes, I guess you could call it that."

"If it is apparent that a guardian's protection is being suppressed, as in this case," added Ariel, "a provisional guardian will be given to the human."

"Wow, you guys have some interesting procedures," Ryan mused.

"Do you think we just float around on clouds, play harps, and arbitrarily visit earth with no *modus operandi*?" laughed Raven. "You earthlings think your instructional manual is lengthy. You should see what ours looks like."

Ryan was puzzled. "Instructional manual?"

Raven threw his head back and laughed boisterously, "I'm talking about the Bible, human!"

"Oh," Ryan said, still a little mystified. "Well, we need to get this guy to the cave, unless one of your 'little helpers' can come here."

"I think the detective in the room needs to be addressed as well," added Samuel.

"Neil and I will attend to that," said Oriel. "The detective's guardian is near."

CHAPTER EIGHTEEN

A Setback

Fear of man will prove to be a snare, but
whoever trusts in the LORD is kept safe.

Proverbs 29:25

Stephen sat across from Neil and Oriel in the family room. He could hear Seth and Solomon in the living room struggling with a large piece of painter's plastic as they tried to cover the newly made hole in the house. He observed again the absence of the sliding glass door, and he could tell that the corner of the family room had just been recently repaired, as it was not yet painted.

Being a churchgoing man, Stephen speculated on the significance of what he had just witnessed upstairs. *Could it be that the two beings sitting in front of him were... no!* He couldn't even finish the thought. It was too crazy. Things like that didn't happen to ordinary people like him.

He was just a low-grade detective in a department that gave him small, unimportant things to investigate. This was supposed to be a simple case of wrongful imprisonment and the perpetrator was already dead. But then, why was the alleged partner or business associate of the perpetrator lying unconscious, upstairs, in the victim's house?

Stephen had never considered himself a super genius, but even he could see that things were not adding up. If those guys were... you know... the real deal, what was he going to write in his report?

Stephen's thoughts were interrupted as China and her brother sat down to his left on the large sectional in the family room.

"Well," said Ryan with a forced smile and an even more forced laugh, "I bet you have a lot of questions for us." He tried to lighten the mood but felt he was failing miserably.

China was looking down at her feet and twisting her hair nervously. Neil decided to break the ice.

"Stephen," he said, smiling at the detective, "I would like to introduce you to a friend of mine. His name is Heath."

Instantaneously, someone was sitting next to Stephen on the couch. The detective jumped up from his spot and whirled around. He looked into the eyes of the newcomer, who had appeared out of nowhere, and realized that this person was not a complete stranger. He squeezed his eyes shut and tried to remember where he had seen him before.

Flashes of memory streamed through his mind like a badly edited movie. He was unable to push the pause button to view any one screen closely. A feeling of warmth and peace spread all over him, and he felt his knees give a little.

Someone whispered his name, "Stephen."

His eyes fluttered open.

"Stephen."

And then he remembered. Heath was with him as a child: when he got lost in the woods on a family camping trip; when he nearly drowned in the city pool; and when he fell off his grandfather's barn roof, breaking his arm and leg. When he was shut in a locker during his freshman year, Heath was the one who let him out. Whenever he and his sister hid in the basement from their dad, Heath held the door shut and took the beating for them.

That night when Stephen picked up the gun... yes, even then Heath was there. Stephen blinked back his tears as he began to realize who Heath was.

"Y-you're m-my... my..."

"Yes," the guardian answered.

"And I am China's," said Neil, who was supporting the weak-kneed detective on his right side.

Oriel was on Stephen's left. He motioned towards Ryan, saying, "Yes, he is mine."

"H-how is all this p-possible? W-why are you all here? And why can we all see you?" the anxious detective asked.

"Well, it's kind of a long story," Ryan began. "Maybe we had all better sit down and I can start from the beginning."

Ryan talked for a half hour straight, relaying all that had happened in the past several weeks. To China's relief, he left out her ordeal with Ezekiel and Joseph the day before her rescue. She had left that part of her story out when she talked with the detective at the hospital. She didn't want to relive even a single moment of the past ten years, especially not in front of Stephen. It was over and done with, and she would never have to talk about it again.

When Ryan was done talking, Stephen sat quietly for a few minutes. Then he stood up and paced up and down the room. He stopped every few steps to look at Ryan, China and the guardians. He opened his mouth, obviously trying to say something, but no words would come out. He closed his mouth and paced a little more, then he sat down again.

China was beginning to get nervous. Maybe Stephen wouldn't want her to go to church with him and his mother after what had happened. It would probably be for the best. She shouldn't have got her hopes up even for a few minutes. Now that Stephen knew about all this angel stuff, on top of her ruinous life, it would just be too much. *She* would be too much. Did she think that this amazing man had come to rescue her from...?

"S-s-so I w-will pick you up at eight?" she heard him ask.

She looked up to see Stephen standing in front of her. "What? Um... tomorrow? Uh... yes. Are you sure you still want to?"

"Absolutely," he said without stuttering.

"Ok. Eight is good."

Stephen shook Ryan's hand. He left the lake house with a smile on his face and a song in his heart.

***

"Well, that went better than expected," said Ryan when Stephen and Heath had left. "I think you might have a keeper there, little Sis."

"Now, wait a minute," Roni said as she came into the family room. "We don't actually know if you are the oldest. I've never been a twin but, from what I've observed over the years, timing is everything. So, how do we know who is older? It's not like we can trust your birth certificate. Who knows what those people at the adoption center made up about us?"

"First of all, Miss Rapunzel, you *are* a twin; and, second, I'm sure the guardians can clear all this up in a few moments." Ryan looked over at Oriel.

"Hey, don't get me involved in all of this! Remember, I wasn't assigned to you until you were twelve. Plus, I was with Roni and Jason when they were born. Ezekiel and Neil were with you and China."

"Oh, yes, I forgot," Ryan said. "How exactly did that happen and how is it that I had to hear about it from Sarah?"

"Sarah? Who's Sarah?" asked Solomon.

A small crowd had gathered in the family room while Ryan was recapping their adventures—in fact, everyone except Seth and Donavon, as the former was still out looking for the latter.

"Another *AIRborn* we ran into at the hospital," Ryan said flatly. "I couldn't save her."

Roni took Ryan by the hand to comfort him. Both were shocked by the gesture, and Roni released his hand immediately. Ryan wasn't sure whether he should be elated that she took his hand or offended that she released it like she had touched a spider. Neil sensed the tension and decided to attend to Ryan's inquiries.

"Ezekiel and I were present at Ryan and China's births; and, yes, Ryan, you were born about five minutes before your sister. Roni and Jason were delivered in a C-section and were born at exactly the same time, like all *AIRborn* twins. The babies are entwined in each other's arms, and a small piece of flesh connects them at the heart. Most of the time, when the heart connection is severed, the males die. But, if they live, the facility uses them to control the females."

"So, there are no male *AIRborns*?" Roni asked.

"Not at this time. Most of the time, only one child is conceived in the proliferation process; but, in about one-third of the pregnancies, twinning occurs. And, of that fraction, only about ten percent of the male twins survive."

Ryan was astonished. "Let me see if I have this right. You are saying that all *AIRborns* are girls but, if twinning does occur, it is always a boy-girl set and the males rarely live?"

"Yes," replied Neil. "The males that do survive are usually weak and don't reach puberty."

"Which explains why Jason was so sickly and so attached to Roni," Ryan added.

"It's easy to understand why Sarah attacked us so passionately," Roni added. "I know what it is to feel protective over a weaker child. I would have done anything for Jason."

133

Though her intent was not to be vicious or accusatory, Roni's words cut Ryan to the heart and his emotions overwhelmed him. His guilt pressed in on him and he slowly turned and left the room.

"Why do I even bother trying to get her to forgive me," he thought. "When all this mess is over, I should just go away and let her get on with her life."

He gathered a few medical supplies and headed for the cave. On his way out of the front door, he saw the Bible that his mom and dad had sent him while he was in Germany.

"How did this get here?" he wondered. He put it in his bag and went outside. It was cold and breezy, even though the sun was shining brightly. He had just rounded the corner of the house when he heard footsteps behind him. He had a feeling Roni would come after him.

"Ryan, wait. Please. I didn't mean to hurt you. Please don't leave."

Ryan turned around and faced her. "I know you didn't. And, even if you did, it wouldn't matter. What you said was the truth and I have to deal with it."

Roni noticed the bag in his hands. "Where are you going?" she inquired.

"To the cave to check on Michael and Jesse."

"Can I come with you?"

"Why?"

"Maybe I can help you."

"I think you should stay and look after Zoei and the boys."

"There are plenty of people to look after them. I want to come with you."

"Well, you can't."

"Why not?"

"Because you just can't." Ryan already knew this conversation was not going to end well.

Roni took a step closer to him, and her face went from concerned to angry.

"You're leaving me again, aren't you?"

"N-no, Roni, I'm..."

"Don't you lie to me, Ryan Allen Miller! I know when you're lying!"

Priscilla and Oriel decided that now would be a good time to make an appearance, before the situation got out of hand. Both reached out to pull their charges back, but something prevented them from doing so.

"Roni, I'm just going to the cave to check on Michael and Jesse, that's all. I'll be back in a few hours."

"You are running away again, and I won't see you! You always leave! You always run!"

Roni's eyes started to glow blue the more she panicked. She lunged forward and grabbed Ryan. Her hands were glowing, and she singed the collar of his shirt. He shoved her away. She flew back about ten feet and hit the ground with a thud.

Ryan's excess strength and fear had caused him to overreact to Roni's emotional state. She sat up dazed and overcome with grief. She reached a glowing hand out to him, but he took a step back.

"Please, don't leave me," she pleaded. "Please don't."

Blue tears were flowing profusely from her eyes, and she realized something was wrong. She tried to stand up but fell to her knees, and her world started spinning. Ryan seemed further and further away. Her eyes began blinking rapidly and the blue glow was changing to grey. And then the pain that had rocked her world a mere six weeks ago returned.

She threw back her head and arched her back acutely as pain ravaged her. She clawed at her chest desperately, as though the pain was something that could be torn away from her body.

Priscilla tried to touch Roni, but she couldn't. She knew the Creator was holding her back, but her protective instinct would not let her stop trying to get to her charge.

Ryan sprinted over to Roni and cradled her in his arms, trying to save her from a head injury as she thrashed around.

"Roni, I'm sorry, I'm here. I'm here! Please don't die. Please don't die, I'm so sorry," he said over and over again.

He laid her back down on the ground and tore open the front of her shirt. The pacemaker was pulsing wildly and burning brightly under her skin. She arched her back again and let out a terrifying scream. Ryan sat her up again and pulled at the back of her shirt. To his horror, he saw that the inky black spot on her back was growing... reaching out with its fingerlike tentacles, as if it intended to wrap around her chest and suffocate her—body, mind and soul.

"JENI!" he screamed with all his might. "JENI!"

Jeni and Juli and everyone else in the house had heard Roni's scream and were already outside trying to find where it had come from. When Jeni heard Ryan calling her, she rushed toward the sound of his voice.

"Jeni," Ryan said, trying to control his shaking voice as he spoke. "Go to the fridge and get the plastic container with the yellow lid; it says 'Roni' on the top. The box of syringes is on top of the fridge. Please go get them quickly."

Jeni tore off back into the house to get Roni's medication. Ryan held Roni close to his chest and rocked her back and forth. She was delirious at this point, and her body was limp. He felt her hands going cold.

Jeni was back in less than a minute. Ryan laid Roni out on the ground again. He opened the box and pulled out a syringe with a four-inch needle on the end. Jeni swallowed hard and tried to be brave. Juli turned her head away and cried softly into Solomon's shoulder.

The liquid was thick and cold, and it took a few moments to fill the syringe.

"Jeni, open an alcohol wipe and disinfect two five-inch square areas on either side of the pacemaker," Ryan said calmly.

Jeni obeyed, though her hands trembled.

After Ryan had filled a second syringe, he leaned in close to Roni's face and whispered, "This is going to hurt, Roni. I'm so sorry to cause you more pain."

He sat back on his heels and looked at Jared and Solomon. "I might need you guys for this one." His voice quivered, and a tear spilled over his golden eyelashes.

The young men nodded and took their positions beside Roni—Jared on her right and Solomon on her left. They knelt and put their hands on her arms. Seth headed for Roni's legs. Jeni cradled her sister's head and kissed her forehead.

All the helpers held their breath as Ryan inserted the first needle. Roni moaned a little. After the first medication was in, Ryan picked up the second needle.

"Ok, is everyone ready?"

All of them nodded in Ryan's direction and braced themselves. He closed his eyes and asked the Creator to give him strength. Then he laid his hand on Roni's chest. A faint yellow light could be seen glowing between his fingers. He touched the tip of the needle to her chest and, in one smooth motion, inserted it directly into her heart.

As soon as he began to depress the syringe, Roni's whole body stiffened. Her eyes opened, and they were blazing with a fiery blue light.

"Make sure her hands are palm-side down," Ryan reminded Jared and Solomon. But the boys were already ahead of him. They had both seen Michael's wounds.

Roni began to thrash around, but Solomon and Jared held her arms. Seth was having a more difficult time and, when one of her legs jerked free, she kicked him in the chest.

"Donavon! Get over here and help me!" Seth yelled at his idle friend.

"Fine," Donavon mumbled. "But, if she kicks me, I'm gonna..."

"You're gonna what?" shouted Ryan as he glared back at Donavon. "Either help or leave, but I'd better not hear anything useless come out of your mouth again!"

As soon as Donavon took hold of Roni's other leg, she began to scream.

"Almost done," shouted Ryan over Roni's voice.

When he pulled the needle out, she was still struggling and crying, but in a little while she started to quieten down. Ryan signaled to the others to let go of her.

He picked her up and cradled her small form. After another minute, she opened her eyes and looked at him. She reached up and, with her cold fingers, brushed a curl back on his forehead.

"Oh, you've come back," she murmured. Then she closed her eyes and plunged into a deep, cataleptic sleep.

CHAPTER NINETEEN

Responsibility

If we confess our sins, he is faithful and just and will forgive us our sins and purify us from all unrighteousness.

1 John 1:9

"She's going to need a healer," Jared said, almost matter-of-factly.

Ryan looked up at him. The two boys had become close, but Jared's knack for badly timed remarks irritated Ryan.

"Really, Jared, don't you think I'd have thought of that?"

Jared shrugged his shoulders and took a step back. He knew his friend was distressed, so he decided to let the comment go.

"What happened?" asked Juli with tears in her eyes. She was trying to fix her sister's shirt. Ryan had carried Roni into the house and laid her on the couch. He looked a little uncomfortable with Juli's question, and Jeni got a sense that she knew exactly what had happened. She moved in front of him, hands on her hips and a glare in her eyes that would have melted the ice off the front door.

"You did it, didn't you?" she asked him in an accusatory tone.

"What?"

"You were going to leave?"

"No, I wasn't. She... Roni got the wrong idea.'

"Well, I don't know where she would get an idea like that," Jeni said sardonically. "Now, why would Roni think that you would leave her?"

"Please, Jeni, this isn't productive," sighed Ryan quietly.

"Productive!" screamed Jeni, and she shoved Ryan against the wall.

Jared moved to intervene, but Oriel stopped him.

"Productive! You left my sister and your dead brother out in the middle of the woods, at night, with a thunderstorm blowing in, and took off to a foreign country so you wouldn't have to face up to what you had done—or rather... hadn't done!"

"Stop, stop, stop," cried Juli. "You're not helping anyone with this fighting."

Jeni was breathing heavily. She had that fight-to-the-death look on her face. Ryan hung his head.

"I can only imagine what a coward you all must think I am," he said slowly. "Yes, I left Roni and my brother—her brother—out in the middle of the woods with a storm coming in. He was dead and I didn't know what to do. I- I- I couldn't save him. I swear I tried, but I couldn't.

"I ran because I thought my jealousy killed Jason. I know now it didn't, but it doesn't mean I don't feel that it did. Trust me, I have tormented myself much more than you all can possibly imagine... and you know what? You know the irony of all of this? I love her. Yes! I love her and... and she'll NEVER have me. Never. I might as well have stabbed Jason in the heart myself."

Ryan was weeping now, and Jeni let loose of him and stepped back. "I'm sorry, Ryan. I-I just got scared," she said, hugging him.

"I'm so sorry I don't know what's wrong. She isn't due for her shot until tomorrow. The pacemaker has been running flawlessly for over a month now. Something must have changed," he cried.

"Maybe the well water?" said Jeni.

"Well, she is really stressed out," Juli said, "but that's been going on for over a year now."

"What about her weight?" Priscilla offered. "She has lost at least ten pounds since you put that thing in her."

"I would say it's closer to fifteen," said Jillian reflectively. "I remember, when we went shopping in Wichita, she told me she had lost ten pounds recently and needed a few new things. And, just yesterday, she commented that her jeans were loose again."

"I don't know," Ryan said, "weight loss is usually good for a person."

"Roni isn't exactly a usual person," said Jared. "She floats through the air and shoots lasers out of her hands."

"I know, but I can't think that losing a few pounds would do this much damage."

"In my vision of Roni's father, all the girl prisoners were a little chubby compared to the boys," Priscilla said, thinking back. "Ryan, I really think you should consider this. Maybe Gabriel can get in contact with Sarah's guardian and see what she knows."

"Ok, ok, but I think we still need to take her to the healers," said Ryan. "If it is a weight thing, we've got to get her conscious so she can eat, or we will have to go back to the hospital and put a feeding tube in her... and I know she wouldn't like that."

***

Roni's sisters had bundled her up in several layers of blankets, and she looked like an angel asleep in Ryan's arms. It was almost 4:00pm and the sun would be setting soon. All the way to the cave, he thought about how he could make it up to her.

"There probably isn't a way. She's never going to be able to forgive me. And why should she? Every time she looks at me, she'll think about Jason and that night. I should just leave."

"Yeah, that worked like a charm the last time," Oriel said.

141

Ryan jumped and almost dropped Roni. "I really wish you guys would stop that."

"What? Appearing out of nowhere or reading your mind?" the guardian laughed.

"Both."

"Well, I can't promise to stop doing either of those things, but I can promise to give you good advice."

"Ok, so what is it?"

"I was just wondering why you would want to run away again," said Oriel. "You hurt everybody and helped no one the last time you took off. Do you not understand the abandonment issues this girl has?"

"Well, yes I do, but..." Ryan started to say, but Oriel interrupted him and put both of his massive hands on Ryan's shoulders.

"No. I don't think you do. She lost her two best friends six years ago and both her parents in the last year. And here you come waltzing back in her life, trying to be her savior... and when things get tough you think about leaving?

"If you want to crush her soul and set her up for a life of misery and mistrust, you go ahead and go. But know this: she will never bond to anyone for the rest of her life if you do."

Ryan stood with his mouth gaping. It did sound incredibly selfish when Oriel put it like that.

"All actions have consequences, Ryan. What are yours going to be?"

They walked on quietly until they reached the cave.

"Maybe Neli can give her some of that light soup," Ryan said wearily. Oriel nodded his head in agreement.

It had taken almost an entire hour to reach the cave this time, and Ryan's back and arms were starting to ache.

Priscilla had offered to carry Roni part of the way, but Ryan wouldn't hear of it. At least he wasn't cold. It was only twenty degrees outside, but he had worked up a good sweat.

As he rounded the corner inside the tunnel, he was met with a wonderful surprise. Michael was sitting up near the fire. He was shirtless, his torso covered with bandages. He smiled to see Oriel and Ryan, but his brow furrowed when he caught sight of the bundle in Ryan's arms. Carefully he rose from his position by the fire and made his way over to his friends.

"Again?" he said as he touched Roni's face. "Who was it this time?" He noticed her hands were also bandaged.

"Actually, it was me," Ryan admitted. "I wanted to leave again, and she called me on it."

Michael instructed him as a father would a son. "You cannot run from your troubles, Ryan. Roni and her sisters are your responsibility now. They have no mother, and soon I fear they will have no father."

Ryan didn't quite understand. "But Roni is eighteen. She can do what she wants. She doesn't need me."

"I would beg to differ on that point," said Oriel. "As to her need, I think her present condition speaks for itself."

A small voice interrupted the angels' counsel.

"Gentlemen, if you wouldn't mind, I have a place for the young lady to rest, and I have made a fresh pot of soup for her." Neli led Ryan over to a small bed of hay covered with several blankets.

He placed Roni's head gently on the pillow. She looked peaceful lying there, and Ryan was reminded of all the summer naps they had taken on the shores of the lake when they were children. He had seen her asleep many times and never wearied of the sight.

"Rest well, Sleeping Beauty," he kissed her on the forehead, then removed his stethoscope from the bag he had brought from the house.

Her heart beat steadily, but her chest was hot to the touch, where her pacemaker and newly mended bone bulged out due to her heart surgeries. He remembered her back and rolled her to her side to get another look at the inky black bruise. It now radiated at least six to eight inches from the center.

"Perhaps this will help," Neli said as she walked up behind him. In her hands was a large, flat stone. It glowed orange, just like her skin.

Ryan knew better than to touch the stone, so he moved aside to let the small creature place it where it needed to go. She put a layer of what looked like lamb's wool over the stone to keep it from coming into direct contact with Roni's skin.

"Now roll her back over, so that the center of the bruise is over the center of the stone," Neli instructed.

As soon as Roni's back came into contact with the lamb's wool, her body jumped slightly, causing Ryan and Oriel to jump as well.

"No worries," the little angel said. "That's a normal response when one comes into contact with the Lamb's wool."

"What do you mean, the Lamb's wool?" Ryan asked. "Isn't lamb's wool just lamb's wool, or do you have one particular sheep that you like to use?" Ryan laughed at his own joke, but Neli stared at him.

"He was led like a lamb to the slaughter, and as a sheep before her shearers is silent, He did not open His mouth," she said, as if Ryan was supposed to know what that meant.

"Um... ok, that didn't really answer my question."

"It's written in that book right there," Neli said, pointing to Ryan's Bible.

"This book here?"

Neli nodded her head. "*Isaiah 53:7.*"

"Oh, you're talking about the Lamb, as in the Creator's Son."

"Of course, you don't think just any lamb's wool could evoke such a response in a human, do you?"

"Of course... what was I thinking?" Ryan mumbled. He looked over at Roni and noticed a brilliance around her eyes. He lifted her lid and was shocked to see orange light under them.

"It's just the stone doing its work," Neli reassured him. "Look at her hands."

Ryan unraveled the bandages on Roni's hands. Her palms glowed orange, and the scorch marks were healing rapidly.

"How long will this take?" asked Ryan.

"That I do not know," answered Neli. "Sometimes the healing is quick and sometimes not so quick."

"So what do I do now?"

"Wait."

"Wait for what?"

"They that wait upon the Lord shall renew their strength; they shall mount up on wings as eagles."

"Soooo... I should just wait. Right here?" Ryan was completely confused.

"I suggest you read that book in your bag. You seem to be lacking some basic understanding of it."

Ryan sat down by the fire and warmed his hands. He picked up his Bible. When he opened the book cover, a piece of paper fell out. It was a note from John.

> Ryan,
>
> As it happens, me and my buddies—Paul and Luke—were fortunate enough to get our books combined with the rest of these writings. Mine are near the end. Hope you enjoy them.
>
> John
>
> PS: This passage is what we talked about: 1 John 1:5-10. You know, asking for forgiveness and all.
>
> PPS: Dr Luke wrote this: Luke 15:11-32. I thought you might reconsider making amends with your parents.

Ryan was stunned. *Was John, the angel he had met in the cave, actually the same John in the Bible? How was that possible? Wasn't he a human, one of Jesus' twelve disciples?* He remembered some of his Sunday school lessons, but he must have missed the part where people turned into angels.

"He is not an angel," Michael interrupted his train of thought.

"Yes, but he said..."

"He never *said* anything. You assumed he was an angel."

Ryan began rolling the conversation he'd had with John around in his head.

"John was the last of the twelve disciples left on earth after all the others had been martyred for the Creator's cause," Michael explained. "He was sent by the Roman authorities to live in exile on a little island called Patmos. There he communed with the Creator and saw heaven and things that were to come.

"He attempted to write down all he saw and experienced, but there wasn't enough paper in the world to describe all of heaven. It's all written down in the last part of that book in your hand. It's called *The Revelation to John*."

Ryan flipped quickly to the back of his Bible, and there it was—the *Book of Revelation*, written by John.

"What in the world? Wasn't this book written, like 2000 years ago? Why is he still alive?"

"Lots of reasons, I suppose. For one, John is a very endearing soul, if you have not noticed."

Ryan smiled. "Yeah, I noticed."

"The Creator's Son loved him immensely," Michael paused and smiled as he thought of John and his Master.

"So, how is it that John has lived so long, and what's with his glowing eyes?"

"Well, the length of his life... that's under the control of the Creator. Ever heard of Enoch or Elijah?"

"A little. Isn't Enoch the guy in Genesis who never died?"

"Yes. *Genesis 5:24* says, 'Enoch walked with God; then he was no more, because God took him away.'"

"So, if he never died, what's he doing now?"

"Whatever the Creator wants, I suspect."

"You mean, you don't know?" Ryan was shocked.

Michael laughed, "Just because I am an angel doesn't mean I am omniscient."

"Oh," Ryan said, embarrassed. "What about the glowing eyes?"

"You know, when Moses spent a lot of time in the presence of the Creator, his whole face glowed. The Israelites were so terrified that he had to wear a veil over his face until the glow subsided (*Exodus 34:29-35*). Glad it's just the eyes now. The Dark One has tried to duplicate the effect with Roni's eyes."

"Yeah, that's only a little bit terrifying," Ryan mumbled. "You know, Jared mentioned that one of the little boys had glowing eyes too. You think that's the Dark One's doing?"

"Undoubtedly."

"So John never died? What about his family? Did he just not show up for dinner one day, and no one bothered looking for him?"

"I don't know all the details, but I'm sure the Creator worked everything out."

"What about that other guy, Elijah? What's his story? Did he just disappear one day too?"

"Ever heard that song about going down in a blaze of glory?" Michael asked with a grin. "Let's just say Elijah went *up* in a blaze of glory."

"Oh yeah, the fiery chariot story from 1 Kings..."

"2 Kings, Chapter 2."

"Yeah, that's what I meant." Ryan was quiet for a few minutes, then he inquired, "Why do you think the Creator does weird things like that?"

"You mean, defy death, walk on water, part the Red Sea, feed 5000 people with five loaves of bread and two fish?" Michael said. "If I were a human, I'd say it's just because He can. But, since I'm not, I will give you the answer the Creator gave us in the Book of Isaiah: *For my thoughts are not your thoughts, neither are your ways my ways (Isaiah 55:8-9)."*

Once again the human was silent.

"Maybe we aren't meant to know why the Creator does all the things He does," Ryan finally said. "I used to make lists of all the things I was going to ask the Creator when I get to heaven. Like: Why did you make head lice? Why do dogs pee on every blade of grass? And why are girls so difficult to understand? But now I have a feeling that, when I get there, I still won't know but I won't even care."

Michael smiled at Ryan and said, "You have no idea how right you are."

CHAPTER TWENTY

Dreams

I will search for the one my heart loves. So I looked
for him but did not find him. The watchmen found
me as they made their rounds in the city.
"Have you seen the one my heart loves?" Scarcely
had I passed them when I found the one my heart
loves. I held him and would not let him go...

Song of Solomon 3:2b-4a

Back at the lake house, everyone was on high alert. After dinner, Seth, Solomon and Donavon kept a close watch on what was happening outside the house, while Jillian, Juli and China kept the children and the injured comfortable inside. Jeni and Jared were in the basement, sifting through the boxes of papers from Norilsk.

Jeni was frantically trying to find something that might help her sister, but all the new boxes they had opened contained only information about the *copii de aur*, the golden children. The amount of new information they had found on the *AIRborns* was hardly enough to fill a small notebook. Jared scanned each and every page, looking for key words, but by midnight they were still no closer to helping Roni.

"Arg!" Jeni huffed as she plopped down in a chair and threw a pile of papers in the air. "I'm so fagged!"

"What did you just say?" Jared said with a confounded look on his face.

"I said I'm fagged. It means tired and worn out. It's what the sisters in the movie *Pride and Prejudice* said when they came home from a ball. Sorry, I didn't mean to sound rude or inappropriate."

Jared smiled. "What an interesting girl you are, Miss Jeni Arianna Chambers. You're a wealth of contradictions and surprises."

Jeni blushed. "Guess you don't know many girls who love sports and Jane Austen, do you?"

Jared walked over to where she was sitting and knelt down at her feet. "May I?" he asked as he took her hand in his. He pressed his lips tenderly against the back of her hand. Jeni felt a rush from her head to her toes.

Then Jared said, "I cannot fix on the hour, or the spot, or the look, or the words, which laid the foundation. It is too long ago. I was in the middle before I knew that I had begun."

Jeni grinned upon hearing a line from her favorite book. "In the middle of what?" she asked playfully.

"Why love, Jeni," he said very sincerely.

"Love!" Jeni exclaimed, pulling her hand from him. "We hardly know each other."

Jared was sullen for a moment. "I know my sister calls me exocentric, but she is just as big a romantic as I am."

He paused for a moment and looked Jeni in the eyes, as if trying to decide something, before he continued.

"Jillian and I have a secret that we haven't told anyone, not even our parents. There are already too many weird things about us, and we don't want to burden them with anything else."

Jeni sat up and gave him her full attention. She felt like her relationship with Jared was about to take a giant leap forward. After a long pause and a deep breath, Jared continued.

"We dream," he said.

Jeni sat quietly waiting for the punchline. She furrowed her brow after a few silent seconds had gone by and said, "Doesn't everyone?"

"No, no, no! You don't understand. We dream—not just random, meaningless dreams, but dreams that come true."

"Dreams that come true, huh?" Jeni said skeptically. "Like what? You dream about a bike you want for Christmas, and you get it?"

"No. Well, yes, I have had that dream before; but that's not what I'm talking about."

"Then what, Jared?" said Jeni impatiently.

"We've dreamed about what friends we're gonna have, if our aunt is having a boy or girl, who's going to pass their driving test first, the lottery numbers..."

"The lottery!" Jeni laughed. "Really, the lottery? You had me going for a minute there."

"I'm serious, Jacs!"

"Jacs?"

"Sorry, it's a pet name I made up for you. Jeni Arianna Chambers. It's your initials."

"That's cute. I like it. Did you dream that up too?" she teased.

They were both standing now, and Jared took a step and closed the space between them. His face was only inches from hers. He pulled at a curl of her long red hair and wound his finger in it.

"I have dreamed of you since I was ten years old."

Jeni was still. She held her breath for almost a full minute, her heart pounding in her chest. She didn't know what to say. Neither of them moved for what seemed like an eternity. Jared finally broke the silence.

"That day when I finally found you in your kitchen, my heart skipped a beat. I didn't ever want to let go of your hand. Jillian knew it too. My hand may have let go that day, but my heart never did. I know this sounds crazy weird, but I swear

151

I'm not a psycho stalker or anything. I don't expect you to feel for me what I feel for you... I mean, you just met me two weeks ago, but I've loved you for seven years and I can't stop now."

For the first time in her life, Jeni was at a loss for words.

Jared took a step back from her and asked, "Have I offended you, Jeni?"

After a few moments, Jeni grinned shyly. "Call me Jacs."

Jared smiled and kissed her on the forehead. They sat down on the couch together.

"Now, I'm not saying that what you just told me isn't weird," Jeni continued, "because it is. And, if you're lying, it's the best pickup line I've ever heard."

"I'm not, I swear!" Jared exclaimed.

"Ok. But you said Jillian knew who I was too. How does that work?"

Jared squirmed a bit. "Well, it's because we both share the same dreams."

"Meaning, she sees your dreams and you see hers?"

"Basically; but it's usually only the important dreams. Like the ones that are going to happen in real life, which is nice because, when we were kids, she mostly dreamed about pink ponies and rainbows."

"What did *you* dream about?"

"Brown ponies and dirt," he said solemnly. They both laughed.

"So, when you dreamed about me, what did you see?" Jeni asked in a more serious tone of voice.

"I've seen your face many times. Your long, red hair. Your pouty lips." He touched her mouth softly.

"Well, how do you know it's me and not Juli who is your destiny? I mean, we both look exactly alike."

"Green eyes," he whispered. "Like emeralds sparkling on a beach. Bet you can guess what my favorite color is."

Jeni lowered her head. "I hope you're not disappointed with all my freckles."

He lifted her chin. "Sixty-nine on the right cheek and fifty-three on the left. I even have names for all of them, if you care to hear them."

"Do you have OCD as well as an eidetic memory?" she laughed. "I don't think I'm ready for the freckle-naming stage of our relationship just yet."

"Well, what level are you ready for?" he asked bluntly.

Jeni thought about it and then said, "Maybe just the 'hold my hand and we'll see where it goes from there' stage."

Jared lips parted in huge smile. "If I hold your hand, is it ok for me to kiss it occasionally?"

"Yeah, but just don't make it too weird. I'm already going to hear about this from my sisters. Oh, what about your sister? Is she gonna hate me? She's probably sick of seeing me in her dreams."

"Jillian's cool. She knew this was coming. Besides, she has her own relationship to worry about."

"And, what relationship would that be, Mr Jared Dylan Reed?" She said as she ran her hand through his yellow curls.

"Oh, well, I can't really say. But, trust me, her relationship is going to take a whole lot more than a few lines from an old love story to come to fruition."

***

Victor's eyes slowly opened. Where was he? Still in jail, back at the facility? Neither, he supposed, from the feel of the bed and the smell of the room.

"Is that cinnamon I smell?" he said to himself.

His body ached from head to toe. His hand was bandaged, and he remembered how it had been broken. He lifted his left arm to rub the sleep out of his eyes and moaned aloud from the pain. Something next to him moved and made a small sighing sound. His arm froze in midair. He slowly turned his head. When his eyes had adjusted to the moonlight from the window, he saw what was beside him.

It was a girl, a beautiful girl with long, golden hair and flawless, fair skin. She was asleep but her hand was clutching a book. He held his breath and slowly turned himself on his side to look at her. The pain was excruciating, but well worth it, just to look at the perfection of the girl's face.

She looked like one of the girls from the facility. He wondered how she had got there. He wondered how *he* had got there. He pushed himself off the bed, careful not to wake her, and slowly made his way to the bathroom.

He fumbled around for the light switch and flipped it on. The sudden brightness blinded him, and he sat down on the toilet lid hard.

"So much for trying to be quiet," he mumbled.

After relieving himself, which was the best feeling he'd had in days, he looked in the mirror. He had the beginnings of a scraggly beard on his face.

"You look like a street urchin, old man," he said to himself. "Not that you were all that good-looking before."

He lifted the bandage above his eye. "Oh, that's going to leave a mark." He turned the faucet on and splashed some water on his face. It felt good. After he had dried off, he inspected the wrappings on his hand. Good thing he was left-handed or he would be up a creek. Someone with medical knowledge had obviously taken great care to set the three broken fingers in three colored splints. Pink, yellow and blue. Victor thought that was strange.

He looked around for a shirt or something else to wear. He was already wearing a stranger's boxers, but he felt exposed with all his scars showing. He usually wore long-sleeved shirts and pants to cover them, but there was no telling where his clothes were now. A soft knock came from the other side of the door.

"Hello, Victor. Is that you?" a soft female voice asked.

He wasn't sure how to answer. Was he a prisoner, and she, his guard? Not a very good one, though. Reading and falling asleep in your prisoner's bed did not seem the best way to keep your job. Maybe she was his doctor? Still, reading and falling asleep in your patient's bed was not very professional. Maybe she was a janitor come to clean his room. Again, reading and falling asleep in some stranger's bed...

"I-I have some clothes for you, if you like," the voice said.

Maybe she was a seamstress? Well, whoever she was, he figured he had better 'man up' and open the door.

The moonlight shone on her blond hair, giving her the look of an angel with a halo. She was wearing a lacy pink tank top and white lounge pants. Victor thought he had never seen anything more beautiful in his life.

"Hello, I'm Jillian," she said.

"Of course you are," he said with a Russian accent. His smile made her smile. He was leaning heavily on the door frame.

"I have something for you to wear."

"Of course you are... I mean... do," he said again. He was beginning to feel lightheaded and the girl was spinning around him. He leaned forward and would have fallen if Jillian had not hurried to catch him.

"Please, let me help you back to bed," she said.

Jillian managed to get him to sit upright on his own. She took the lounge pants that were in her hand, unfolded them, and shook them out. Then she knelt at his feet and placed one foot in each leg. She shimmied the pants up around his knees.

"You are going to have to stand a little if you want me to pull these up," she said. "Put your hands on my shoulders and steady yourself."

In one smooth motion, Victor stood up, Jillian pulled up the lounge pants, and then Victor sat back down on the bed. He forgot to let go of her shoulders, and she toppled forward and found herself lying on his chest and staring into the most intense blue and orange eyes she had ever seen.

"I'm... I'm so sorry," he said. "I'm not f-feeling like myself today." His eyes rolled back in his head and he was unconscious again.

"Well, this is awkward," Jillian said aloud.

"It most certainly is," said Raven, and he flipped on the bedroom light. The guardian was grinning from ear to ear. Jillian was wedged between the footboard of the bed and Victor's side.

"Exactly how long are you going to let me stay like this?"

"What? You look quite comfortable and relaxed. One might even assume that you had planned for such a close encounter."

"Very funny, ha, ha. Now, please, can you do your job and help me up?"

Raven took her hand and gave her a tug.

"Now, if you're done reveling in my unfortunate landing, would you consider helping me get Victor back into bed?" she said, as soon as she had found her footing.

"Unfortunate landing, huh?"

Raven was still smiling as he and his young charge put Victor back in a comfortable position on the bed. Jillian pulled the blankets over him and tucked him back in. She brushed his hair off his face and tenderly wiped the sweat that had accumulated on his forehead.

"So, how do you feel now that you have seen him?" Raven asked.

"Less apprehensive. Less fearful. More peaceful," she answered.

"I know both you and your brother have dreamt about him for many years now. How is Jared doing?"

"He knew it was him, when he saw him lying on the dining table the other day. I think we have both been preparing our hearts for Victor. I know he has suffered a lot of bad things in his life. I also know he has done some things that most people wouldn't forgive," she said with tears in her eyes.

Raven put his arms around Jillian and said, "I was unsure when the Creator chose him for you. I wanted you to have someone to take care of you, to be strong for you, but you will have to take care of him and be strong for him.

"I see now, how the Creator has been preparing you and Victor for the journey you must walk together. It will not be easy, my sweet one. It will seem horrible at times; but, if you really want him to be yours, you must trust in the Creator with all your heart and never let your love for Victor waver. Of that I am sure."

"As am I," she answered. "I just never imagined him to be so beautiful. I mean, of course I've seen him in my mind; but seeing someone in your mind is very different from seeing him in real life."

She paused for a few minutes as she fixed Victor's blankets again.

"You know, Jared and I have been in love with Victor and Jeni for such a long time. How is it going to be for them? I mean, they have only just met us."

"It will require patience on your part—and Jared's too," Raven replied. "You know you don't have to be with Victor. The Creator allows His children free will. If there's someone else you…"

"No!" Jillian said abruptly. "I've been waiting for him my whole life. I trust the Creator. He knows what will make me the happiest and the most satisfied in a partner."

"You are so young to have so much faith."

"Well, you can thank my parents for that," she said happily and yawned.

"It's late, my sweet one," Raven said and kissed her on the temple. "You have not had your four hours of sleep yet. Go lie down; I will stand watch over you both."

"Ok, but you must wake me if he opens his eyes. Even if it's only for a few seconds." She yawned again and curled up next to Victor. Taking his hand in hers as she drifted back to sleep, she mumbled softly, "I will never let you go. Never."

***

That night, when China laid her head down on her pillow, her mind was full. Full of Stephen and Allyson, and wondering… wondering what she was going to do next. Stephen was going to come get her tomorrow morning. Even after all the weird angel stuff, he said he would come.

"What am I going to wear?" she thought to herself. "What if his mom doesn't like me? What if Allyson cries the whole time? I can't go! When he comes tomorrow, I'll tell him I can't go. But he will have driven all this way. Ok, I'll go, but I'll leave Allyson here. But his mom wants to see her. Oh, what should I do?"

"I think you should go," Neil said as he materialized next to her. She wasn't startled; she was used to the angel showing up unannounced. It made her feel safe. She sat up and turned on the side table lamp.

"And I think you should take Allyson with you."

"Really?" she said sheepishly. "What if I don't know what to say?"

"Then don't say anything," Neil advised. "Too many people talk and have nothing to say. Just listen with your heart. If something touches it, it will know what to say."

China listened to her guardian's advice and took it all in. "How do I know if he is safe? Maybe he is pretending to be nice like Joseph did, and then he will be mean to me and Allyson."

"Do you trust me, China?" Neil asked.

"I suppose I do," China answered, looking down at the floor. She sat quietly for a few minutes and tried to listen with her heart. When she thought of Neil, she felt happiness and safety. He would protect her at all costs.

A smile came to her lips, and she looked up at him like a trusting child. "Yes, I do trust you, Neil."

"Good," he said. "Then I want you to go with Stephen and his mom tomorrow, and I want you to have a wonderful day. I will be close by at all times, so you will not have to worry."

"What about Allyson? Will you watch over her too?"

"I will be there for the baby," said Anastasia from near Allyson's crib. "Both of us will have ourselves ready to protect you, should anyone or anything try to hurt you or Allyson."

"China," Neil said as he stood up and walked over to Anastasia. He turned to face his charge and spoke softly, "I want you to know that Anastasia and I fought night and day to get you and Trinity released from Joseph's prison.

159

"I am sorry it took so long. The forces of the Dark One were strong in that place. A virtual stronghold of despair had wrapped its arms around that house. We were able to sneak in and be with you but, when we tried to get you out of there, there were just too many of them. Finally, when Michael and your brother showed up, we had the advantage. The demons were distracted long enough for us to deliver aid to you and get you out."

"What about Trinity? Why couldn't you save her?"

"I'm sorry, my darling, that we could not. She was very weak. She was ready to go home to her father, and she had fulfilled her purpose."

"That doesn't sound like a very good purpose. Just to have a baby and then die," China said quietly.

Anastasia knelt down next to her and said, "She saved your life, China. What greater purpose can there be, than to save the life of another? Did the Creator's Son not do the very same for all His children?"

China ran her hands over the long scars on her wrists. She remembered how she had felt after the loss of her second baby. She had wanted to end her life. Trinity did save her, but still it didn't seem quite fair; Trinity was only a little girl, and she had died so young. Sometimes China wished that it had been her who had died and not her friend. Then she wouldn't have to worry about staying safe and protecting Allyson.

She lay down in her bed and closed her eyes. Countless thoughts of Trinity and Neil and the Creator swam around in her mind, but eventually she fell asleep... and dreamt of Trinity in heaven with the Creator's Son.

CHAPTER TWENTY-ONE

The Plan

*"For my thoughts are not your thoughts, neither
are your ways my ways," declares the LORD.*

Isaiah 55:8

Sunday, 17th November

Ryan stretched and yawned as he sat up in his sleeping bag. With all the straw the healers had brought into the cave, it had been quite comfortable sleeping on the ground. He looked at his watch. It was just over five hours since he had gone to bed. He figured his body must have needed more than his usual four hours of sleep when it was injured. He looked at his foot and was pleased that it was healing nicely.

Michael, Oriel and Neli were sitting around the fire talking with two more healers he didn't recognize. Ryan noticed a familiar figure standing over Roni, who was still unconscious. It was John, and he looked like he was praying. Ryan stood up and gingerly made his way over to him.

John looked up when he heard the hay shifting around under Ryan's feet. He smiled and embraced the young man. "Hello, friend. It is good to see you again."

"It is good to see you as well." Ryan wasn't sure how to respond to such a long, unmanly hug. Then he remembered that John wasn't just a man; he was *the* John of the Gospel.

"So, how have you been since we last talked?" he asked Ryan as he pulled an apple out of his pocket.

"Good," Ryan blurted out immediately. "Well, ok. Not really that good. Honestly, I'm in a mess with Roni again."

"What did you do this time?"

"Tried to run. Again."

"Haven't you figured out that running..."

"I know, I know, I've already been lectured by Jeni, Oriel and Michael." Ryan decided to change the subject. "So, what exactly do you do?" he asked.

"Oh, this and that. Usually, when there's a war of some kind, I get assigned to a ship, since I have a lot of experience on the water."

"So, you are a guardian like Oriel?"

"Oh no, let's just say I'm someone with a little more than average knowledge of how the spiritual world works, and I use that knowledge to help people navigate their way around it."

"Well, what about super powers?" asked Ryan.

"What about them?" John replied.

"Do you have any?"

"Not really. Except for the glowing eyes—which I guess is a side effect of my hanging out with my Master—I just end up where the Creator wants me to be, when he wants me to be there. Sometimes I can hear what people are thinking, which is really nice. Cuts down on all the questions."

"Oh, really?" Ryan smiled. "You know this cave isn't exactly open water, so what are you doing here?"

"I'm between assignments now, but I'm going to be sailing across the Pacific Ocean with some naval newbies very soon."

"Sounds like fun."

"It should be," John winked at Ryan.

The winking was still awkward, but Ryan quickly turned his attentions to Roni. She looked peaceful. Ryan felt her pulse and listened to her heart. Her eyes weren't glowing anymore, and he wondered if Neli's stone had done the trick. He tried to roll Roni onto her side to look at her back, but he met with some resistance as she started to wake up.

"Good morning," he said to her. She didn't smile. "How are you feeling?"

"Fine," she answered dryly, then added, "I'm surprised you're still here."

"I know, and I'm sorry."

"It's fine. What happened to me?"

"I'm not completely sure," he said. "Gabriel's trying to get in touch with Sarah's guardian to check on a theory that Priscilla came up with."

"Oh yeah, and what is that?"

"Well, Priscilla thinks your condition may require you to keep your... uh... body weight up above a certain... uh... you know... uh... number," Ryan was tense as he told her the hypothesis. He knew Roni's weight had always been a sore point with her. She had been teased mercilessly in school by her classmates.

"Isn't that just peachy? Just when I finally start losing some weight, I find out I have to keep it in order to survive."

"I'm not completely sure that's the problem, but it's... um... likely."

They sat quietly for a while. Roni stared up at the ceiling of the cave and Ryan down at the ground.

"I was wondering if I could... um... look at your back," Ryan finally spoke. "The last time I looked at it, the bruise had spread out a bit farther than it was at the hospital."

Roni rolled her eyes and turned her body away from Ryan. He gingerly lifted up her shirt and was surprised to see that the bruise had shrunk down to just two inches in diameter. He stroked the area softly, and Roni shivered. She turned back abruptly.

"Are you done yet?"

"Ah, yeah, it looks a lot better."

163

"Good, I need to get back to the house to check on Zoei and the boys."

She tried to sit up but immediately felt nauseous. Ryan wrapped his arms around her shoulders to help her lie back down, but he was too late. Everything Roni had eaten the night before came up and hit Ryan in the face. He closed his eyes and mouth just in time. He didn't push her away. He wasn't going to make that mistake again. By the time she had emptied her stomach, she was crying.

John had seen what happened and brought a bowl of water and a cloth to wash Ryan's face. When he could open his eyes again, Ryan looked down at Roni, and he could see that she wasn't completely coherent.

"I-I-I'm sorry, Ryan, I didn't..." and then she was mumbling, and no one could figure out what she was saying.

"It's ok, Roni," said Ryan, trying to reach her, but she acted as if she couldn't even hear him.

"She's delirious," said John, and he placed a hand on her forehead. "She feels a little feverish too."

Ryan touched her and agreed with John.

Neli brought a bowl of soup over. "How are we going to get her to eat this? She needs it to gain strength."

"Let's get her cleaned up, and then we can try to get some of that in her," said Ryan.

"You go and get a shower," said Neli. "I will take care of her. Garnet and Opal will help me." She pointed to the red and iridescent-colored healers who were sitting near the fire.

Ryan hesitated. "I don't want her waking up and thinking I've left her."

"We'll tell her," John reassured him.

Reluctantly Ryan left the cave.

Oriel accompanied him on the thirty-minute hike back to the lake house. After making their way through the dense foliage around the cave opening, the two were able to walk side by side.

"Ryan," Oriel said, "I need to speak to you about the plan that Michael and I have come up with. We think it will be the best and most unobtrusive way to rescue John Chambers."

This news caught Ryan off guard, as the topic of Roni's father had not come up since Thursday, when they had all returned from the hospital. And, in the last few hours, thoughts of Roni had crowded out any other issue that might have needed his attention.

"Oh really?" was his response.

"Yes, and it will require all your patience and trust."

Ryan was curious now, and he gave full attention to what Oriel had to say.

"Michael thinks that you and Roni should make your way over to Russia by boat and pretend to tour Krasnoyarsk along with some other couples. There is a tour of the Norilsk Nickel plant and a camping and hiking expedition that goes through a good portion of the Siberian Traps."

Ryan stopped suddenly, and his mouth hung open for a moment. He blinked hard several times before he spoke.

"Oriel, are you telling me that you want Roni and me to get on a boat and sail over to Russia and then go camping and hiking and touring near Norilsk?"

"Yes."

Ryan smiled. "You *are* funny. For a second there, I thought you were serious."

"I am perfectly serious," Oriel said in earnest.

Ryan's eyes widened as he realized Oriel meant exactly what he had said.

"You two are crazy if you think I'm going to be able to make Roni get on a boat and travel halfway around the world, let alone go hiking and camping with me."

"I disagree. I think, with her father's life at stake, she would consent to almost anything," Oriel interjected.

"How are we supposed to get into the country? I have a passport, but I'm sure Roni doesn't."

"Michael is working on that."

"Oh, Michael is working on that, is he? Well, what's our cover going to be? Why would two American teenagers go camping and hiking in Siberia?"

"For your honeymoon."

"Our what!" Ryan exclaimed.

"Your honeymoon. You and Roni will marry and go on a couples' cruise in California. Most of the other passengers will be on their honeymoons as well. You will then travel to Norilsk, where you will go on a five-day hiking expedition in the Siberian Traps."

Ryan was stunned. His mind raced and his heart trembled. *You and Roni will marry.* Those words kept playing over and over in his head.

"How am I going to get her to marry me?" he thought. "She hates me, and she doesn't trust me. What am I thinking? I don't trust myself either!"

"Ryan, Ryan," Oriel tried to get his attention. "Ryan!"

"Huh? Oh? This will never work!" he exclaimed. "Roni will NEVER consent to marry me."

He took several steps toward the lake house and then stopped abruptly.

"Unless it is a fake marriage. We could just pretend to be married, right?"

Oriel shook his head. "No, it has to be real and legal."

166

"Can't you just use your angel powers and make up fake documents or something?"

"Angelic powers always leave a little residue that can be picked up by the enemy. We can't risk your safety or Roni's."

"Oh man, this isn't how I imagined getting Roni to marry me. I'm telling you, she's not going to go for this."

"I think you underestimate Roni's love for her father."

"What happens after we return to the States?" Ryan asked. "Do we divorce or get the marriage annulled? Because you know we won't... um... you know, officially... um..."

"Consummate the marriage," Oriel finished Ryan's statement for him.

"Yes, consummate, that's what I..." Ryan stopped talking and started stressing out.

They made it back to the house, and Ryan hurried downstairs to take a quick shower. He was dressed and ready to go in twenty minutes. When he came back upstairs, he ran into Jeni and Jared, who were in the kitchen trying to find something to eat.

"Where's Roni?" Jeni was worried. "Is she ok?"

"She's fine for now," Ryan answered. "She got a little sick to her stomach and... well, let's just say I'm here for a shower."

"So she's conscious?" asked Jared.

"Well, she was... but, I think, when we get some food into her, she will be good," Ryan said reassuringly. "Hey, I was wondering if you could run upstairs and get your sister a change of clothes and maybe a toothbrush..."

"Oh sure," said Jeni, and she took off up the stairs.

Ryan turned to Jared, "Oh, man, you are not going to believe what Oriel and Michael have cooked up for me and Roni."

"What?" Jared asked.

167

Ryan quickly relayed the conversation he had had with Oriel.

"Holy cow!" Jared couldn't believe what he was hearing. "Does she know yet?"

"I don't know, but I'm kind of hoping that Priscilla will tell her before I get back."

"Tell who what?" asked Jeni as she came down the stairs.

"I'll tell you later, Jacs," said Jared.

"Oh, it's Jacs, is it?" Ryan teased.

Jeni blushed. "I... ah... packed her a couple of outfits and some bathroom stuff."

"That's great, Jeni. Thanks. I've got to get back to the cave. Hopefully we'll see you later today."

"Tell Roni I love and miss her," Jeni said, choking back a tear.

"I will," Ryan assured her.

Then he remembered what Michael had said about him being responsible for Roni and her sisters. He hugged Jeni and reassured her that he would take good care of her big sister. This seemed to make Jeni feel better, so he turned and left.

The walk back across the field was quiet. Oriel let the news of the plan continue to roll around in Ryan's head, hoping that he would be able to find peace in his heart.

When they reached the cave, white smoke was coming from the entrance. Oriel froze and put his arm out to stop Ryan. He did not sense any unfriendly angels or spirits, but he drew his sword anyway and approached cautiously.

After rounding the turn in the tunnel, they could see that the fire had been put out and it looked like everyone was preparing to leave. Michael and John were dressed for cold weather and Priscilla was bundling Roni up in more blankets.

"What's going on?" Ryan asked.

Michael made his way over to them.

"We have to leave. Bryn and her followers have joined with Ezekiel and are planning another assault on the lake house."

"Can't we just fight them off, like the last time?" Ryan questioned the archangel.

"No," Michael replied. "The last time, we only fought the scouts. This time, Bryn and Katrina are bringing a whole legion of angels, demons, and only the Creator knows what else."

"I would count on a few Nephilim as well," added John.

"Don't you mean Misty?" Ryan commented. "She got pretty mad when you called her Katrina."

"Katrina was the name given to her by the Creator. It means 'pure'. She changed it when she decided to join the Dark One. She has lured many men into inappropriate relationships with herself and other young women.

"Did you notice China's reaction to her when she first appeared at the lake house? It is obvious that China has been raped many times, due to Katrina's influence on Joseph and other men."

Ryan's heart raced as he felt the weight of his sister's sad life.

"What about China and the other girls and everyone else back at the house? What are they going to do?" he inquired.

"We need to get back to the house and warn everyone. I think we will have to divide up. You and Roni will go to Dodge City and marry, then continue on to Russia with John to recover her father."

"Does Roni even know about this plan you have drummed up for us?"

"Not yet," John answered. "She hasn't regained consciousness. We'll have to tell her later."

Ryan's mind was going a hundred miles an hour.

"It's not safe for her to travel yet, her heart could stop again and she needs her medication!" he protested.

Oriel tried to calm him. "There is an old bomb shelter about five miles from here. If we hurry, we can make it before the sun rises."

"You mean, we have to walk there?"

"Running would be preferable," Michael said as he handed Ryan his backpack of medical supplies.

"I think we're ready," said Priscilla, scooping Roni and all her blankets up into her arms. With her human form being so small and the bundle of human so large, the guardian looked almost comical.

Ryan walked with determination in his step and took Roni from her protector.

"She is my responsibility," he said.

Priscilla started to protest, but one look from Michael cut her off. She knew Ryan needed to take responsibility and, though turning Roni over to him was difficult, she was happy that the human seemed to be accepting his God-given purpose.

"All's ready here," John announced.

Michael and John stood facing one another, knowing it could be a long time before they would see each other again. They locked arms.

"Until we meet again, my brother," Michael said to John.

A tear glistened in John's glowing eyes as he looked up at the archangel.

"Until we meet again."

CHAPTER TWENTY-TWO

Traitor

Then Samuel took a stone and set it up between
Mizpah and Shen. He named it Ebenezer,
saying, "Thus far has the LORD helped us."

1 Samuel 7:12

Jared and Jeni were in the kitchen, sharing a pint of mint chocolate-chip ice cream, when Michael unexpectedly appeared. Samuel and Camiel revealed themselves as well.

"It's time," Michael said to the guardians.

"Time for what?" Jared and Jeni asked simultaneously.

"We have been expecting an all-out assault since the Valkyries were here," Michael explained. "I thought we might have a little more time, but it seems that someone has been informing the enemy about our status here. They know Roni isn't well and I am still recovering from my injuries."

"Who would do such a thing!" cried Jeni. "We are all on the same side, aren't we?"

Michael looked at Jared, who gasped as he realized who the traitor was.

"There is a reason why there are so few of you assembled here. I chose only those selectively bred who had a heart for the Creator and an inclination for doing good.

"Humans with angelic DNA tend to be proud and self-serving. They show little or no regard for their fellowmen. They rebel against the Creator and are sometimes violent. Most human brains cannot cope with the rush of power their special abilities give them. Sadly, they usually end up in prison as violent offenders."

"But, if you handpicked us all, then you must have made a mistake," said Jeni.

"No, I did not."

"Jeni, it's Donavon," Jared said softly, placing his hand on her shoulder. "Remember, he wasn't chosen to come with us; he's a friend of Seth and Solomon's. He came over with them to help with the repairs to the house while we were at the hospital."

"Oh no," Jeni covered her mouth. "What are we going to tell them? Seth will be heartbroken."

"The first thing we need to do is find Seth and Solomon," said Michael. "They will be able to influence their friend more than the rest of us. I have sent Uriel to get a message to Heath and the detective. I think China, Allyson and John will be safest with them. I will take James to my friend Madeline. She has a cabin in Missouri. Hopefully she will help us."

"Why would you want to split up the boys?" Jeni asked.

"Twins have a very strong link with one another. The closer they are, the more likely they will try to connect mentally with each other. In so doing, they will inadvertently send out signals that will lead the enemy right to them."

Jeni was quiet for a moment and her lip began to quiver. "Does that mean I will have to be separated from Juli too?"

"Yes," Michael touched her face gently. "I am sorry, but it's for your safety as well as hers."

"Don't worry, Jacs, I'll be with you," Jared said tenderly to her. Then he realized that he and Jillian would have to be separated too.

"Yes," said Michael. "Jared will go with you as well as Seth. Solomon, Juli and Jillian will leave together. Victor..."

Jared interjected, "I'm telling you right now, Jillian will not leave Victor."

Michael relented. "Very well, he will have to go with them as well. Take Seth and Solomon's truck and drive south. Your guardians will lead you to a safe house near Oklahoma City. The others will drive Roni's minivan north toward North Dakota."

"What about Zoei?" Jeni asked apprehensively.

"I will take her to Madeline's with James," said Michael.

"How long do you think we have until Bryn and her army get here?" asked Jared.

"Not long, maybe till sun up. The first thing we need to do, Jared, is to wake Seth and Solomon so we can deal with Donavon.

"Jeni, you go upstairs and quietly wake up the girls and tell them to pack lightly. Only necessities, please. Remember, your guardians have to be able to ride in your vehicles with you in their human forms, or the Valkyries will find them."

As Jeni made her way up the stairs, Jared leaned over to Michael and said, "You do know you just asked for a minor miracle, right? I can't remember going away for even one night without Jillian packing at least half her wardrobe and the entire contents of her bathroom."

Michael smiled slightly. "The Creator made a beautiful and mysterious thing when He formed a woman."

***

Jeni knocked softly on China's bedroom door. The sleeping girl was startled awake and answered the door quickly. Not wanting to wake the baby up, Jeni closed the door behind her softly. She quickly told China what was going on.

Immediately, China began pulling clothes out of her drawers. Jeni hauled down a couple of old suitcases from the top shelf in the closet, for China to pack stuff for herself and Allyson. Anastasia helped China, while Jeni went to awaken Juli and Jillian; but the two girls were already up and packing. Their guardians had wasted no time in rousing their charges as soon as Michael had sent out the distress alert.

Zoei sat up in her bed and rubbed her eyes.

"This is not fabulous!" she exclaimed. "It's still dark outside, and I'm supposed to be asleep."

Jeni tried to calm her little sister down.

"Zo Bear, it's ok, we have to get ready to go on a trip. You and James are going with Michael to stay with that nice lady from the hospital. Remember her name was Madeline?"

Zoei's eyes grew wide. "What about you and Juli and Roni? Aren't you coming too?"

"Well, sweetie, it's like this; we all have to split up, but just for a little while. I have to go with Jared and Seth, and Juli has to go with Jillian, Victor and Solomon, but I promise it won't be for long." Jeni's eyes began to water, and she choked back her tears. "Now, I expect you to be a big helper to Michael and Madeline. You are older than James, and you will have to be his big sister."

"But what about Roni? Where is she going?"

Jeni's mind drew a blank as she hadn't heard what was happening with her older sister down at the cave. "You know what? I know that Ryan is with Roni, and he will take good care of her. Plus, she will have Priscilla there too."

"I know, I know. James said that Ryan will always take care of Roni and Juli and you."

Jeni looked startled. "Oh, he did?"

"Yes, and he also said that I would take care of all of you too," added the little girl.

Jeni wasn't sure what to make of Zoei's comments, but she decided to put it out of her mind for the moment. She headed over to the closet to get Zoei's backpack.

"Zo Bear, I need you to get a few toys and books that you would like to read on your trip and put them in your backpack. I'll put some clothes on your bed for you to put on and—oh!"

Jeni jumped back as a little fur ball came tumbling out of Zoei's backpack.

"Zoei Anne Chambers! What in the world…"

Zoei jumped out of her bed and scooped up the little grey fur ball. It gave a squeal and dug its sharp claws into Zoei's nightgown and hung on for dear life.

"It's just a baby, and it needed a home," Zoei said as she stroked the kitten's back. "It was really cold outside, and they were hungry."

"They? You're telling me there are more in your closet?"

"No, James and John have the other two."

"Oh, wow, I bet Jared is having fun with that right now," she said as she stroked the kitten's head. "What's her name?"

"Francesca Bastali, and James named his Bert, and John named his Ernie."

"Priel! Where is that guardian? Pri…"

"I am here."

"Oh," Jeni was startled. "Please watch over my sister until it's time to go."

Priel looked gravely at Jeni and took her by the hand.

"I will never leave her," he said reassuringly.

"Ok," Jeni said slowly and then looked at Zoei.

"Let's get you and Francesca ready to go. I hope Madeline isn't allergic to cats.

***

175

Jillian and Raven were trying to get a shirt on Victor when the young man began to revive. When he opened his eyes, he saw Jillian's face above him.

"Hello again," he said softly. "I was hoping you were real and not a dream."

Jillian smiled. She was already in love with the sound of his voice.

"It's Jillian, right?"

"Yes, Victor, that is right." Her cheeks were turning pink.

Raven interrupted the two. "I hate to intrude on what looks like a promising relationship, but we need to hurry up and get out of here. Remember Bryn, Misty... the Valkyries? They will be here by sun up."

Victor's face turned white. "I... we have to get out of here."

He tried to get out of bed too quickly and fell to the floor. Jillian knelt down beside him.

"It's ok, Victor, we're going to make you safe."

Victor allowed Raven to help him finish getting dressed. Jillian ran over to her room and grabbed her travel make-up, hair and nail kit, along with a few well-coordinated outfits and matching shoes. She made it back to Victor's room in fifteen minutes.

"That has to be some kind of record," Raven said, as Jillian placed her three-piece matching luggage set on the floor, just inside the bedroom door. "I'm pretty sure I've never seen you pack that fast in your whole life."

"No reason I shouldn't look amazing when I'm running for my life."

Raven smiled as he finished tying an old pair of tennis shoes on Victor. He had found them in the closet, along with a few items of clothing that used to belong to John Chambers.

As Jillian and her guardian started to help Victor to his feet, another guardian appeared.

"Jesse!" Raven was surprised to see his friend looking so much better so soon.

"In the flesh," the high-spirited angel replied. "And I mean literally in the flesh."

The last time Jillian and Raven had seen Jesse, he had been beaten to a bloody pulp, but now he looked quite recovered. Jillian noticed the scar above Jesse's left eye was very much like the one on Victor's forehead.

"Let me get him, little lady," Jesse said to Jillian as he took her place beneath Victor's arm. "You grab the luggage."

***

Downstairs, things weren't going quite so smoothly. James and John had completed their four-hour sleep cycle and were running around the basement and jumping from chair to chair with Bert and Ernie, as Michael and Raphael tried to pack up all the research materials from Norilsk. Jared had thrown his few personal items into his suitcase before going to the kitchen to pack some travel snacks.

Seth went to search for Donavon, while Solomon quickly packed up their belongings. Both brothers were grief-stricken to learn that their childhood friend was a traitor. After completing a thorough search of the house, Seth put on his heavy coat and a thick pair of gloves and went outside.

It had begun to rain, and the ground was covered with a thin layer of sleet. The partially frozen snow made the grass very slippery, and Seth had to catch himself several times so he wouldn't fall. He called out Donavon's name, but the wind was blowing too hard for his voice to carry.

As he made his way around the back of the house, he saw a faint glimmer of light coming from the storm shelter door.

No one had gone down there since the battle against Ezekiel and the Nephilim. Slowly, Seth crept toward the light. When he was almost to the door he heard voices. He couldn't make out what was being said, but he recognized Donavon's voice.

Carefully, he put one hand on the door and his eye to the crack, where the light was shining through. He could see Donavon talking with two very tall men. One was facing the door, but Seth didn't recognize him; the other had his back turned towards him. He put his ear up to the crack and tried to eavesdrop on their conversation. The only words he could make out were "*AIRborn*", "the doctor", and "Valkyries".

Seth put his eye back up to the crack, just as the other man turned around. Ezekiel! Seth covered his mouth and backed away from the shelter door, doing the crabwalk for about twenty feet. He reached out with his mind to Solomon and, immediately, the shelter door flew open. Ezekiel came soaring out into the open, landing with a thud that shook the whole house.

"So, I see we have a spy," he bellowed. "It looks like one of your friends, Master Donavon."

Donavon inched his way slowly up the stairs and peeked over the edge of the door. He looked terrified.

"I find it quite interesting," Ezekiel continued, "that, even though you stole this boy's girl, he still wants to save you."

Seth was scared and confused. "What are you talking about? You mean Anita? Donavon, what is going on here? What have you been telling this demon?"

"Just that you Martinez brothers always get what you want." Ezekiel pulled his sword, H'imesh-Dagon (the arm of Dagon), slowly from his sheath. "But today we are going to settle that score! Right, Master Donavon?"

Donavon pulled himself together. He walked up the last few steps of the storm shelter with his hand on a sword that hung from his hip. He was wearing armor and a red dragon was on his breastplate.

"No," whispered Seth. "Please, no, Donavon! What are you doing? You can't fight for the Dark One. Remember our Sunday school teacher? She told us that the bad guys can seem to be good. You don't want to go against the Creator!"

Donavon spoke in a voice that was half confidence, half fear. "The Creator? What Creator? I know the truth, Seth. There is no Creator. There's just us and them." He pointed at Ezekiel.

"And who do you think he is?" Seth stood up and pointed at the fallen angel.

"One of them, you know," said Donavon, pointing upwards. "He's an alien."

Seth wasn't sure what to say. He just stood there with his mouth open. Ezekiel watched the pair, the corners of his mouth curled up in a sinister grin. His plan to break up the friendship was nearing fruition.

Seth finally broke the silence.

"Come on, Don, we've been friends forever. Don't let this liar convince you otherwise. He's not an alien; he's an angel, a fallen angel. The alien stuff is just to distract you from the truth."

"Truth, huh! Well, if he's lying, then I don't want to believe in a god who lets little kids and their moms get beaten up by their drunken, churchgoing dads."

"You think God let you get abused by your dad? You're wrong! He tried to save you, and He's still trying to save you. Come with me now. Don't let the bad guys win."

Donavon looked down at his feet for a few moments, and a tear slid down his cheek and fell on the toe of his boot. He looked up and took a step toward Seth's outstretched hand.

"You know, all the years we went to that church, everybody—and I mean *everybody*—knew what was going on at my house. And did anyone lift a finger to help? No. Not a single deacon or elder or choir member. Your dad..."

"Yeah, my dad," Seth interrupted. "Be careful what you say about my dad. He was the one who stood up in that congregational meeting and put our family's reputation and business on the line for you and your mom. You know he got arrested, right, for conspiracy to kidnap? Who do you think he was trying to kidnap, Donavon? You. Your mom was the one who turned him in."

"He tried to save you, but your mom..." Seth began to weep heavily. "Your mom wouldn't let us take you. We were going to take you back to Mexico to keep you safe. Instead, your mom turned my parents in, and Solomon and I almost got taken by child services."

"You're lying!" screamed Donavon.

"I'm not! You know I'm not! Disengage your heart from these monsters, and you will know I'm telling the truth."

Solomon and Jared came crashing through the plastic that covered the hole where the sliding glass door used to be. They were already dressed for battle. Jared held his two short swords and Solomon was holding what at first Seth thought to be a pitchfork; but, upon closer examination, he saw that his brother was wielding a golden trident.

"Thought you could sneak up on us again, Ezekiel?" Jared yelled over the wind.

"Oh no, my boy," Ezekiel sneered, "I knew I could."

CHAPTER TWENTY-THREE

Exit Strategy

Reckless words pierce like a sword, but
the tongue of the wise brings healing.

Proverbs 12:18

When the lake house shook, all the occupants knew the battle had started.

Stephen arrived just as Ezekiel made his grand entrance. He had driven up in a large white van that said *First Baptist Church* on the side. He was able to get China and the baby in the van just fine, but trying to convince John to leave his brother was another matter entirely. The boys had never been apart from each other. John started crying, and he kicked Stephen in the shin in a bid to escape. But Stephen was a detective and had dealt with people trying to get away from him almost on a daily basis; so a small kick in the shins didn't faze him at all.

Michael could see that it would be no small task to separate the boys, so he knelt down in front of them. He put his hands on their heads.

"Listen, my sons. You will only be away from each other for a little while. James, look into the future and see if I speak the truth."

James closed his eyes and began to smile.

"Now, share what you see with your brother."

John began to smile too. The little boys hugged each other, and then John took the detective's hand, and Stephen was able to lead him safely to the van. Neil, Anastasia and John's guardian Daniel took their seats next to Heath in the rear of the vehicle.

Daniel, who rarely spoke, wondered how all the guardians were going to be able to keep their human forms for so long. Michael answered his question aloud, so that the others could hear him.

"Since you will have to hold your human form indefinitely, you will need to consume adequate amounts of food and water and get at least six hours of sleep in a twenty-four hour period. Practice talking as much as you can and, for the sake of the humans, only transform if there is absolutely no other option." The guardians nodded in agreement.

Before Stephen got into the driver's seat, Michael stuffed a thick envelope into the detective's inner coat pocket.

"There's $15,000.00 in there," he said to the detective. "Try to live as inconspicuously as possible at your residence in town but, if you should need to run, that should cover your expenses. I have included birth certificates and social security numbers for everyone, also driver's licenses for the adults.

"China has a bank account at a small bank in Mulvane. You know where that is, just south of Wichita? Good, there are some papers for you and her to sign. Only use that account in a dire emergency. It isn't linked to any main computer networks, but it might still be traceable."

Stephen took in everything Michael was saying. The angel knew he was asking a lot of the human, but he felt that Stephen would rise to the occasion.

"Do you have any questions?" Michael asked the detective.

"J-just one. H-h-ow or w-what did you mean when y-y-you told James to see the f-f-future?"

"James can see future events, while John can see the past. It is their gift."

"S-some g-gift."

"Yes, indeed, and Ezekiel would like nothing better than to get his hands on the two of them. Please watch over John carefully... and one more thing."

"Yes?"

"Be careful what you ask."

"Will do," Stephen said as he held his hand out to Michael.

Michael grabbed the detective by the shoulders and kissed him on the forehead.

"May the God of Peace go with you, my son."

***

As the detective and his precious cargo left the lake house, Michael headed back inside. He could hear a fight going on in the backyard, but he needed to get the other humans to safety. Juli met him at the door.

"E-Ezekiel!" was the only word she could get out.

"I know. Get Victor and Jillian to the minivan. Wait for Solomon." He handed Juli an envelope similar to the one he had given Stephen. "There are instructions inside. Please don't draw attention to yourselves on the road. Always do the speed limit and watch out for careless drivers."

Juli looked wide-eyed at Michael. "Me? Why are you giving this to me? I-I-I'm not a leader. I'm not brave. You meant to give this to Jeni." She tried to push the envelope back at Michael.

"No, it is meant for you. You must trust in the Creator and allow Him to help you fulfill your purpose."

"But... but..." she tried to dispute Michael's command but found herself alone, still holding the envelope. She looked around for him, but he was gone.

"A-alright, Juli Noelle Chambers, you got this. You *are* brave. You *can* lead like Jeni—" a loud crash from outside startled her, "—or not!"

She screamed and started to run up the stairs, but then she stopped because Jillian was on her way down with her hands full of luggage—and Raven was right behind her with Victor and Jesse.

"Let's go, Juli," Jillian tried to sound calm. "Michael says you're driving."

The group made it to the garage and piled into Roni's minivan. It was a good thing that Juli's guardian, Ariel, was small. She would have to sit on the floor between the two front seats.

"Where are Solomon and Saffron?" she asked.

"Michael said to wait for them."

***

Out on the lawn, Seth, Solomon, Jared and their guardians were locked in a fight with Ezekiel, Donavon and his keeper Bak. It would have been a quick fight, since the former outnumbered the latter two to one; but a high-pitched war cry cut through the night air and suddenly they were fighting four of the Valkyries. Misty, Eir, Prima and Rota lunged towards the guardians, taking over from the already-winded Donavon and Bak.

"Where is Bryn?" Ezekiel bellowed.

Misty ducked under Camiel's sword. "She got held up somewhere around Dodge City. It seemed our attack was anticipated."

"At least the fight is a little fairer," said Donavon.

Ezekiel put the tip of his sword up to the boy's neck. "Fair? You think a fair fight is what I want?" A trickle of blood ran down Donavon's neck.

"I want to annihilate all of them! Humans and guardians alike! And then, when I rule the world, no God on high is going to tell me how to run this place!"

Ezekiel put his sword down and regained his composure. "Now, where is that girl? And the good doctor?"

"Someplace you will never find them," came a voice from behind him.

"Ah, Michael, so nice of you to join us," Ezekiel turned around. "How's the back? Any better? I hear you are a little under the weather these days."

"I still have enough strength in me to fight you."

"Michael, Michael, Michael, all this fighting. Aren't you tired of it? Why don't you learn to play nice? I know you would enjoy not having to save the world every time you turn around."

"There's only ever been One who could save this world, and He is my Master."

"Very well, have it your way," said Ezekiel, flicking a knife at Michael. The archangel winced as the sharp weapon sliced his leg open.

"I really should save you for Bryn. She's been looking forward to a rematch, but she's late and there's no one left to challenge me, so…"

Ezekiel lifted his sword and walked toward his enemy. When he was only a few feet away, he felt a pinprick, and something went whooshing by his ear. He reached his hand up to his head. It was wet. He looked at his hand and saw blood.

"Must be one of those Ginger Twins again! I had a feeling you would be trouble the moment I saw the first little red ringlet sprout from your head," he called out. "We never would have sent you out had we known you were trash, like the other rejects."

Jeni's second arrow found its mark right between Ezekiel's shoulder blades. This infuriated the fallen angel, and he whirled around to see where she had fired from.

Whoosh! Another arrow hit him in the back of his leg.

Ezekiel cursed and dropped to one knee. He looked around frantically, trying to find out where the arrows were coming from. Bak, who was being pressed back by Seth, tripped over Ezekiel's leg.

"Idiot!" he screamed at the clumsy keeper.

Seth saw a chance to get to Donavon, and he took it. He grabbed his friend by the arm.

"Come on, let's get you out of here!"

Donavon pushed him away and crouched into an at-ready stance, with his sword in one hand and a knife in the other. "I'm not going anywhere with you!"

"Please, Don, you can't mean that," Seth put down his trident and pulled off his helmet. He unlatched his breastplate and dropped it on the ground in an attempt to appear less threatening to his friend.

"Please, my brother, I don't want to fight you. You don't want to be with the wrong side, do you?"

"Who says it's the wrong side? Just because you're not on it doesn't make it the wrong side."

"He has tricked you. Don't you see that?"

"What, now I'm too dumb to understand what's going on? I just can't win with you!" The anger in Donavon grew like an out-of-control fire and he lunged at Seth. It suddenly grew quiet. Donavon found himself looking into Seth's blue eyes for what seemed like an eternity, and then slowly his friend sank to the ground. Like a blooming flower, a deep red stain began spreading across Seth's chest.

"He's bleeding. Seth's bleeding! Someone has stabbed Seth!" his mind was screaming. "Who was it?"

And then he looked at his hand. It was covered in blood, and so was the knife he was holding.

He couldn't move at first. Then, he felt his body lurch toward the house. Jared slammed into him, and Donavon saw him tearing off his armor to get to his shirt.

Jared pulled his blue polo off and pressed it against Seth's chest to try to stop the bleeding around his heart; but it was too late. The knife had slashed Seth's heart and punctured his lung. Jared screamed out Ryan's name helplessly, in the vain hope that his friend might hear him.

Lorrel was being hammered by Prima and Eir but, when his charge fell, he felt the knife go through his own heart. The guardian dropped to his knees. Prima was just about to run him through when Camiel struck her in the head with his sword. The sword bounced off her helmet and the reverberations stunned him long enough for Prima and Eir to get away. Solomon and Saffron had driven Rota back beyond the tree line, and the two were jogging back when they saw that the others were gone.

"That's good work, my friend," Solomon said to Saffron.

"It was indeed," she said slowly, as she looked around at the other guardians.

All eyes were on Solomon. He saw Jared and Jeni leaning over someone, and his heart quickened.

"Where is Seth?" He reached out with his mind and sensed that his brother was failing fast.

He pushed Jared and Jeni aside. "No, no, no," he wept as he gathered his brother into his arms. "Who did this to you?"

"You must not hurt him, little brother, he may yet believe."

"Who? Who did this? Donavon? I will kill him!"

"No, don't," Seth grabbed his brother's collar and tried to speak, but his chest cavity was filling with blood. Blood began to run down the corners of his mouth as he choked out, "He... he is your brother now."

And then he was gone.

CHAPTER TWENTY-FOUR

Oblivion

All go unto one place; all are of the dust,
and all turn to dust again.

Ecclesiastes 3:20, KJV

Ezekiel pulled the last of Jeni's arrows out of his back and staggered to his feet. He leaned his massive frame against the house.

"What's happened?" he asked Donavon, who was standing nearby in the shadows.

"He... he's dead. My friend is dead, and I-I killed him."

Ezekiel grinned. "They'll never forgive you now. You'd better run. Run fast and far away."

Donavon was shaking as he backed away from the huddled group of people. As soon as he reached the corner of the house, he took off like a rocket. But he only made it about ten feet when he hit something waist high with his knife. He tumbled head over heels and fell into a bush.

"What the..." he exclaimed but stopped short when he saw what had blocked his way—a little girl in a pink nightgown, with a doll tucked under one arm. The contents of an unzipped backpack were spilled out onto the icy sidewalk. A little grey kitten crawled out of the backpack and onto the girl's head.

Donavon watched the animal scamper away, leaving tiny paw prints in the sleet. As he moved toward the still child, he activated a motion sensor light and, to his horror, saw that the little paw prints were made with blood. He was speechless. He turned the girl over and tried to revive her. She wasn't breathing, so he tried to do CPR but stopped when he felt one of her ribs break.

Her head was soaked in blood and her body was limp. Donavon could do nothing but cry out, "Please, somebody, help me!"

"That's the first smart thing you've said in months." The voice came from a young woman who had appeared amid a faint flash of light. She squatted down next to Donavon and the girl. "Do you know this child?"

"Y-yes, she is the little sister of the girl who owns this place. I think her name is Zoei."

"Well, she's going to die."

"No, no, she can't die! Her sisters need her. Their parents are gone, and they only have each other."

"Since when have you cared about anybody's problems but your own?"

"Since right now! Can't you help her?"

"No," she said, tossing her long, dark braid over her shoulder, "but this might be your lucky day."

"Lucky?" Donavon frowned. He couldn't think of anything lucky about the day at all. He had killed two people within ten minutes of each other.

"Yes, lucky. Are you hard of hearing?"

The woman stood up and walked around Donavon and Zoei, examining the girl closely. She bent over and lifted Zoei's eyelid. A pale light shone dimly beneath them. Donavon threw his hands up and let out a high pitched squeak. Zoei rolled off his lap, back onto the pavement.

"You sure have gotten skittish," said the woman.

"What? You know me?"

"Yes, and you knew me too—up until six months ago."

"What? I don't know you. What's your name?"

"Delanny," she replied, crossing her arms and staring at Donavon. Though she was only five feet tall, he was getting uncomfortable under her intimidating glare.

She shifted her weight and huffed. "You don't know me? Really? You sure seemed to know me when I saved your bacon with your science teacher. Remember the paper you had due, on tropical birds? The one you thought your dog ate? Well, he did eat it, and I saved it."

"How'd you do that?"

"You don't want to know. Anyway, the point is, I was always with you—until you pulled that lame brained stunt with the McAllister boy."

Donavon looked quizzically at her.

"Last Easter, when you idiots tried to summon some aliens from the far side of the universe, I believe the moment of truth came when you said—and I quote—'Aliens from the deep, guard us; aliens from the deep, guide us; keep us from all others, show us the way to go.'"

The expression on Donavon's face went from confusion to terror. He wondered how she could possibly have known that.

"Yes, it sounds just as stupid when I say it."

"Are... are you an alien?"

Delanny rolled her eyes. "Of course I'm not an alien." She stared hard at Donavon. "Do I look like an alien? Do aliens wear jeans and black leather jackets? You're not very clever, are you? Puberty did nothing for you. Don't worry, around twenty-seven or so, you'll start making sense again."

"Are you psychic?"

"You know, children often make more sense and have more imagination than some of the teenagers I know. I'll give you one more guess, and then OFF WITH YOUR HEAD!" she yelled. Donavon's face went pale.

"Just kidding! But, seriously, you don't know who I am?"

The boy shook his head slowly.

"Well, ok, looks like I'm just going to have to spell it out for you. I'm your guardian angel. At least, I was—until you traded me in for Bak the alien."

Donavon felt really confused. He sat staring at Delanny for a long time. He seemed to remember her slightly. He stood up and walked within a yard of her. He sniffed the air and took a step closer. Her lavender scent was very familiar. She held one hand out to him. He took it. She walked around and behind him and embraced him. Her human form melted away, and he was covered in her soft white feathers.

Donavon looked at Delanny's hands, which were locked together in front of him. He touched her wrists; they were scarred with several layers of rope burns. He put his hand next to hers, and he could see that their ligature marks were identical. He turned around and backed away from her.

"What... how did you get this? W-who did it?"

"It was your father, Donavon," Delanny said gravely.

"My father did it? I don't remember anyone else being there when he tied me to the pole in the basement."

"Don't you?" she asked softly, cupping his cheek in her hands. He breathed her scent in deeply and closed his eyes.

He remembered her. It seemed like time stood still with Delanny near him. When he opened his eyes, he could see Priel hovering over Zoei's body.

"What's happening?" he asked, somewhat terrified.

"The child's guardian is petitioning the Creator to spare her life."

"W-what if He says no?" Donavon said nervously.

"Then she will go to be with her Heavenly Father forever. You sure seem concerned about this child. Maybe you should be in charge of her," Delanny grinned, and then she closed her eyes. Donavon stared at her, wondering what she was doing.

"I'm speaking with the Creator," she said in answer to his thoughts.

"W-well, what is He saying?" the boy asked skeptically.

"Just a minute," she said, with her eyes still closed and her head lifted to the heavens. When she was done, she smiled and looked at Donavon. "So, that was easy."

"What was easy?"

"Well, I just got you a new mission in life."

"What!?"

"Yeah, you are going to be taking on some new responsibilities. Call it a new purpose."

"A new purpose? What's that supposed to mean?"

"You wanted to save this child's life, right?" Delanny asked shrewdly.

"Yes," Donavon replied. He was getting the feeling that he had just walked into something he wasn't going to like.

"Well, the Creator has decided that you will be personally responsible for this child's life."

"What! I can't be in charge of a kid. I'm only sixteen years old!" he bellowed. "Besides, she already has a house full of 'parents'." He emphasized the word "parents" with his hands.

"Things are about to change," said Delanny gravely. "This group of humans are about to be scattered in every direction."

Zoei began to stir, and Donavon rushed to her side. Priel stood next to Delanny; he was back in his human form. The child's hazel eyes fluttered open.

"Zoei, Zoei, are you alright?"

"I'm ok, I'm ok," she whispered.

She looked up at Donavon. He was startled by the glow in her eyes.

"What happened?" Donavon looked at Delanny with uncertainty.

"I-I was just with Jesus," the little girl said.

Delanny stooped down. She looked the little girl in the eyes and said, "Zoei, do you remember Donavon?"

Zoei rubbed her eyes and peered up at the nervous teenager. "Oh, him," she said, sounding annoyed. She stood up and collected her backpack and its contents. Then she picked up her kitten and nuzzled her.

"Jesus told me you were going to be taking care of me." She looked him over, somewhat smugly for a five-year-old.

"Well," she finally said, "I guess we all have our crosses to bear. Come on, let's get back inside before you run someone else through with that knife."

Donavon's mouth hung open as Zoei led the way back into the house. Priel and Delanny had a hard time keeping a straight face.

"I knew I was going to love this assignment," Delanny said.

When they were safely inside, Zoei said, "We have to get out of here. But, first, Jesus said we had to find James."

***

A faint glow on the horizon reminded everyone outside the house that the day was upon them. Ariel and Saffron had to drag Solomon away from Seth's body. Lorrel had already guided Seth's soul to the Creator, but the sight of the lifeless body was more than his twin brother could bear. He couldn't breathe; he felt as though his heart was being ripped in two. Finally, Saffron laid her hand gently on his forehead and Solomon fell into a deep sleep.

Jeni and Juli gave each other a tearful goodbye hug, as did Jillian and Jared. The unconscious Victor and Solomon were buckled into the back seats of Roni's van, with Jesse sandwiched in between. Juli and Jillian took the middle two seats, while Raven got in the driver's chair and Saffron rode shotgun. Ariel sat on the floor between Raven and Saffron, facing the back of the vehicle.

"I don't envy you your long journey," Camiel said when everyone was settled in the van.

"We'll manage," Raven replied.

"May the Creator guide you."

"And you as well, my brother."

***

Jeni waved until the van was out of sight. Jared put his arm around her shoulder, but she needed more than a one-armed side hug. She turned and captured his neck with her arms. He lifted her up, and she wrapped her legs around his waist. Jeni let out a colossal wave of emotion and her soul melded into his. She let herself be the weak one for a few moments.

The ground beneath Jared's feet began to shake.

"The rest of the army is near," Jared said, gently lowering Jeni down to let her stand on her own feet again.

"Seth left the keys to his truck on the front seat. He wasn't—," she choked, "he wasn't sure who was going to drive." A second wave of emotion almost consumed her, but Jeni held it firmly in check. She needed to stick with the task at hand.

Michael came through the garage door. He looked weary and ragged. "You must leave now before the road south is cut off. All the papers from Norilsk are in the back of this truck," he informed them. "Guard them well."

Jeni suddenly remembered her baby sister. "You have Zoei, right?"

"She is in good hands," Michael reassured her.

194

Jeni, Jared and their guardians piled into Seth and Solomon's truck. It wasn't a king cab, but it had a small camper top attached to its bed. Michael handed Jared an envelope similar to the one he had given to the other two groups and cautioned them on the importance of not drawing attention to themselves.

"When will I see my sisters again?" Jeni asked.

"Only heaven knows," Michael said. "You must go. The Lord above be with you till we meet again."

Jared spun the tires as he exited the driveway.

Michael shook his head and said to himself, "Did I not say to go unnoticed?" He prayed for protection as the truck disappeared behind the trees.

A small voice brought Michael back. "We haven't been able to find James."

Michael turned around and saw Zoei, Priel, Donavon and Delanny standing in the doorway that led into the house. He walked up to Zoei, who was holding Donavon's hand, and squatted in front of her.

"I see you have spent time with my Master," he said to Zoei as he looked into her glowing eyes. Then he turned to Delanny.

"It's a long story," the angel said to her superior.

"I see." The archangel placed his hand on Zoei's head. "Well, we don't have time for long stories right now. Has James been found?"

"No, sir," answered Delanny. "He isn't in the house."

Michael thought for a moment. "Zoei, are there any hiding places you and the boys would go to when you played?"

"We've already checked those," Zoei replied. Beginning to feel a little faint, she leaned against Donavon's leg.

"She needs to rest," Michael said to the teen.

Donavon looked down at Zoei, and the child reached her arms up to him. He gingerly picked her up, and she immediately snuggled against his chest.

"Do you have any idea where James might be?" Michael asked Donavon.

Donavon thought for a second and then said, "What about the storm shelter? He tried to get in there a few times while I was talking with the ali-" he almost said aliens, but he caught himself, "I mean, with Ezekiel and Bak."

The small group headed to the back of the house. The sun was still orange on the horizon, but there was enough light to see what looked like a massive storm approaching.

"Bryn will be here soon. If we can make it to the tree line by the lake, we have a chance. Delanny, Priel—take Zoei and Donavon and hide yourselves in the garage. I will retrieve James, and then we will make our escape along the bank of the lake. The brush should give us enough cover to get a good distance from the house.

"Madeline is supposed to meet us at the fuel station on the highway. It's about two miles from here but, if we carry the children, we should be able to make it."

"What about Seth?" Donavon asked timidly. Someone had laid Seth's body on the family room couch. "I... we can't just leave him here."

"The one who is Seth is no longer here on earth. This physical body was born of this earth; and all that are born of this earth, to the earth they shall return."

Delanny pulled Donavon and Zoei to the garage, with Priel following closely behind. Michael went through the living room into the dining room. Not knowing if any enemy angels were near, he slowly climbed through the one remaining window and inched his way to the opening of the storm shelter on his elbows.

"James, James," he whispered.

"We are here," Clayton, James' guardian, answered.

"It is time to leave. We must hurry, the storm approaches."

"The child is frightened and will not come."

"He is not of age; you must override his free will."

Within seconds, Clayton and James appeared on the steps of the storm shelter. The boy clung to his guardian's back, and Clayton had James' small grey kitten tucked in the front of his coat. The child had chased it down into the cellar and had then been too afraid to come back up.

"We must get back to the other side of the house without using any..." Michael was cut short as a knife buried itself into his shoulder. Clayton immediately transformed himself into a warrior angel as Michael fell to his knees. He put his charge into the archangel's arms.

"Here, take James and get to safety. I will find you!" Clayton turned around and rushed towards Ezekiel, who was still in a weakened state but had mustered enough strength to throw the knife that had injured Michael. Clayton beat him down until he had no life force left. Ezekiel evaporated and his essence returned to his master.

When the angel turned around, Michael and James were gone. Clayton looked toward the west and saw that the storm was almost upon him. With the kitten still nestled inside his coat, he ran back into the house and towards the garage. He was about to make his way to the lake when two things caught his eye.

One was a large black tarp alongside the garage wall. The second was a gas line. It ran along the wall next to the tarp. When he lifted the tarp, a grin appeared on his face.

"A motorcycle," he said aloud. Hoping the bike would still run, he rolled it away from the wall.

He walked over to the pipe and carefully twisted it until a fissure developed, allowing gas to escape the line. Darting back to the motorcycle—which was no more than a dirt bike for twelve-year-olds—he tried to start it, but it sputtered and died. He focused all his angelic powers on the machine, and it roared to life. As he rode the bike out of the garage, he leaned over and picked up a piece of ice and threw it at the automatic door button.

"Bullseye."

Clayton sped along the shore of the lake for about sixty seconds before the bike began sputtering. Then it died, and he turned it towards the lake, crashing it through the brush.

When he had picked himself up off the ground, he turned back to face the house. The storm clouds had settled right over it. Bolts of lightning were hitting the rods on the roof, but they soon became useless because there were too many hits.

Clayton kept watching and waiting, hoping that his last-minute plan would work. In another minute, an enormous thunderbolt lit up the morning sky. It was as bright as the middle of the day. Electricity sparked and ran along the old metal guttering of the house. When it finally neared the garage, Clayton held his breath.

At first there was no sound, just a small spark, and then fire consumed all the air around the house and beyond. The lake house, along with all the Chambers family's past hopes and dreams, was blown into oblivion.

CHAPTER TWENTY-FIVE

Gone

"Do not worry about tomorrow, for tomorrow will worry
about itself. Each day has enough trouble of its own."

Matthew 6:34

Ryan felt the explosion from the fallout shelter five miles northwest of the lake house. He ran outside, just in time to see the last fragments of Roni's life float bit by bit to the ground. He hoped and prayed that nobody had been hurt.

They had made it to the shelter in good time. The terrain was mostly dead prairie grass and leaves. Only a few clumps of naked elm trees dotted the rolling hills, so there wasn't much cover for the small band of refugees. They had to hurry as the darkness of the night was giving way to the rays of the rising sun.

Ryan had carried Roni the whole way. He wouldn't let Priscilla or Oriel help. She was his responsibility, and he was going to start acting like it. No more running. No more hiding.

The shelter was roomy enough for the five of them. The dreary grey walls were lined with old wooden shelves that carried a variety of canned food, green woolen blankets, and an old radio from the 1960s. John found a decrepit oil lamp and matches. Thankfully, the matches were dry and the wick caught fire right away. Priscilla made up the two sets of bunk beds for the weary band.

Ryan laid Roni on one of the bottom beds. He brushed back the strands of hair that covered her face.

"I'll take the first watch," he said.

John, Oriel and Priscilla began the first of their many sleep cycles.

Ryan had been sitting on the ground next to Roni's bunk when the lake house exploded. Fear and sadness gripped his heart as he walked back down into the shelter, after dashing out to watch the fallout. Coming through the doorway, his eyes met Roni's. He turned away from her quickly, to close the door and try to get himself together. When he turned around, she was close to him.

"What's happened?" she asked.

He knew he couldn't conceal what had happened from her for very long, so he decided to go with the truth.

"I-I think your house just blew up."

"What?"

He repeated himself. Roni walked back over to her bed and sat down. She was handling the news better than Ryan thought she would.

"Gone, all gone?" she asked.

"I'm sure everybody got out," Ryan offered.

"Yes, I'm sure they did," said Roni, clutching the crystal on her necklace.

Ryan took hold of her other hand. It was cold and clammy. Her pulse was rapid, and her breathing was quick and shallow. Ryan knelt in front of her and touched her face.

"Roni, look at me," he said in earnest. "Roni, let me have your eyes."

She tried to focus on his eyes but, as the blood began to drain from her face, her lips grew pale and her body went limp. He laid her back on her bed and covered her with blankets.

She stared up at the bunk above her, repeating one word over and over.

"Gone."

***

Stephen caught a glimpse of the explosion in his rearview mirror as he traveled east on Highway 54. A huge fireball rivaling the brightness of the rising sun was followed by thick smoke that was instantly carried away by a biting northerly wind. The current of air took hold of the smoke and etched delicate black lines into the horizon.

Stephen looked over at Daniel, who was petitioning the Creator for the safety of the ones left behind. Anastasia and Heath were in the third row of seats; they also looked as if they were offering up a prayer. Allyson and John were in the second row, with China seated in between them.

"Are you my new mommy?" John asked, looking up at China.

Caught off-guard, China wasn't sure how to answer. She looked from the little boy to Stephen, who shrugged his shoulders, as if he too was at a loss for words.

"I'm not sure," she said.

"Oh well, James is pretty sure you are," the child replied.

"Oh, I..." China stumbled around for the right words to say, but nothing came to mind. He was a cute little boy, and she had enjoyed watching him playing with his brother and Zoei. But what would she do with two more children? She was barely able to hold on to the one she had. How could she provide a safe place for Allyson and the two little boys to live?

Stephen could see the wheels in China's mind turning. Her brow was furrowed and she was biting her nails.

"How about a little music?" he offered, trying to lighten the mood.

He turned on the radio just as the artist Plumb started singing "Only Takes One Drop". After the first verse and chorus, John chimed in. He sang the song remarkably well.

"Have you heard that song before?" asked China when the singing was over.

She asked, because she figured that he and his brother had lived a sheltered life like herself. She was never allowed to listen to music in all the years she was with Joseph. Her nurse had taught her a few Russian folk songs, and Victor had taught her the teapot song; but, other than that, her musical experience was extremely limited.

"No, I just looked it up in my brain," he said, pointing to his head.

"What... how?" she looked up at Stephen and could tell by his facial expression that he knew what was up. They would have to talk about it later.

When the next song started to play, John once again was able to start singing along after hearing only thirty seconds of the music. The child continued in this way until Stephen pulled up in front of a little blue house in a rundown neighborhood in Wichita.

"It's not much, but it is home," Stephen said as everyone piled out of the van.

Anastasia carried Allyson, who was fast asleep in her car seat, while China grabbed what was left of all the baby items Roni and Jillian had bought just a few days ago. Everything she left behind had gone up with the house. She had only packed a couple of outfits for herself, and she hoped they would look alright when she put them on. Jillian had given her a lesson on fashion just yesterday, but China was still unsure of her ability to select a "killer outfit".

China and the guardians followed Stephen up the porch stairs and through the front door. As soon as they entered the house, everyone became aware of the small woman sitting in an old, worn-out recliner in the corner of the living room. The CD player next to her was playing a dramatized version of the Bible.

The little woman had a halo of white hair piled on top of her head, and she was holding a little poodle of the same color. As soon as her warm brown eyes caught sight of China, she smiled and said, "Oh, Stephen, you've brought home a princess."

***

The force of the blast rocked the minivan as it traveled down the highway. Juli started crying when she saw the huge fireball consuming her family's vacation home. She held her necklace tightly and whispered softly, "Gone."

She was a young child the last time she had been there; but she had begun to feel a long-lost connection to her past as she spent the last few days there. Now it was all gone. Ariel touched her charge's hand to comfort her, and Juli welcomed the kind gesture.

Victor stirred in his seat, and Jillian unbuckled her seatbelt so that she could turn around to get to him.

"Victor," she said, stroking his face softly. "Victor, it's Jillian. Are you ready to wake up? We are in the van, and you are safe."

Slowly he opened his eyes. He looked at Jillian and blinked a few more times to make sure he wasn't dreaming.

"Oh, you're still here," he said sheepishly as he touched her hand. "That's good."

Jillian smiled at her beautiful patient. Her devotion to him would be unwavering, but she wondered if he would ever feel the same towards her.

"I've loved you all my life," she thought to herself. "Can you love me?"

Putting her own thoughts aside, she asked him, "Would you like something to drink?"

"Certainly."

203

Jillian pulled a bottle of flavored water out of her purse and broke the seal around the top of it.

"This is some water I brought from my dad's spa. It has lots of vitamins and minerals in it. I hope you like strawberry."

"I do now," he said with a smile.

He put the bottle to his lips, but his eyes never left hers. He adored her already, but he knew he could never have her. She was a kind and thoughtful person and gorgeous as well. What would she want with him—a vile, used-up man whose body was disfigured beyond belief?

The prisoner John had told him that he believed the Creator had someone special in mind for him. Victor wanted to believe this, but his faith was still at the infancy stage. He had not learnt to rely on the Creator for anything. He looked outside the window and asked where they were headed.

"North Dakota, I think," said Jillian.

"Oh, ok," said Victor slowly, and he leaned back against the seat. His mind began spinning involuntarily, as if searching for a memory... a lost memory. Putting his hand to his head, he tried to reach down into the depths of his mind to find it.

"Are you ok, Victor?" Jillian asked, touching him on the shoulder.

He was reaching out with all his might when the figure of a young girl exploded to the front of his mind. He stretched out further in his mind and saw her lying on the floor of a barn. Straw covered the floor, and she shivered from the cold. A glowing man with a sword was fighting three other men whose facial expressions reminded Victor of some of the guards who had taken away his innocence as a child.

It looked like the glowing man was protecting the girl. After a while, the three wicked men gave up and went away.

The glowing man knelt down next to the girl and cradled her in his arms. Suddenly Victor's mind focused on the man.

"Victor, please hurry, she doesn't have much time left," the man said.

"Who?" Victor said with his mouth and mind. His mind flashed back to the girl's face.

"Esperanza!"

***

Jared and Jeni had been driving only fifteen minutes when the lake house exploded. Jeni screamed out Zoei's name and succeeded in opening the passenger door in an attempt to get to her. Thankfully, her seatbelt held her in place. Jared slammed on the brakes and grabbed at Jeni's shirt to pull her back. She was still struggling to get out when Jared made it around to her door. Samuel and Camiel had got out of the back of the truck to offer their assistance.

"Jeni, Jeni!" Jared exclaimed as he held her tightly.

Jeni had reached the end of her emotional reserve. She had nothing left as her knees gave way and she collapsed into Jared's strong arms. One word escaped her lips: "Gone."

"Zoei is with Michael," Jared tried to reassure her. But she could no longer hear him, as thoughts of loss consumed her. Jared and the guardians laid her on a mattress in the back of the truck. Jared covered her with all the blankets he could find, and then he put his arm over her. Camiel and Samuel took over the driving as they made their way south.

***

Madeline wondered what in the world she was doing, getting out of bed at five o'clock in the morning for a man who clearly wasn't interested in her. They had known each other for seven years now; if she hadn't been able to attract him by now, she might as well give up. But he did seem to like her.

205

He gave her his undivided attention and looked her straight in the eye when they talked. He wasn't married and had never mentioned a girlfriend. So what was the hold up?

"I'd better not get the 'it's not you, it's me' speech from him," she said as she looked at her reflection in the rearview mirror, inspecting her ten-minute hair and makeup job.

As she pulled into the gas station, the lake house burst into a giant ball of flames. She ducked behind her dashboard as debris hit the windshield of her car. She waited five minutes before she lifted her head and peered out of her windshield, which was now cracked.

Slowly she opened the door and got out of her car. Small pieces of ash were coming down and settling in her brown hair. She walked around to the front of her car and saw that the headlights had been blown out. The front tag, which said "Maddy", had been destroyed by a brick that had once been part of the Chambers' fireplace.

"Great, just great," she said. "More money that I don't have."

She turned her attention back in the direction of the house and wondered what had happened. Then a sick feeling came over her. Michael. Was he in the house? She covered her mouth with her hands and her eyes began to water.

Just then, she heard a rustle down in the ravine that ran along the east side of the gas station parking area. She looked down into the fifteen-foot ditch and saw an unexpected sight. Michael, three men, two children, and a beautiful woman were looking up at her.

"Madeline, can you help us?" Michael said, looking up at her. She stood frozen, not knowing what to say.

"Maddy... please..." was the furthest he got, before he collapsed.

CHAPTER TWENTY-SIX

Surrender

"Where were you when I laid the earth's foundation?
Tell me, if you understand. Who marked off its dimensions?
Surely you know! Who stretched a measuring line across it?
On what were its footings set, or who laid its cornerstone—
while the morning stars sang together and all the
angels shouted for joy?"

Job 38:4-7

Priel, Delanny and Clayton tried not to move around too much in the backseat of Madeline's forest green Honda CR-V.

"If I'd known I was going to be transporting half of a professional basketball team, I would have brought a bigger vehicle," Madeline thought, when she and the guardians had finally got Michael into the front seat.

James played quietly with his kitten, Bert, as he sat between Delanny and Clayton, who had fallen asleep after about an hour on the road. They were in their human forms now and would have to learn to sleep at regular intervals.

Zoei was asleep on Donavon's lap in the very back of the vehicle. A narrow bench seat had been pulled out for him and the little girl, along with her guardian Priel, who kept staring at Donavon. Zoei's kitten slept in a tight ball right up next to Donavon's neck.

"Ugh! I hate cats," he said to himself. But, once he was settled in with Zoei and her kitten, he had more pressing matters to think about.

"I killed my best friend," he said to himself over and over again. "I wasn't even holding a knife when I was talking to him. Or was I? Solomon is never going to forgive me. In fact, he probably wants to kill me. If he doesn't, Jared or Ryan will do the job for him. Why does stuff like this always happen to me?"

"Maybe the better question for you to be asking is, why do you keep allowing yourself to get into situations where you can be used by others?"

The voice in his head startled Donavon.

"What? Who said that?" Donavon's body jerked slightly in his sleep. He had drifted off to sleep and was dreaming, which seemed to be a good opportunity for the Creator's Son to speak to him—since, when he was awake, he was usually more concerned about an alien invasion. He looked around for the owner of the quiet voice.

"It's just me, your Father."

Donavon turned around and saw a man with shoulder-length hair pulled back in a ponytail. His beard and clothes rivaled the look of the Brawny Towel man. From the scars on the man's hands, Donavon had a sneaking suspicion that he knew who this Man was.

As he took in his surroundings, he realized that he was in a forest. A small campfire was burning in a homemade pit surrounded by rocks. A red tent for two was pitched a short way off. Something wet touched his hand and, when the boy looked down, he saw a medium-sized dog licking his fingers.

"That's Lady," said the man. "She's a Red Heeler; great herding dog, never saw a cow she couldn't wrangle."

Donavon leaned over and patted the dog on her side. She responded with a yip and nuzzled him affectionately. Donavon smiled. He had always wanted a dog. He turned his attention back to the man.

"How did I get here, and why do you claim to be my father? I know who you are."

"You do, huh?" said the Man, as He threw another log on the fire. "I am here to offer you a chance at redemption."

"Redemption?" sneered Donavon as he sat down on an upturned log. "Redemption for what?"

"Well, rejecting me for one thing; and then there is the matter of the murder you just committed."

Donavon's heart sank. He had murdered Seth. His anger had taken hold of him again and he had killed his best friend.

"How can I make up for taking a life? I can't bring him back! I-I will just have to run, like Ezekiel said."

"Ezekiel would use you for his own evil purposes. I am offering you a way to heal your soul."

Donavon thought for a minute as he continued to pet Lady. Something began to stir in his heart. Maybe Bak and Ezekiel were wrong. *Maybe there is a God and aliens aren't real!*

"What's your idea?" he finally said.

"Well, first I would like you to surrender your life to me."

Donavon raised his eyebrows. "What?"

"Surrender your life to me," the Man said. "Give up all the plans you have set for yourself. Let me guide you, show you a new way to go." The Man stooped down and put His hand on Donavon's shoulder. "Let me adopt you as my son."

"Your son!" Donavon jumped up and pushed the man away from where he was sitting. He walked to the other side of the campfire. "Your son? I'm already somebody's son and it's not going so well, for your information."

"I know," said the Man.

"You know? Then why haven't you done something about it!"

"I am. Right now." The Creator's Son walked over to the boy and placed His hands on either side of his face. Donavon squirmed, as the close contact made him nervous.

"Your earthly father has not been able to break free of the abusive cycle in his family. His father abused him, and his father before that. You, Donavon, can break the cycle right now, if you choose me."

"B-but my father, he..."

"I have given your father sixteen years of chances with you, and he has refused me every time," he said, releasing Donavon's head. "He has squandered the gift I gave him."

Here he paused and added, "Not that he is beyond redemption. He may yet surrender his life to me, but his relationship with you is over, for now.

"But we will not discuss him; I want to know what *your* decision will be."

Donavon pondered over the Man's words for a minute.

"So, you want me to give up the rest of my life to you, with no say in how things will turn out?"

"You will always have a choice in how things turn out."

"What about the little kid you and Delanny just dropped in my lap? Seems to me I didn't have much choice in that."

"Sure you do. When you wake up, you can choose to leave her. It's your choice."

"You mean, at any time, if I want out of the deal, I can get out?"

"You can. I wouldn't advise it, but you can."

"How do I know I can trust you to do what's best for me?"

"Can I tell you a story about a friend of mine?"

Donavon was caught off guard for a moment, but he nodded his head. The Creator's Son began His story.

"I had a friend... oh, about four thousand years back. This guy was awesome. His name was Job. He trusted me for everything, and I couldn't do enough to reward him for his obedience. I gave him a beautiful wife, ten kids, all the animals he could handle, and the best property there was. We were like this," the Man crossed His fingers to illustrate His point.

"So, one day, my arch enemy sneaked in to talk to me...

210

"I asked him what he was doing, and he said he was just wandering around the earth and decided to stop by. I knew what he was up to, but I let him talk.

"He was whining about how I protected my children—especially this friend of mine, Job. He said, if I were to let bad things happen to Job, my friend would curse me. So I let my enemy do whatever he wanted to Job; everything but kill him."

"Wow, some friend you are!" Donavon interjected.

"Just wait, the story gets better. My enemy took everything from Job: his kids, animals, servants, even his health. His wife lost it. She wanted him to reject me and then kill himself. But Job said something quite profound. He said, 'Shall we accept good from God and not trouble?'"

"So, you made trouble for your friend, and he liked it?" Donavon asked. "Weird."

"Yeah, maybe," said the Man, "but sometimes weird is good. Anyway, three of Job's friends came by, and they tried to figure out what their friend had done wrong to deserve such disaster in his life. They talked for hours and hours.

"When I'd finally had enough, I asked them some very pointed questions. I won't tell you every one of them, but I wanted to know what gave them the right to give such horrible advice to Job.

"Had they laid the foundations of the earth? Had they hung the stars in the sky? Had they formed the great dinosaurs that were on the land and in the sea? No, they had only lived for a very short time on earth, and I had already lived forever. I do not begin. I do not end."

The Creator's Son had become a little red-faced as He told the story. His eyes glowed like fire, and Donavon was getting anxious.

"W-well, was that it? You made Job's life suck, and you let him suffer and die?"

The Creator's Son looked kindly at the boy. "Of course not, I gave him back everything he had and more. Sheep, camels, oxen, servants, even ten more kids. Including three of the most beautiful daughters I ever created. Job lived happily until he was a hundred and forty years old. He got to see his great, great, great grandchildren."

"So, what's this story got to do with our arrangement?" Donavon finally asked.

"It's about trust," the Man answered. "Job trusted me for everything. He even trusted me when he had nothing left. I want you to trust me in the same way."

"Yeah, ok, but Job never killed anybody," Donavon said.

"True, but I want you to trust me in that too. Give that situation over to me and trust that I can use it for good."

"For good? Me murdering my best friend...? How are you going to use *that* for good?"

"Trust me, and you will see."

Donavon was deep in thought for several minutes. He stroked Lady's spotted fur and considered the choices before him. Run and live his life in constant fear—or trust this guy to work out his problems for him.

He thought about his Sunday school teacher. She had told him that God would always love him and give him strength to do the right thing. He knew in his heart that surrendering his life was the right thing to do. He stood up and held out his hand.

"I-I surrender," he said sheepishly.

The Creator's Son shook his hand and pulled him close to Himself.

"Welcome home, my son."

CHAPTER TWENTY-SEVEN

Clara and Jordan

"For I know the plans I have for you," declares the LORD,
*"plans to prosper you and not to harm you, plans to
give you hope and a future."*

Jeremiah 29:11

China looked around the little room that Stephen had led her
to. The patchwork quilt on the bed made the bedroom look
cozy. It was hand-sewn from scraps of material that were all
different shades of blue. She picked up a pillow with the
name "Darla" embroidered onto it. The doll sitting next to it
had yellow hair and a bonnet that matched the bedspread.
She wondered who Darla was and if this was her room.

She unpacked the few possessions she had brought along
for Allyson and herself and placed them in the little white
dresser near the window. There was no crib for the baby to
sleep in, so Allyson would probably have to share her bed.

A light knock on the door made China jump. She tiptoed
over to it and opened it a little. Stephen was standing there,
with a laundry basket filled to the top with blankets and
pillows. She opened the door the rest of the way to let him in.

"I-I... w-we don't have a-a crib f-f-for the baby, b-but m-
my mom thought we could m-make this old laundry basket
into a b-bed for her until we get s-s-something else."

China thought that was a great idea and smiled sweetly at
Stephen. He grinned back and set the basket down on the bed.

"Th-this room used t-to belong to my sister. H-her name
is D-Darla."

"Yes, I figured that out from the little pillow here on the
bed," she said and sat down. The bed was nice and springy,
and China allowed herself to bounce a little on it.

He loved to hear her talk. Her voice was like a beautiful Russian melody that took you back to a time and place of sweet innocence.

"Where is she now?" China asked. "Won't she need her bed tonight?"

Stephen rubbed the back of his neck nervously. "W-w-well, she doesn't c-come around much any m-m-more. She has her own l-l-life."

China could see that there was much more to the story, but Stephen didn't seem to want to talk about it, so she changed the subject.

"Where's Allyson?"

"Oh, m-my mom has her. S-she just loves babies."

China got up from the bed and walked toward the living room. Stephen followed. Stephen's mother was glowing as she held the sweet little baby. Allyson was wide awake and cooing at the elderly woman.

"What a little darling you are," she said to the baby, and then she looked at China. "Your daughter is beautiful."

China smiled and sat down on a worn-out couch across from her.

"People around here call me Grandma Sanderson. I don't have young grandchildren anymore. My Stephen is all grown up. What's your name, dear?"

"I am called China," she answered and then added, "I'm sorry, but I thought you were Stephen's mother."

"What a lovely name for a beautiful princess," Grandma Sanderson said.

China blushed. "Thank you, ma'am."

"I've been Stephen's mother since my daughter and her husband died."

"Oh, I'm sorry," China looked at Stephen, who was staring nervously at the floor.

"It's ok, dear," Grandma Sanderson said, smiling as she took hold of her grandson's hand. "I've not been sorry one day since I was given this wonderful boy."

When the old woman reached her right hand out to Stephen, China noticed that one of her arms was deformed. It was at least six inches shorter than the other one and was tucked up close to her body, like an injured bird's wing.

Stephen introduced the guardians Neil, Anastasia and Heath to his mother. He said they were some friends from work and would be staying in the basement for a while.

Just then, John came running into the house with Daniel right on his heels.

"Oh," Grandma Sanderson exclaimed, "and who is this handsome prince I see here?"

John ran right up to the woman. He was out of breath as he tried to speak. "I'm Jo-John," he said with intermittent breaths.

"Well, John-John, it's nice to meet you. Are you going to be staying here too?"

John shook his head yes.

"That is wonderful. If you ask my grandson Stephen here, I bet he can round you up a few toys to play with."

John's eyes got big. "What about Ally? Do you have some toys for her too?"

"Oh no, my precious boy," she touched his face, "she's too little to play with toys right now. But she probably would like to look at some brightly colored pictures."

"Where do you get those from?" asked the boy.

"You have to color them for her."

She reached down next to a pocket on the side of her chair and pulled out a coloring book. She handed it to John and then reached back into the pocket and retrieved a plastic container of crayons.

215

John noticed the woman's short arm, and his eyes grew wide. "It's your t-rex arm!" exclaimed the boy.

"My what?" she inquired.

"You have a-an arm like a t-rex!" cried the young boy excitedly; but then his voice got very low and serious, "Do you use it to fight off the velociraptors?"

The old woman laughed. "Well, I guess you could say I've fought off something like a dinosaur before; but you know my arm doesn't work so well unless I have my armor on. It just sits up close to my belly until I need it."

John touched the old woman's good arm. He could see the moment of her birth and how the doctors had grabbed her head with forceps in the delivery process. The forceps damaged the right side of her brain, causing her to become crippled on her left side. Her seemingly lifeless body was placed under a sheet and she was left for dead. The infant struggled for life under the sheet, and only when a nurse passing by happened to look in her direction was she saved.

"The velociraptors didn't want you to live, did they?" John asked in the same serious tone of voice.

"No, they didn't," she said to the child. "But the Creator had a plan, didn't He?"

John smiled back, and the two of them shared a knowing look.

"E-everything looks in order h-here," said Stephen, not sure of what had just happened. "I-I'll show the g-guar... I mean... our guests... to the basement."

Grandma Sanderson's eyes twinkled as she looked at the guardians and a perceptive look came across her face.

"Yes, the guardians... I mean, our guests must get their rest."

Stephen looked a little confused as he made his way to the basement. He felt a hand on his shoulder.

"It surprises you that your grandmother recognizes us?" Heath asked the bewildered detective.

"W-w-well, yes."

"At your grandmother's age, she has fought many spiritual battles. It is easy for her to identify spiritual beings," Heath said, "good and evil ones."

"S-s-some detective I am," Stephen murmured.

"Don't worry about it, Stephen," his guardian said. "Some people never recognize us. Spiritual warriors are few and far between."

"W-w-warriors? I-I don't see my grandmother as a w-warrior."

"Oh, you'd be surprised at what Miss Clara is capable of," Heath laughed. "If you're going up against a hellish horde of demon-velociraptors," he added with a smile, "you definitely want her on your side. It's been a while since I've seen Petra in action, but I have a feeling the time is drawing near when her sword will be needed."

"W-w-who's P-Petra and why are we needing a s-s-sword?" Stephen was feeling very much out of the information loop.

"Petra is your grandmother's spiritual weapon," a voice came from the stairway. "It means 'rock'."

Stephen peered up to see a youngster with shoulder-length blond hair descending the staircase. He looked no older than fifteen.

"I'm Jordan, your grandmother's guardian," he said.

"N-no, you're J-Jordan the p-p-paper boy," Stephen was alarmed at the teen's presumptuous behavior.

"No, I'm Jordan, your grandmother's guardian," the boy said again, with almost no emotion.

"N-no, y-you're... Jordan the paper b-boy."

217

"No, I'm…"

"Ok, stop!" Heath exclaimed. "This could go on all day. Stephen, this is Jordan, your grandmother's guardian."

"B-but he's j-j-just a k-kid," Stephen said.

"It is not our outward appearance that determines if we are powerful," Anastasia explained. "It is the devotion of our soul to our Master that establishes our strength."

"B-but I t-thought you w-were just that w-weird kid who l-liked t-to come over and eat m-m-my grandmother's snickerdoodles."

"Weird, huh!" Jordan raised an eyebrow.

"Jordan, relax," Heath interjected, seeing that the situation was about five seconds from escalating. "Stephen, what you call weird is simply what humans have diagnosed as ASD, Autism Spectrum Disorder. The way Jordan processes information is different—unique—from the way you do. Many guardians come off this way to humans."

"S-so, are you s-saying that all autistic p-people are guardian angels?" Stephen asked.

"No, certainly not," Heath replied. "Most cases of autism on earth are genetic and neurological disorders. Once sin entered the world, the Creator's perfect human DNA began to be corrupted. What you have now is a large percentage of the population trying to cope with mutated genes and the problem is only going to get worse.

"One in eighty-eight kids are diagnosed with ASD. And that's just the ones with access to diagnosticians. In underdeveloped countries and poor sections of modern society, humans with this disorder are oftentimes discarded or, even worse, exploited for sexual purposes or for their exceptional problem-solving and computer skills."

Stephen stared at Jordan closely and then said, "C-come to think of it, y-you have been fifteen f-for a very l-long time."

The other guardians burst out laughing, while Jordan looked straight-faced at Stephen. He offered his hand to the detective and Stephen shook it, though he was still suspicious of such a young-looking boy being sent to protect his grandmother.

***

John was snoring softly. He rolled over in his bunk and Ryan thought he heard the apostle mumble something about "fishing" and "men". Roni was sleeping serenely too. He wondered how in the world he was going to talk her into marrying him. She didn't even trust him. Hadn't he almost abandoned her? Again?!

Why couldn't they just pretend to be married? Who would know? It's not like they were going to have to show proof of marriage to get on the boat. Wouldn't a couple of rings and a few well-rehearsed kisses convince people of their sincerity? With his luck, probably not.

He paced back and forth across the floor, practicing in his mind what he would say to her. *Hey Roni, Michael thinks we should get married, go on a honeymoon/cruise/camping trip to the coldest city on the planet, and then rescue your father. What do you think?*

He had unknowingly said the last sentence out loud, and he heard a faint giggle from the other side of the room. Roni's brown eyes peered out from underneath her blanket.

"What do I think about what?" she asked playfully.

Ryan almost wanted to grin as the pleasing tone of her voice reached his ears, but he held back.

"Well, you see, Michael has this plan and... um... it's... ah... going to require you to kind of... sort of... marry... um... me."

"Kind of sort of marry you?" she asked impishly. "How do you 'kind of sort of' marry someone?"

219

Ryan had made his way over to her and sat on her bed. He was trying to be serious, but he could not get away from the mischievous look in her eyes.

"Michael says we need to get married. Married for real. I tried to talk him out of it, but he says it has to be a legitimate, real marriage..."

"Ok."

"Now, I know you don't want to marry me, but to... um... tell you the truth, I-I really do want to marry you..."

"Ok."

"I know I've been a real jerk and..."

"Ryan!"

"What?" he said with a start.

"*O-Kay*," she enunciated each syllable.

"Ok what?"

"Ok, I'll marry you."

"You will?"

"Yes."

"Why?"

Roni rolled her eyes. "Because it's the best way to save my dad and..."

"And?" Ryan asked hopefully.

Roni paused and her eyes glance down at the floor.

"A-and I know you... care about me and my sisters."

"Oh... yeah." He did care about her and her sisters, but Ryan was disappointed that she didn't realize he also loved her more than anything.

"Why are you so calm about this?" he asked. "I expected you to be full of all the reasons why we can't get married."

Roni's face turned a little red. "Well, I haven't only been sleeping here. I kind of have this thing with God."

Ryan stood up abruptly. "Oh, I see, a *thing* with the Creator. Would you like to explain this *thing* you have with the Maker of the universe?" He was a little peeved at this new insight into Roni's spiritual life.

Roni frowned. "You don't have to get snotty about it. It's just that, whenever I get upset and start questioning *things*," she paused, "He talks to me, in my head. He tries to set me straight on things."

"Well, then, I'm assuming He set you straight on marrying me. I wouldn't want you to get upset or question my l-loyalty to you." He corrected himself at the end of his little rant.

"Why are you acting like this?" her voice was strained. "I-I-thought you... I thought you..." she was quiet for a few seconds. "No, you don't."

"Roni, I do, but..."

"You're still thinking about running," she interrupted him. "You're still trying to get away from anyone you might lose."

"No, I..." he tried to explain.

"That's ok," she said matter-of-factly. "I know you don't want to be stuck with Dr Frankenstein's monster for a wife. I mean, I could implode on you at any moment. We can just marry, for the trip over to get my dad, and then you can have it annulled, as we won't be consummating *anything*."

Roni's face was red from anger and embarrassment. She should have known that the good-looking doctor wouldn't want a short, fat, psychotic robot for a wife. Her tears burned hot down her cheeks as she rolled back over in her bed and faced the wall.

After a few minutes, Ryan approached her bed. He put his hand on her shoulder and could feel her shaking.

"Roni, I'm sorry. That came out all wrong. I was—"

"It's fine. You don't have to explain. I just need one thing right now."

"What's that?"

"A bathroom."

CHAPTER TWENTY-EIGHT

Seeds

Jesus loves me! This I know, for the Bible tells me so.
Little ones to Him belong; they are weak, but He is strong.
Yes, Jesus loves me! Yes, Jesus loves me!
Yes, Jesus loves me! The Bible tells me so.

Anna Bartlett Warner

"We have to go back!" shouted Victor.

Raven slammed on the brakes of the minivan, and it skidded to a halt on Highway 281. Most of the passengers were restrained by their seat belts, but Jillian and Ariel were thrown to the front of the vehicle. The guardian took the brunt of the impact as her first thought was to protect the human. Jillian felt terrible as Raven and Saffron pulled the petite angel from the front seat and sat her down on the ground off the shoulder of the highway.

"Are you in pain?" Saffron asked Ariel.

"My back," she answered. "But I think it's just a bruise."

Raven examined her back closely and could see the imprint of the instrument panel on it. Several switches and knobs had jabbed her hard enough to draw blood. She had a bloody nose and a small gash on her lower lip from the impact of Jillian's head hitting her in the face as well.

"Juli, hand me the first aid kit," Raven said.

Juli searched the pockets behind the front seat and found the little blue box that Roni always made sure was well stocked with Band-Aids and triple antibiotic ointment for Zoei's owies.

After cleaning the half-dozen wounds on Ariel's back, Saffron covered each of them with a colorful Band-Aid.

"You look like a Disney Princess advertisement," Raven said, trying to lighten the mood. "I especially like the Little Mermaid ones, Ariel."

Saffron looked at him curiously. She had the same amusement meter that the guardian Jordan did.

"Never mind," he said and helped Ariel to her feet.

Meanwhile, in the van, Jesse and Jillian were trying to get Victor to stay in his seat.

"I have to get her," cried Victor. "She is in danger! I promised her I wouldn't let anything happen to her."

Victor was so distressed that Jesse finally let him out of the vehicle. He made it about ten steps, and then his knees buckled. Jillian ran to him.

"You are not strong enough yet," she said, kneeling in front of him. "Please tell us what you need. Maybe we can help."

"I-I-I have been delivering children from the facility to dealers in southwest Kansas for the past year and a half," he said bluntly. "But I have been working on a plan for the last six months to try to get the children to safety instead of to the dealers. The other day—when you got me arrested at Joseph's—that was supposed to be my first try."

"Well, we have the boys," said Raven. "They are safe, you don't have to worry."

"I am worried!" cried Victor. "The boys weren't my only delivery for the day. I dropped off a thirteen-year-old girl at a farmhouse only an hour before I met Joseph. I was going to take the money from Joseph and the other dealer and wait until nightfall to go back and get the children.

"I wasn't completely sure how I was going to get the boys, but I knew that Esperanza would be kept in a cage in the dealer's barn. I was supposed to get her that night. No one has touched her, she is still a virgin and is going to be sold to the highest bidder at a skin auction very soon."

"Skin auction? What's that?" asked Juli, but she regretted it almost immediately.

"A skin auction is where young people, boys and girls only twelve or thirteen, are stripped so they can be examined by potential buyers. It's horrible and demeaning and..." Victor could say no more as he wept openly before the group of angels and humans.

The guardians all looked at the distressed young man and then at each other, and they knew what had to be done.

"We have to do this in our human form and not as angels," Saffron said. "If we start some kind of battle and use our weapons, we will be discovered very quickly."

"What about Solomon?" Juli interjected. "He is in no condition to fight anyone." Everyone turned to look at the still-unconscious young man.

"We will drive back to Pratt," Saffron said. "I know someone who will shelter him until we have rescued the girl."

"We should probably try to get a larger vehicle too," Ariel added. "It's already crowded enough, and now we will be taking on another passenger."

"My contact is a minister. She will have a larger vehicle."

"Ok then," said Raven. "Let's get back to Pratt and come up with a plan."

**

Grandma Sanderson led the way out the door at 10:00am. She had never missed a Sunday at church since she was a child, and she wasn't going to start now. Earlier that morning, Stephen had wondered aloud if it would be better for them to skip church, considering all the events that had taken place in the last few hours.

"Nonsense," Grandma Sanderson had said, "When your life is being turned upside down, that's when you need to be with your church family the most. You can get more peace in a one-hour church service than you can in a bottle of whiskey."

224

"What's whiskey?" John asked as he took hold of the old lady's gloved hand.

"Something you should never drink," she answered. "It tastes awful and makes you do terrible things."

"Ooohh, I don't want to do terrible things, Grandma."

She smiled at the boy. "Of course you don't, child."

Everyone piled into the church van. It was a good thing Stephen had brought it home the night before. His old Saturn wouldn't have held so many people. His glasses fogged up when he got into the warm vehicle. He wiped them clear and set them back on his nose. When he looked up to check his rearview mirror, he caught China's eye, and she blushed when he smiled at her.

She was wearing a light blue sweater that brought out the azure blue of her eyes. His mom had given her a matching crocheted hat with a large pink flower on the side. Allyson had one to match as well. As soon as Stephen told his mom about China and Allyson, she had started to knit the hats.

It took them about an hour to drive to church.

"W-we used to live in Pratt a-a-a few years back," Stephen explained, "but we had to move to Wichita w-when mom got sick. We have a h-h-house out here, but the water pipes all burst a c-couple of winters ago, and we h-haven't been able to get them fixed. M-mom s-s-still likes to go to church out here, though."

"It's very good of you to drive her all the way out here every weekend," China said. "You are a good son."

Now it was Stephen's turn to go red in the face.

"He certainly is," Grandma Sanderson exclaimed.

On the way to Pratt, Grandma Sanderson taught John as many Sunday school songs as she could remember. "The B-i-b-l-e", "Father Abraham", and "Jesus Loves Me" were the favorites. All the guardians and Stephen sang along.

China sat quietly and pondered over the words to each song. She wondered about this Jesus that everyone was singing about. She remembered the Man in her dream at the hospital. He was very kind and had given her an apple. That night, a seed had been planted in her heart, and now the words of a simple child's song were causing it to grow.

Jesus loves me! This I know, for the Bible tells me so.
Little ones to Him belong; they are weak, but He is strong.
Yes, Jesus loves me! Yes, Jesus loves me!
Yes, Jesus loves me! The Bible tells me so.

"He loves me," she thought to herself. "Somebody really loves me?"

She had no idea what a Bible was and decided to ask Stephen later. If it was written down somewhere about this Man's love, she wanted to read it.

They pulled up to a little white church building. It had a steeple with a cross on the top. When they entered the building, China saw row upon row of seats. She had never been in a place like this before. Another cross was hanging on the wall at the front of the room. She figured out very quickly that this symbol was very important to the people there. Grandma Sanderson had a gold one hanging from a chain around her neck, as did several of the other ladies. A young boy had a cross on his t-shirt, and a young girl was wearing them in her ears as earrings.

When they were all seated, China leaned over to Stephen, who had of course sat next to her, and asked, "What is the meaning of the two sticks that everyone is wearing around their necks?"

"That's a c-cross," Stephen said. "I-it is what Jesus d-died on, to save us from our sins."

"Oh," she said quietly. "What are sins?"

"It's w-when you d-do something you know i-is wrong but y-y-you do it anyway."

She thought for a few moments and then asked, "How do you know if you have sins?"

"I-it's written down in the B-Bible. You know the t-ten commandments; thou shalt not k-kill, thou shalt not steal, thou sh-shalt not bear false witness, honor thy f-father and thy mother."

"Oh."

"H-have you ever read the Bible?"

She shook her head.

"Oh well, w-we will have to fix that," he said with a smile. "Tomorrow we can go to the Christian bookstore and get you one, b-but you can sh-share mine for today."

He shifted his weight toward her until his arm lightly touched hers. China wasn't sure what to do. She wondered if it was appropriate for her to allow him to get so close. Stephen was a good and kind man. He had never given her cause to fear him. He knew almost all her secrets and he didn't seem to care about her past. He acted like he wanted to help her. Joseph had told her that nobody decent would ever want to be with a girl like her. But for the first time she thought that maybe Joseph had been wrong.

***

It was 11:17am when the minivan pulled into the parking lot of the little white church in Pratt, Kansas. The small brick parsonage where the minister lived was only a short distance away. The van's passengers disembarked, and Saffron led the way to the back of the house, to a set of steps that led into the basement. She opened the door quietly.

"We don't want to startle Gibson," she whispered before calling out the name into the dark of the basement.

227

"Who's Gibson?" Raven asked.

"A very large..." was all Saffron was able to say before the sound of large paws could be heard coming from around a corner.

A loud "WOOF", and the band of humans and guardians all took a step back.

"Hello Gibson," Saffron said to a nearly 100lb brindled bull mastiff. "He is very friendly, except he doesn't like men very much. I suggest you allow the dog to come to you, Victor. Do not reach out to him or he may strike."

"Strike?" The tone of Victor's voice revealed his aversion to dogs. He backed up as far as he could without knocking anyone over.

Gibson stood in front of the group. He sniffed and nudged his way forward through the humans and angels until he came within a foot of Victor. He gave a low growl as he approached the terrified human. The large dog stared Victor down for several minutes and everyone, including Victor, held their breath until Gibson relaxed his gaze and nuzzled Victor's hand.

"Apparently he likes you," Saffron stated.

Victor gingerly patted the dog on the head and stepped around the massive animal.

Saffron continued. "Cassandra is still in the service right now. We will wait here until she is available."

Saffron had been supporting the unconscious Solomon with Jesse's help. They made their way over to a couch and propped him up on it.

"Don't you think we should wake him up?" Jesse asked.

"He is very troubled by the passing of his brother," Saffron replied. "I am not sure if it is the right thing to do just yet."

"Well, he can't stay asleep forever," Juli interrupted the two guardians. "He will have to deal with it eventually."

Saffron was quiet for a moment as she considered Juli's argument. "Very well," she said at last.

She approached the sleeping young man and tenderly touched his forehead. Solomon's eyes began to flutter, and he mumbled softly. Juli sat next to him and held his hand.

"Solomon," she said softly. "Solomon, wake up."

He finally opened his eyes. He looked around at his unfamiliar surroundings and then back at Juli.

"Wow, I just had the most bizarre dream. I dreamed Ezekiel came to the house and Donavon killed Seth and..."

His voice trailed off as he became aware that what had occurred was not a dream. The tears in Juli's eyes confirmed what he was grappling with—the horrible reality of his twin brother's death. Solomon jumped off the couch. He was still a little lightheaded from his angel-induced sleep as he grabbed Saffron's arm.

"Where is he?" Solomon demanded. "Where is that good-for-nothing murderer? I will kill him for what he has done!" He sank to his knees and lamented the loss of his twin.

Juli tried to console him, but to no avail. Saffron decided it was time to distract Solomon with the mission at hand. She briefly informed him of Victor's interrupted rescue mission and requested his help in rescuing Esperanza. Solomon reluctantly agreed.

Victor explained where the farm was located and the best way to get to it. He also told them of the vision he had, of someone fighting to keep Espe safe.

"You are one of the *copii de aur*, the golden children," Saffron said. "You can communicate telepathically with angels and other selectively bred humans. It is your gift."

"You mean my curse," Victor scoffed.

"You may choose to look at it either way," Saffron countered.

"If he's one of us, then how come he doesn't look like us?" Jillian asked. "You know—blond hair, blue eyes?"

"Not all the golden children turned out the way the Dark One designed," Saffron answered. "For instance, Victor was born with dark brown hair and a birthmark on his neck; so he was not deemed suitable for the enemy's purposes. China was born with a cleft lip, so she was not considered valuable either. Juli and Jeni have red hair instead of blond, and Jeni has green eyes. If the Dark One had known of their defects, they too would have been put on the market."

"Can we stop talking, and get back to rescuing Espe?" Victor was becoming very agitated, as he felt he was the only one with a sense of urgency where Esperanza was concerned.

"Very well," Saffron said.

After hatching a somewhat ambitious plan for rescuing Espe, Juli sat down next to Solomon, who was trying to hold back tears.

"I am sorry about Seth," she said quietly. "I can only imagine what it must be like to lose your twin. I'm sure I couldn't bear it if I lost Jeni."

Solomon was hardly listening. His mind was clouded with rage and hate. He felt like he was missing half of his soul. His heart was ripped in two. This boy, who had been his brother's best friend, had killed him. Betrayed and murdered him. The seeds of revenge had been sown, and Solomon began to nurture them in his heart.

His guardian could feel his charge's sorrow, and she mourned inwardly. She was going to do everything she could to prevent revenge from taking over his life.

CHAPTER TWENTY-NINE

The Archangel

*Then Pharaoh said to Joseph, "Since God has made all this
known to you, there is no one so discerning and wise as you.
You shall be in charge of my palace, and all my people
are to submit to your orders. Only with respect to the
throne will I be greater than you."*

Genesis 41:39-40

Madeline tried to wipe the sweat from Michael's forehead
with a napkin she had taken from the gas station diner. The
angel had not stopped shivering since Clayton and Delanny
lifted him from the ravine and put him in the social worker's
car. Madeline tried to keep one eye on the road and the other
on Michael. A million thoughts were racing through her mind.

"Who are these strangers?" she wondered as she looked
in her rearview mirror. She knew James, and the little girl
had to be Zoei, Roni's youngest sister; she had seen a picture
of her when she met Roni at the hospital. But the frightened
teenager and the other three people—she had never seen
them before.

The girl was stunning, with her porcelain white skin and
grey eyes. She wore her lustrous brown hair in a massive
braid that rivaled Princess Jasmine's tresses from Disney's
Aladdin. Maybe she was Michael's girlfriend.

"No wonder he wasn't interested in me," she thought to
herself.

The two men in the back of the vehicle looked like they
were bodybuilders, and the way they hovered over James
and Zoei caused Madeline to wonder what exactly their
relationships were with the children. The one called Priel
was having a hard time letting Zoei sit with the teenage boy.

The boy looked extremely stressed out. He was like a weasel trapped in a cage, wanting to bolt the second the door was opened. But, though frazzled, he soon fell asleep and didn't awaken until Madeline pulled up to her Ozark Mountain log cabin.

The cabin had belonged to her parents, who had passed away a few years earlier. It was surrounded by a dense forest that came right up to the sides of the driveway. Both leaf-bearing trees and conifers stood erect in a canopy over the house. No sky could be seen when you looked up, even though it was winter and all the leaves from the deciduous trees had fallen months ago.

The chilly November wind was whisking its way through the never-ending forest, and Donavon and Clayton held the children close as they made their way up the front porch and into the house. Zoei clung to Francesca, and James to Bert.

Priel helped Delanny move Michael into the house. Madeline showed them to a bedroom with a large bed. She pulled off the protective cloth that covered all the furniture in the cabin. Dust flew everywhere and Priel sneezed. He and Delanny looked at each other in surprise.

"What?" Madeline asked inquisitively. "You look like it's the first time you've ever sneezed."

"Well, yes," Priel said analytically.

"How was it?" Delanny asked.

Priel thought for a moment. "Terrifying and amazing! I thought my head was exploding!"

Madeline stared at the guardians. "What an odd couple," she thought.

"Oh, we can explain," Delanny said.

"Explain what?" Madeline asked.

"Why we appear to be so odd."

"Oh…ah… did I say that out loud?" she put her hand over her mouth.

"Coffee," Priel changed the subject. "Let's make coffee."

"That sounds like a good idea," Delanny said in agreement.

Madeline brought in the few bags of groceries she had purchased in the last town they had stopped at. She pulled out an old coffee pot. The pipes groaned and spit at first, when she turned on the faucet, but eventually they gave up their liquid treasure. Surprisingly, the water was clear when it came out.

The coffee began to drip, and the house was filled with its aroma. It reminded Madeline of her parents; coffee and cinnamon rolls were her dad's favorites—and hers too—and her mom had indulged them more often than she ought too.

Michael had come over many times for breakfast with them. They had shared many laughs, and she would have liked to share many other things with him; but he wouldn't get close. He always listened to her and knew when she needed encouragement. He was kind and helpful and always generous to the children they rescued, and his connections were incredible. He could always find just the right living situation for the children they had rescued.

Delanny entered the kitchen to inquire after some medical supplies. Seeing Michael's injuries, Madeline had also purchased replenishments for her first aid kit. She handed everything over to Delanny.

"I've… um… never heard Michael talk about you," she said timidly.

Delanny furrowed her brow. "Why would he?"

"I thought that maybe you and he were… um… together."

Delanny smiled. "No, we are not together in that way. Let me look after his wounds, and then we can have a talk."

Delanny and Priel spent the next forty-five minutes cleaning and bandaging up the archangel. Most of the wounds were superficial, but the burn marks on his back were giving the guardians cause for alarm.

"I think we are going to have to call on the healers again," Priel said gravely.

"I agree, but it's a big risk and, if the Valkyries detect us…" Delanny hit her hand with her fist. "Argh, those angels are such a pain! Ever since Michael killed Lilly and Jade, Bryn has been quite a handful."

"True, but we may just have to take the risk. So who's going to call on the healers?" Priel asked with a slight grin.

Delanny rolled her eyes. "Come on, Priel. Not again!"

"Alright, I'll go. But you get the privilege of explaining to the human why Michael isn't romantically interested in her. Have fun," he smiled as he headed out the door.

"Oh great, just what I wanted, another emotional human."

"Oh, and keep an eye on Zoei. I don't trust that kid yet."

"Will do," Delanny said and saluted her fellow guardian.

***

Madeline sat on the couch in the living room, watching the children as they played with their kittens. Delanny sat in an old rocking chair across the room from her.

"So I guess you're wondering what's going on here."

Madeline pulled her attention away from the children.

"Trust me when I tell you that it's not you, it's him."

"How did I know this conversation was going to go this way," thought Madeline.

"I know what you're thinking," Delanny said as Madeline stared blankly at her. "I mean, I literally know what you're thinking."

Madeline still made no response.

"I can prove it. You were just thinking that you knew I was going to say it's him, not you."

The blood began to drain from Madeline's face and her heart started beating rapidly.

"Don't freak out, please. There's a reason I know what you're thinking. I'm an angel." After a short pause, Delanny continued, "I know you are thinking that this is impossible, but it isn't. I can't really prove it to you right now, because I don't want those crazy Valkyrie ladies to find us; but I assure you that Michael and I—and Clayton and Priel too—are all angels, and we only want to help you. But right now we really need your help."

Madeline wasn't sure what to say. Of all the farfetched scenarios she had thought of as to the reason Michael didn't want to get together with her, she had to admit that the angel angle was not something she had considered.

"Well, if you're angels, then why do you need my help? Can't you just... I don't know... make whatever you want to happen, happen?"

"It's not quite that simple. Angels are not limitless like the Creator. Our powers are not absolute; they are finite. They have rules and restrictions."

Madeline wasn't sure what to think. Using her natural ability to read people, she could see that the girl was sincere.

"I don't understand," she said, "I thought angels could do anything and be anything they wanted."

"Yeah, I wish! If I could wipe the Dark One off the expanse of the universe with just a word, or create life where there is none—that would be awesome. But can you imagine how bad it would be, if the Creator had made all the angels that way? Just visualize the carnage! We would have destroyed ourselves and you guys a long time ago."

Madeline was beginning to understand.

"You know, there have been many times when I've wanted to kill a human for one reason or another, but the Creator has stayed my hand. He wants all of His children to spend eternity with Him, so He gives them as many chances as He can.

"Do you realize that, while Noah was building the Ark, he was also preaching to the people for almost a hundred years, to try to save more than just his own family? One hundred years! That is more generous than I would have been. Guess that's why He gets to be called God and I don't."

"So, you're telling me that the man I have been working with for over seven years is an angel?" Madeline asked.

"Yes, but not just any angel, the archangel Michael. Only the Creator, the Lord God and His Son, are above him."

Madeline's eyes grew wide. "You mean, he's the Michael from the book of Daniel? Wow." She stood up and began pacing the floor.

"You really know how to pick them, Maddy," she said to herself. "So, are you saying that you guys aren't allowed to have relationships and families and stuff?"

"That is correct. We were not designed for that. It is not our purpose. We only appear in human form for your sake. We are neither male nor female."

"Oh," Madeline said, "I never really thought about angels that deeply before. So, basically, you guys are monumentally unavailable?"

"Yes. It is against the Creator's design for His angels to have inappropriate mental or physical relationships with people. Some of the Watchers tried it a while back; trust me, it did not turn out well."

"What happened?"

"Let's just say things got so out of hand that the Creator ended up nearly destroying His entire creation. Ever heard of the Great Flood?"

Madeline nodded.

"I know many people think it was just man's wickedness that made that whole thing go down; but, trust me, they had help. It got pretty ugly. The kids that the angels and humans had were just... woe insane! Genesis chapter 6 gives a quick overview of the Nephilim but, believe me, the true significance of what they were is definitely lost in translation."

"So, who or what are you and what are you doing here?"

"I'm a guardian."

"Like a guardian angel?"

"Yep, in the flesh," the guardian tried to be comical, but Madeline was too distracted to notice.

"I thought that entire 'everyone has their own angel' thing was just something adults say to kids so they won't be afraid of the dark?"

"Nope, it's true."

"So," Madeline asked slowly, "are you my guardian angel?"

"No. That boy we brought with us is my charge. He's a funny one. Thinks I'm an alien, but I'm hoping that his conversation with the Creator has opened his spiritual eyes."

"So, where is mine?"

At that moment, there was a knock at the front door. Madeline went to answer it.

"Oh George," she was surprised to see her older brother standing outside on the porch.

"Hello, Madeline."

He came into the room, and she introduced him to Delanny, Clayton and the children.

"What are you doing here?" she inquired.

"You did ask who your guardian angel was. Well, here I am."

***

237

Roni was up and about around 3:00pm. She made her bunk and started to look through the canned goods for some meal combinations that might be appetizing.

"Pork and beans with peaches or mixed veggies and pears?"

None of it looked all that appealing. She was definitely missing Priscilla's southern cooking about now, but there would be no fried chicken with homemade biscuits for dinner tonight. The guardians were stuck in human form indefinitely, so no one could make a quick, invisible trip to get supplies. They were stuck eating 1950s bomb shelter cuisine.

Ryan was sleeping on the floor just below her bunk. She started thinking about the conversation they had had a few hours ago.

"I really thought he loved me," she said to herself. "Jason said he did. Maybe Jason was wrong. After all, Ryan is tall, well-built, with blond hair and blue eyes; plus he's smart. I mean, he's a doctor at 18 years old!

"I bet the girls in Germany were falling all over him. Bet he didn't want to run away from them. He probably jumped right into bed with them. No doubt he had a whole line of them waiting outside his bedroom door! *Oh Inga, you're so cute in your little, tight, short dress. And, Gretchen, what a nice tiny little waist you have, and your bosoms are so wonderful, hanging halfway out of your shirt and...*"

"Now, don't you think that's going a bit too far?" Priscilla had heard just about enough of Roni's ranting.

"What's going too far?" she said, red-faced.

"What you were saying about Ryan."

"Well... I.... was just... Hey! You aren't supposed to be using your angel powers!"

"Those aren't angel powers, baby. The ability to hear your thoughts comes with our human forms. It's as much a part of our makeup as your sight and hearing. Ever heard of a sixth sense? Well, we angels have it. But, getting back to you, why are you saying all those impolite things about Ryan?"

"I didn't say anything about him, I was just *thinking* it."

Priscilla got very solemn. "Do you know when Cain murdered his brother?"

Roni was taken aback by the sudden change in subject, but she answered sarcastically, "Well, no; no one knows exactly, except you guys and the Creator, I suppose."

"It wasn't the moment he hit him on the head with the rock; it was in the instant he thought bad things about his brother. You see, a crime always has its roots in envy, jealousy, hatred and resentment. Murder almost always happens in the mind, a long time before it happens with your hands."

"Are you calling me a murderer?" Roni was offended.

"I am," her guardian said quietly but firmly. "You are at the beginning stages of murdering a beautiful love that could exist far beyond your lifetime and Ryan's."

"Why does Priscilla always have to get so dramatic?" she thought and then remembered her guardian could hear her thoughts.

"I'm sorry, Priscilla. I'm just so tired of all the fighting; fighting with Ryan, fighting Ezekiel, fighting for my life. Sometimes I wish life could get a little easier for just a week or two. We've all been running around like crazy since the beginning of October. I need a break. I need my sisters!" she cried.

Priscilla put her arms around Roni and comforted her.

"Everyone has trials, baby. Yours are just bigger than you think you can handle. I know some people say that God will never give you more than you can handle, but I'm telling you that's wrong.

"So many things that happen in life are way too hard for us to handle; but that's the moment when you need to give those huge problems over to the Creator. If you never had a problem too hard for you to handle, then you would never need Him. Do you understand?"

Roni wiped the tears from her eyes. "But what about Ryan? Jason says he loves me, but it seems like he just wants to get away from me. Besides, he does probably have a line of women waiting for him back in Germany."

Priscilla smiled. "Would it surprise you to know that Ryan has one of the most sexually pure minds I have ever heard?"

Roni was startled at Priscilla's use of the "s-word" but she was even more surprised to be informed of Ryan's pure mind.

"I... well... I didn't... no."

"In all the time he was away, he thought only of you—and, even in that, he has kept his thoughts pure. M-m-m," Priscilla mused, "what a man!"

Now Roni felt stupid for having thought so badly of Ryan. She had thought it almost impossible for a boy to love her like that.

"And, just for the record, it wasn't Inga and Gretchen who were trying to get Ryan into bed; it was Olga and Christine."

CHAPTER THIRTY

He'll Leave the Light on

And we know that in all things God works for
the good of those who love him, who have
been called according to his purpose.

Romans 8:28

After Samuel had driven south for two hours, Jared started banging on the window between the cab and the camper at the back. Even though he and Jeni were huddled under a pile of blankets they had found in the truck, it was still freezing in the camper. Jeni's teeth were chattering as she mumbled in her sleep, and Jared knew they had better stop and get her warm before hypothermia set in.

Samuel pulled off the highway and backtracked about a mile and a half. He turned into the parking lot of an old, run-down motel. The vacancy light was on, and smoke appeared from the top of the chimney. Camiel knocked on the door of the front office.

A middle-aged man with a long beard opened the door.

"You'd better get in here before you get blown away by the storm that's developing over there," he said, pointing to billowing storm clouds that were moving towards the motel. His voice was soft and smooth and sounded very big city.

Jared carried Jeni inside and sat her up on a couch near the fireplace. He pulled off her boots and socks and rubbed her feet swiftly, hoping that a little friction might help her blood circulate better.

Three small children and a puppy were playing on a rug nearby, and an old lady with a basket of yarn sat in a rickety rocking chair, knitting what Jared thought looked like a red stocking cap.

Suddenly a swinging door opened and a young blond woman came through, singing and carrying a large platter of warm blueberry muffins. She looked about nine months pregnant.

"Come an' git it, ya'll," she said sweetly.

The puppy and the children began to jump up and down around the lady's legs; and an old hunting dog, which had been lying in a corner of the room, began bellowing at the top of its lungs.

"O Sheba, hush. You children git yer hands washed up and to the table fer prayers. There'll be no eatin' till ya thank the good Lord for what He provided fer ya. Oh, I see we have guests. Allen-Honey, did you tell them the heater was out?"

"I was just about to, Pansy-Darlin', but I was distracted by your sweet singing." He walked over to his wife, wrapped one arm around her, and kissed her on the lips. His other hand made a landing onto the platter of blueberry muffins, but she pushed her husband away from her.

"My sweet singing, huh," she smiled. "More like my sweet muffins!"

"You are a sweet muffin, Pansy-Darlin'. My sweet muffin," he said and smacked her lightly on her behind.

"Daddy gave mommy a spankin'!" one of the children called out with a heavy droll. The others squealed with joy, and their father picked up all three of them in one big bear hug.

It was plain to see that the half-frozen travelers had stumbled onto a very happy family. Camiel and Samuel smiled at the family, which were obviously warmed by the Creator's love.

There was a loud bang on the front door, and Jared and the guardians jumped. "It's just my dad with the wood," Allen said as he opened the door.

The man who stood outside the door had a long beard too, but his was more grey than brown.

"My goodness, it looks like it's gonna be a bad'n," he said, depositing a pile of firewood on the floor. "One of them northern fellers that's sure to drop a lotta snow on us. Hope you city folks got a warm place to stay tonight 'cos the heater's gone and tuckered out on us ag'in."

Jared looked at Allen. "Ah yes, we just heard. Is there another motel around here for us to stay at?"

"About thirty miles or so due north, there's a nice little place. But I see you all just came from that way. There's nothing south for at least a hundred miles."

"But you all are welcome to batten down the hatches with us right here," Pansy said in her thick backwoods accent. "We got plenty of food and blankets."

"And a never-ending pile of wood me and my dad chopped up this past summer and fall," Allen added. "It might not be as private as you'd want, but it'll be warm and dry."

"We have some mattresses in the back of the truck," Camiel offered. "And a few extra blankets as well." He looked at Jared. "We need to get Jeni warm before a fever sets in."

Jared was leery of staying in a place so under-furnished, but he knew that Camiel was right. Plus, if Jeni got sick, the guardians wouldn't be able to use any of their angel powers to heal her. And the people seemed nice; and honestly he was having a hard time focusing on anything but the smell of fresh blueberry muffins. He and Jeni hadn't eaten in many hours.

Pansy got the children and the old woman up to a small folding table to eat, while the men brought in some of the bedding from the truck and a few mattresses from the empty motel rooms as well. Jeni sat on the couch and continued to thaw out from her ride in the back of the truck.

243

She was still a little numb from seeing her family's house explode. There were so many memories that had been blown away in the blast, but she knew her sisters were safe. She could still feel them as she held her necklace between her fingers. Her thoughts were interrupted by a little hand pulling at her foot. The child was no older than two and had blueberry-stained cheeks. He held out his tiny hand to her and she took hold of it. With his other hand, he offered her a slightly smashed muffin.

"Muffin?" he said.

"Thank you," Jeni smiled as she took the offering and separated the muffin paper from her smashed breakfast.

"Jeb, you git yerself right back up to this here table," Pansy said in her best "I mean business" voice. "I'm gonna set yer pa after you."

The little boy waved sheepishly at Jeni and toddled back over to his mother, with the puppy in tow cleaning up all the crumbs he had dropped.

Pansy walked over and sat on the couch by Jeni. "How are you feelin' sweetie?" she said gently as she brushed some of Jeni's hair out of her eyes.

Jeni stared back at the woman, who had startlingly blue eyes. Her wavy blond hair was swept back in a ponytail, but small strands had found their way out and made their way down to her shoulders. She looked at Pansy's swollen belly and then back at her face.

"Jillian?" she whispered softly.

Jeni's eyes were brimming with fear, but the woman touched her cheek and Jeni felt a wave of serenity washing over her. At once, the guardians sensed Pansy using her power, and they dropped what they were carrying, rushed to Jeni, and pulled her from Pansy's hand.

Allen went to his wife, who looked a little faint.

"Pansy! Pansy!" Allen said, trying not to alarm the children in the room. "I'm sorry. I try to tell her not to do this when she's pregnant, but she just gets so caught up in the moment, she forgets."

"Charlie, Sissy, come help mommy," Allen said.

The two older children ran over to their mother. Charlie, who looked about six years old, gently put his hand on his mother's cheek and Sissy, who was five, kissed her on the forehead. "It's ok, mommy," they said, and Pansy began to come around.

"I'm really sorry to alarm you and the young lady here," Allen apologized again. "Please let me get her to bed and I can explain. Please, you are in no danger."

His sincerity was genuine, and Jared and the angels let him tend to his wife. They talked in hushed tones until he came back to them.

"Well, you've probably noticed I'm the misfit here," Allen began with a half-smile. "My sweet Pansy is from this area, but I am from Kansas City. I was a lawyer, and I was traveling to Amarillo, and I got lost. I stopped here to ask for directions from a beautiful Oklahoma girl.

"I was a big-time city lawyer with a career that was on the up and up. I had a seven-figure income and houses in Chicago, California and New York. I had more women than a man could ever dream of, but something was still missing. I had a hole in my life, and I looked for many—and, when I say many, I'm not exaggerating—ways to fill it. Drugs, alcohol, sex, pornography; my life sounded like the lyrics to a heavy metal rock song.

"When I met Pansy, I was on my way to the one thing I hadn't tried yet—marriage. I had met this other rich lawyer online, and she was looking to get married for some tax advantages. She wanted an open, noncommittal marriage, and I thought I wanted the same thing; but then I met Pansy.

"While my car was being fixed from overheating, I sat down at that picnic table out front and had lunch with this young woman, this perfect soul," he glanced back at his sleeping bride. "She had something I wanted—peace. So I married her. I sold everything I had and moved out here to this little motel her family had been running for years.

"I had enough money to take them anywhere, buy them anything they wanted; but they were content to stay right here and serve the people of this small town. Have you ever felt that, Jared? True contentment? That's a feeling that can't be bought or sold. These people had it, and I was going to be the last person in the world to take it from them."

"What about your wife?" Jared asked. "Where is she from?"

"Well, I told you," Allen said nervously, avoiding eye contact with Jared. "Right here in Oklahoma."

"Before that, I mean. Was she... well, I mean, was she... adopted?"

Allen got very nervous and began wringing his hands. He lowered his voice, "Who are you and what do you want? Is it money? I still have some. I'll give it to you, but you have to promise not to hurt Pansy or the children or her parents."

"No, Allen, that's not what I mean. Look at me," Jared said. "Look at me. I have a twin sister who could pass as a younger sibling of Pansy's." He held out his wallet and Allen stared down in disbelief at the picture in it.

"Why do you have a picture of my wife?" he demanded.

"That's my sister, Jillian," Jared said, but Allen couldn't believe it.

"That's my wife Pansy. I'll prove it," he pulled out his wallet and showed Jared a wedding picture. "That was taken eight years ago at our wedding."

"I believe you," Jared said, getting heated, "but this is my sister Jillian. We grew up in Kansas with our adoptive parents. Before that, we came from an adoption agency in Russia. A baby mill for a selectively bred superhuman race, and now the people who 'invented' us want to kill us," he said, trying to calm himself down. "Now, was your wife adopted?"

Allen was stunned. Jared's outpouring of information had almost put him in a state of shock. He stood up to face Jared and then sat down, motioning for Jared to do the same.

"Pansy's dad told me that her parents were murdered," Allen kept his voice low. "That was another reason it was safer for her to stay in this little town. Her mom is a distant cousin of Pansy's birth mother. Everyone thought she had died in the explosion, but somehow she made it out safely."

"Explosion?" Jared hadn't expected to hear that. "How do you know it was murder then?"

Allen looked sad. "The detectives found evidence that her parents had been bound before the house went up."

"What about the remains of the baby?"

"The epicenter of the explosion was... was the baby's cradle. Any remains there might have been were blown into oblivion."

Jared, Jeni and the guardians looked at each other in amazement. It was too convenient that they should just happen to ask for help at this little rundown motel out in the middle of nowhere. Allen was thinking the same thing.

"Why did you guys even stop here?" Allen asked.

"We saw your vacancy light on," Camiel offered.

"Ha, what light? That light hasn't worked since I married Pansy," Allen laughed, but he got serious as he looked out the window and saw the vacancy light lit up like a Christmas tree.

"Wow. I guess He'll leave the light on for you."

***

247

Pastor Langdon gave a relatively short sermon. It was about someone China had never heard of. A woman named Mary was told by an angel that she was going to have a baby and it would be God's Son. China wondered why the Creator would want to leave a place as beautiful and peaceful as heaven to come down to earth and be born in a barn. He was a king in heaven, and now He would be a servant. He would be hungry and thirsty and not have a home. He would be beaten up and tossed aside by the very people He had come to rescue. China thought that maybe she and the Creator's Son had a lot more in common than she used to think.

At the end of the service, the choir began to sing. The hymn they sang moved China deeply:

When peace like a river attendeth my way;
When sorrows like sea billows roll.
Whatever my lot, thou has taught me to say,
It is well, it is well with my soul.

China's lot had been a tragic one. She had been created to be a scientific blight on humanity, but her face wasn't good enough. The only human love she had ever had was from an old woman and a boy as mutilated as she was. She was bought and sold like a piece of meat—a little rag doll passed around to man after man. Her own two children had died in a darkened cellar, and even Trinity had been taken from her.

And now, when love was within an arm's reach, a new feeling began to take hold of her heart. Hope. As the seed of hope burst through the fallow soil of her heart, a pain more wonderful and terrible pierced her whole body. She wanted to say it was well with her soul, no matter what. She wanted to be able to give love and receive it. She turned toward Stephen and smiled. He touched her hand gently. Happiness exuded from deep within her soul, and her physical body collapsed.

CHAPTER THIRTY-ONE

Perfect Love

*There is no fear in love. But perfect love drives out fear,
because fear has to do with punishment. The one
who fears is not made perfect in love.*

1 John 4:18

Ryan stretched and yawned as he awakened from his power nap. The air smelled of pork and beans and peaches. He wrinkled up his nose.

"Yeah I know, it smells lovely," Roni handed him a metal plate. "It was this or asparagus and pears." She sat cross-legged in front of him.

"The texture of a peach is very similar, whether it is canned or fresh," Oriel observed.

"I disagree," John interjected, "fresh peaches are always best. These genetically-altered foods taste nothing like they used to, though. They are half as big and much less tasty."

"Tasty," Priscilla exclaimed. "Tasty! Everyone knows the best way to eat a peach is in a cobbler."

John and Oriel eyed one another and grinned.

"Well, I don't know... a can of peaches over a waffle or meatloaf is extra delicious," Oriel said slyly.

"Oh, for sure," John added, "there's nothing like peaches and meatloaf. They're good with baked Alaska too."

"Meatloaf!" shouted Priscilla. "Baked Alaska! You two have no—"

John and Oriel could barely contain themselves. Ryan and Roni tried to keep their faces straight too, but the sight of the angel getting her wings ruffled was just too much. All four were red-faced and trying to keep from spitting peaches and pork and beans everywhere.

"All right, that's it," Priscilla huffed. "When we get back to a kitchen, no peach cobbler for any of you."

That was sobering for everyone in the room.

"Except for you," she said, pointing at Roni. "You know I would never deprive my girl. But the rest of you... better watch out!"

Roni grinned from ear to ear. Ryan was happy to see it.

"Now, I believe you two have a few things to discuss while we clean up," Priscilla looked at Roni and Ryan.

It was quiet between the two for a few minutes. Ryan spoke up first. "Roni, I'm really sorry for thinking of running again. I'm... I'm just so..."

"Soooo..."

"So... so... afraid," he finally said.

"Of what, Ryan?" she could see that he was uneasy, so she scooted herself up next to him. She was so close she could smell his day-old aftershave.

He breathed in heavily and wiped the sweat from his face and put his hand on hers. "Of losing you, and I don't mean you dying, although that has been worrying me a great deal lately."

"You and me both," she replied.

"When we were growing up, you and Jason were always so close, and I was jealous. I always felt connected to you somehow, but my brother was always in the way. Of course, now we know why; but all the time growing up and even when I was in Germany, I... I..." Tears flowed freely down Ryan's cheeks.

Roni reached up and touched his tear-streaked face. She balanced one tear drop on her finger and then let it fall on her necklace. The necklace glowed red for a few moments, and then the radiance died out. Ryan was amazed.

"It's something I learned from the Creator," Roni said.

"What does it mean?" Ryan inquired.

"I learned a few things the last time I spoke to the Creator," Roni reflected. "A few things about love."

Ryan was intrigued. "Like what?"

"Like fear and love can't exist in the same space."

"I thought the fear of the Lord is the beginning of wisdom," said Ryan, quoting a line from the Book of Proverbs.

"Not that kind of fear," Roni said. "That's talking more about respect, not about being afraid. There is no fear in love, because fear has to do with punishment, and love has to do with the character of the Creator. When He created us, He did not fear that we would someday reject Him. He was not afraid to love us; He charged in full force and without hesitation, and that's what He has in mind for all His children.

"You know the Creator loved us before He even created the first people, Adam and Eve. He loved us even when He knew we would reject him. He loved us even though He knew He would have to send His one and only Son to die, to redeem us all."

"Yah, that's a little crazy to think about; already knowing you're going to get rejected, but still going ahead with the plan."

"It gets even crazier than that. Just imagine knowing that one of your kids is going to be a murderer. Wouldn't you think twice about even having him? How would you treat him if you knew his future? Would you think he was just a waste of space because he was going to end up in jail, anyway?"

"Ok, stop. You are blowing my mind with all this spiritual insight!" Ryan exclaimed.

"I know, my mind was blown away too, when I took on the nature of the Creator. For an instant, He allowed me to feel what He felt when one of His children broke His heart. I could only stand it for a moment because it was like no sorrow I had ever experienced.

"Even when my mom and dad died, the pain I felt then could not be compared with what the Creator feels when even one soul is lost. I know one day I will see my parents again in heaven; but, when someone dies in slavery to the Dark One..." here she paused as she remembered the Creator's grief, then she whispered, "they are lost forever."

Ryan tried to comfort her. He turned the crystal on the end of her necklace and, for a moment, it turned slightly red. He released it at once.

"You haven't told me about your necklace yet," he said.

"Oh yes," she composed herself. "My necklace turns red when it comes into contact with love."

"Love? How does that work?"

"Here's how it was explained to me. Love isn't just a thing we do, it's a living thing. It's a part of the Creator that's in all of us. It's in our blood, our sweat, and our tears. When we truly turn our lives over to the Creator, His love flows out of us spiritually and physically. If we could only love each other without conditions and without fear..." she reached up and swept a lock of his hair away from his forehead.

He turned his head into her hand and closed his eyes. He cupped her hand in his and pressed a kiss into her palm, and a shiver went down to her toes. A random thought crossed her mind. "My mother always said you looked like Chris Hemsworth," she said softly.

He smiled and asked, "What do you think I look like?"

"Perfect love."

All at once, the fear that had held them both back was released. Ryan put his hand behind Roni's neck and pulled her to himself. He pressed his lips to hers and kissed her softly. Her passion for him was awakened, and she knew in that moment that she would never love another man.

She had tears in her eyes, but she was smiling. Her tears slid down her cheeks and neck until they reached the crystal that hung from her necklace. When her tears made contact with the crystal, it glowed with such intensity that even the guardians were surprised by its brilliance.

Ryan handled the crystal again. "Red for love. That's a little cheesy, don't you think?" he teased.

Roni put her arms around Ryan again. "Who says I don't like cheesy?"

"Well, if you like cheesy, then you are really going to love this," said Ryan. He backed away from her and knelt down on one knee. Roni gasped, and her heart fluttered.

"Oh, wait!" he jumped up, fumbled around in his medical bag, and pulled out a small box that said *Norilsk Nickel* on the lid. Opening the box, he presented her with a small ring. The band was a nickel rose branch with delicate copper roses.

"It's from our birthplace," he said. "One of the people I helped gave it to me. I thought of you when I saw it."

"It's beautiful," she beamed. "I-I love it."

"I love you, Roni Susan Chambers, and I was... um... wondering if you'd like to spend the rest of your life with me."

"The rest of my life," she said the words over and over to herself. Somewhere in the back of her mind, thoughts of rejection and abandonment loomed; but, for now, the power of love prevailed and she found herself saying yes to the blond-haired, blue-eyed boy who had turned into the man of her dreams. He kissed her again.

"You've made me so happy, Rapunzel!"

Roni rolled her eyes. "Really, Ryan, do you have to call me that?"

"You're my princess, Roni. You always have been and you always will be."

Now, who could argue with that?

CHAPTER THIRTY-TWO

Trust

*Set me as a seal over your heart, like a seal on your arm; for
love is as strong as death, its jealousy unyielding as the
grave. It burns like blazing fire, like a mighty flame.*

Song of Solomon 8:6

China heard a knock on the door and, when she opened it, the
Man who had shared the apple with her was standing at the
threshold. He smiled and asked if He could come in. Looking
around, she saw that the house was filthy. It wasn't dust and
dirt that polluted the room, but all the shame and heartache
that had accumulated over her eighteen years of life.

A pile of loss crowded out a stack of humiliation in every
corner. Fear hung from the ceiling, and despondency
shrouded every window. Her own clothes were grey and
shabby and barely covered her body. In the center of the
room lay her virtue, like a tattered wedding dress, singed and
frayed and covered in blood. She walked over to the dress
and knelt before it. A wave of emotion swept over her as she
picked it up. She clutched the dress violently and wept with
an intensity that shook her to her core.

Between her sobs, she could hear the Man at the door
imploring her to let Him come in. When she finally turned
her head towards Him, her eyes met His. She recognized
Him. It was Jesus, whose picture she had seen on the wall at
the hospital—the same Man who had shared the apple with
her beside the stream.

"Won't you let me in, child?" He asked.

"It's... it's such a mess in here," she answered. "I... I need
to clean up first." She stood up and began to look for a place
where she could hide her soiled dress.

A battered trunk sat at the back of the house, but she couldn't get it open, so she stuffed the dress down the gap between it and the wall. She picked up a broom and tried to sweep the floor with it, but the grey dust whirled around her. She was making no progress. Every time she pulled down a tattered curtain, another would appear in its place. Finally she sank down to the ground in utter frustration.

"I can help you with that," said the Man at the door, as He pointed to the pile of fabric on the floor.

It was the dress again. She wondered how it had gotten back onto the floor. She looked over to where the trunk was supposed to be, but it wasn't there. It was across the room, under a window. China was bewildered by what was happening. She looked up at the man.

"You can never truly hide your pain and sorrow from me. I know everything about you," He said tenderly.

"Well, then, why would you want to come in here?"

"Because I love you."

China felt her heart skip a beat. He loved her? How could that be? She looked around the room again and felt the weight of her shame once more.

"You... you can't love me. Look at this place, it's... it's so ugly," she stammered. "I'm so ugly," she said, as a tear slid down her cheek.

Tears welled up in the Man's eyes. "I know what you have been through, my daughter. I want to help you, to heal you."

"But you don't understand..." was all she could get out.

"Oh, but I do."

Suddenly the Man's appearance changed. He stood before her wearing only a loin cloth, and He had so many cuts and bruises on His skin that He was barely recognizable. A circle of thorns had been crushed into His skull, and He had holes in His hands and feet. A huge gash on His side

255

almost exposed His ribs, and blood was flowing from every part of His body onto the ground.

"W-what happened?"

"On my last day as a human, this is what I looked like," He said. "The very people I came to save did this to me because they were afraid. They couldn't accept my message of grace. They chose to fumble around in rooms like this one, trying to earn the Creator's love and forgiveness, rather than just letting me into their hearts. I brought them a message of love, and they responded with fear and hate."

A large wound on the man's shoulder was bleeding profusely. She watched the red stream as it flowed down the man's arm and onto the ground. As it hit the ground, it seemed to take on a life of its own. It began to swirl and take the shape of letters; first a "C", then an "h". As the "ina" appeared, she recognized her name. She reached up and felt the scar on her shoulder.

"I can take that," He said gently, "if you will let me."

As she was considering the Man's offer, she noticed His blood beginning to pool at the entrance to her house. Somehow, she knew that it would not flow over the threshold until she gave permission for the Man to enter.

"What did you do to the people who did this to you?" she whispered.

"I forgave them."

He stretched out His hand and she took hold of it. As she pulled Him in, a rushing wind blew through the room like a small tornado. The dust and dirt and cobwebs were blown away. As the man's blood poured into the house, whatever it touched became white. Even her soiled dress became beautiful and, when His blood enveloped her body, the rags she had been wearing melted away. She was exquisitely dressed and her soul overflowed with joy.

The Man was now wearing a white robe, just like the one He had worn in the hospital painting. He reached into the folds of His garment and pulled out what looked like an old rusty nail. He began to carve something onto His hand with it. Blood flowed once again, and China stepped closer to the Man to see what He was inscribing into His skin. When He had finished, He held out His palm, and she could see her name once again written in His blood.

She was troubled by what He had done and asked, "Why would you do that?"

"Watch," He said in delight. He opened up His robe to expose a small part of His chest. China noticed faint scars on His skin. He placed His palm, with her name on it, right over His heart. A searing sound and what appeared to be steam came from His chest and, when He removed His hand, she could see her name once again—only this time it was written, not in blood, but in gold. Her name seemed to float on His skin momentarily, and then it sank into His flesh.

"I have burnt your name into my heart. I have sealed you forever with my love, and nothing can separate you from me for as long as you wish. Your past is gone, and you are clean in my eyes." He took up the nail and began to write on His palm again. She looked at His hand. It had squiggles on it, but she couldn't make out a word.

"What does it say?" she asked.

"It's my name," He said, "to complete the bond between us. You must have my name in your heart as well. Do you wish my name to be in your heart?"

She nodded slowly.

"Then you must take it."

She put her hand under His and guided it to her chest. She pressed it to her heart, and the same searing sound and steam came from His hand. When He removed it, His name was in gold, absorbed into her skin, as hers had done to his.

A happiness she had never known before welled up in her, and she smiled, truly smiled, for the first time in her life.

"What do I do now?" she asked.

"Trust me."

His words echoed in China's mind as she felt herself waking up. Her eyes fluttered open, and she saw a nurse standing over her.

"Oh, there you are," the nurse said. "I'll just go get the doctor."

Stephen was sitting in a chair next to her bed. He stood up and walked over to her. He took her by the hand.

"What happened?" she asked. "The last thing I remember is singing, and then a bump on my head." She could feel a knot just under the skin on her forehead.

"Y-y-you f-f-fainted," Stephen could barely get the words out. "Y-you bumped your h-head on the pew."

Something was wrong. China could see it all over Stephen's face. His eyes were brimming with tears and his hands were shaking.

"What is it, Stephen? Is it Allyson? What has happened to her?" she began to cry. "Tell me, Stephen!"

"A-Allyson is fine. Sh-she is w-with A-A-Anas-stasia."

"Then why are you so upset?"

"S-s-something h-has h-h-happened, China."

"To who? Your mother? John?"

"N-no, t-to you," he finally got out.

"To me? What's the matter with me?"

Stephen tried to clear his voice. He turned his face away from her for a moment, trying to compose himself. Then he turned back to face her and, as his mouth formed the next two words, he saw her blue eyes go from helpless to hopeless.

"You're pregnant."

THE END

Made in United States
Orlando, FL
18 February 2023